The Girls' Guide to Homemaking

Amy Bratley lives in London with her husband and
two children. This is her first novel.

THE GIRLS' GUIDE TO HOMEMAKING

AMY BRATLEY

PAN BOOKS

First published 2011 by Pan Books
an imprint of Pan Macmillan, a division of Macmillan Publishers Limited
Pan Macmillan, 20 New Wharf Road, London N1 9RR
Basingstoke and Oxford
Associated companies throughout the world
www.panmacmillan.com

ISBN 978-1-447-20022-2

1 3 5 7 9 8 6 4 2

A CIP catalogue record for this book is available from
the British Library.

Typeset by CPI Typesetting
Printed in the UK by CPI Mackays, Chatham ME5 8TD

Visit **www.panmacmillan.com** to read more about all our books
and to buy them. You will also find features, author interviews and
news of any author events, and you can sign up for e-newsletters
so that you're always first to hear about our new releases.

For Jimmy, Sonny and Audrey

Acknowledgements

For unrelenting support and encouragement, my sincere thanks to Veronique Baxter and Laura West. Thanks to Jenny Geras and everyone at Pan Macmillan for their belief in the book. Thanks to my lifelong friends, Karen Cudmore and Caroline Mitchell, for their fantastic friendship. Thanks to Melissa Four and Kitty Beamish for Craft Club, Judy Spikings and Helen McNeive for character inspiration, and to my loving family, especially Isabel Cook, for the writing room. I have tried to seek permission from any sources I have used, but in the cases where I haven't been able to find the original author, I say thank you for your inspiration. Thanks to *www.countryliving.com* which inspired some homely ideas. Heartfelt thanks to my wonderful mum, Anne Cook, who will always be my 'home', and lots of love to little Audrey and to Jimmy and Sonny – my two most favourite boys.

Where thou art, that is home

Emily Dickinson

Chapter One

The goal: try to make your home a place of peace and
order where your husband can renew himself in body
and spirit.

Housekeeping Monthly, May 1955

Tonight, when Simon and I were kissing, lying naked together
in our new king-size bed, he called me Hanna.

My name is Juliet.

I sat bolt upright and pulled the duvet up to my chin. A fox
shrieked in the communal gardens outside our window.
Simon scratched his ear.

'Simon,' I said. 'Did you just call me Hanna?'

Hanna was our ex-housemate, a friend from university.
Hanna was Swedish and hideously attractive. We'd shared a
maisonette near Greenwich with her for a year. We had been
in this flat, our first home together, since seven p.m. Exactly
five hours and fourteen minutes.

'No,' he said quickly. 'No, of course I didn't.'

'Yes, you did,' I said. 'I heard you say her name.'

'No,' he said. 'I didn't.'

'Simon,' I said. 'I heard you call me Hanna. Admit it.'

He sighed and began stroking my thigh, his hand creeping upwards.

'Look, I was only imagining the three of us together,' he said quietly. 'A harmless fantasy, that's all. It's no big deal is it?'

My eyes were perfect circles in the dark. I pushed his hand away, reached for the lamp switch and clicked it on. Simon froze, an errant stag caught in headlights.

Simon and I had found our new flat in *Loot*. I was sold on the address before we'd even viewed the property: Lovelace Avenue, Gipsy Hill, London. How could we not be blissfully happy there? I imagined the house as an impressive four-storey Victorian building halfway up a quiet, tree-lined street. Our flat would be on the top floor, with spectacular views of London's skyline and apricot sunsets. The shared garden would boast sweet-smelling rosemary, blackberry bushes and honeysuckle. Maybe even a robin. There would definitely not be yellow police tape cordoning off crime scenes, sirens blazing or murder weapons strewn about the pavement. It would be a real home, with a hearth and a heart. Our hearts.

'Ju-li-et, he-ll-o-o-o-o,' Simon said, waving his hand in front of my face. 'So shall I call the landlord?'

We were devouring almond croissants and drinking coffee in a cosy café in Greenwich, circling adverts on the 'Flats to Rent' page. Simon was wearing Jarvis Cocker-style glasses, stubble and a blue checked shirt. He had wide cheeks and eyes as dark as caves, but fluffy light hair. Pen in mouth, he studied *Loot* in a serious, concentrated way. Very arty. I liked him in this guise. (Dare I say, preferred?) Normally, for his job as a PE teacher, he wore clothes made of fabric that repelled rain and absorbed sweat, more suitable for mountaineering than café society. As a rule we made an incongruous couple, Simon in his practical outdoor gear prepared to abseil a cliff or hurdle at a moment's notice, me in a flowery tea-dress and red sandals, my hair an unruly hedge of brown curls. Simon was far more beautiful naked. Under that viscose he had the chest and thighs of Hercules. And just above his right bum cheek, he had a strawberry-shaped birthmark that I adored.

'Yes, call him,' I said. 'With an address like that, as long as the place has a roof, I'll be happy.'

Simon raised his right eyebrow. That was one of his party pieces – tilting one eyebrow higher than the other, like Gregory Peck. I'd seen him do it many times, but it still made me smile. (My party piece, fitting a whole orange into my mouth, was equally impressive.) I chewed on my thumbnail as Simon called the landlord of Lovelace Avenue, trying to look more casual than I felt. I listened with relief as he booked an appointment, reverting to teacher type with a formal 'Yes, sir!' before hanging up.

'Job done,' he said as a crowd of Italian students filed into the café, followed by their rucksacks. They'd just been staring blankly at the shop opposite selling maritime paraphernalia. The shop was called 'Nauticalia', and if it was edible, I'd have eaten it. Second to the antiques market – where I'd once bought an old mannequin that now stood spellbound in my wardrobe – it was my favourite place in Greenwich. Even though there was never a reason to buy a barometer, I could browse the cornucopia of curious model ships in glass bottles and telescopes for an embarrassingly long time.

'Lovelace Avenue,' I smiled, testing out the name on my tongue and nudging Simon's foot with mine. 'The perfect name for our love nest, don't you think?'

Simon turned abruptly away from me and looked over at the noisy students, taking a bite from his croissant. Sunshine and dust cast fizzy columns around us. I picked a white daisy out of the vase on the table and sniffed. It was plastic and I snapped off a leaf. I watched Simon's profile, waiting for a reply. He liked to make me wait. I was used to long pauses and vacant staring. Some days this made me want to scream at the top of my lungs or tear my hair out in clumps. Be patient, I told myself – he's just filing through all that grey matter, chasing the right words. Even though Simon could sprint a hundred metres in thirteen seconds, he didn't like to be rushed for an answer.

'My dad's doctor is called Dr Death,' he eventually said, grinning. 'It's true, I promise. It's actually spelt the same as the word, too. I've checked in the phone book.'

I gave him a doubting look, hiding my irritation that he'd sidestepped my question.

'Did you know that the bra was invented by Otto Titzling?' I replied with a wry smile.

As we laughed, I let a rare feeling of contentment wash over me. I focused on my Technicolor snapshot of our future together: an old couple, wrinkled as raisins, chuckling by the fireside in our rocking chairs, photographs of our children adorning the walls, our wedding bands as worn and familiar as our bones, a loyal mutt asleep across my slippers, an embroidered quilt over our knees, lovingly stitched by my own hand, sun gleaming through our thatched cottage window. There together with nothing and no one to disturb us. I asked myself, could life really be that way? I yearned to confess my romantic dreams, but I stayed quiet. I guessed they wouldn't be especially well received.

'Don't be ridiculous,' Simon said, hitting me on the head with the rolled-up *Loot*. 'That's fiction.'

Reaching the decision to move out of our shared maisonette and into a 'love nest' of our own had taken several months of careful negotiation. I had found myself attempting to lure Simon with promises of sex-on-loop, quality cooked breakfasts, fluffy white towels, a Smeg fridge filled with cold Stella. I tucked paper notes inside his trainers and sports bag telling him how wonderful he was, so that he'd realize how wonderful I was. I baked vanilla meringues and served them with dollops of clotted cream, wafting them under his nose fresh out of the oven (who could resist that?), rubbed his feet with my expensive Molton Brown foot cream, let him play on his Nintendo Wii thingy when I longed to watch *Relocation, Relocation*, hoping to absorb Kirstie Allsopp's sense of style. Shameless, I know. But having our own home had become ridiculously important to me. Some girls covet Vivienne Westwood; for me a real home is the real thing. Perhaps I was ignoring the fine but visible splinters in our relationship, was trying to believe it was OK because everyone has faults, no one's perfect. But I went bullishly on with my plan, regardless. I had to.

'Why are you so desperate to move in with him?' Hanna, our flatmate, had asked me one night, her eyebrows knotted. 'You're young. Why not check out the options first? Experiment and enjoy your freedom. We don't just buy one dress and wear it for ever, do we? Shop around.'

Hanna annoyed me. I shook my head angrily. How did sleeping with a handful of men constitute freedom? I don't want to sound too Amish here, but wasn't there some kind of freedom in sleeping with just one man? Having to be intimate with a sequence of strangers I knew nothing about had felt like hell. I shuddered at the dim and distant memories of groping sessions with various unknowns.

'Is that so strange?' I asked Hanna, my voice quivering. 'To want to live with the man I love? It's a natural step for us, you know.'

I knew I sounded naïve, like the pink-cheeked heroine in a period drama. I knew deep inside that I was clutching at the idea like a life raft. The cynic in me was shaking her head in disbelief at my own words.

'Look, I'm sure that Simon and I are meant for each other,' I said, vaguely aware I might be protesting too much. 'Why wait until I'm thirty before making a proper commitment? Just because that's what everyone else does? God, people are obsessed with not settling down until they've got their careers sorted, but I want to get on with it.'

Hanna shrugged and told me I was old before my years and that I should be more cautious. But she didn't understand.

'I'm not old before my time,' I told her. 'I adore living in London, but I want somewhere and someone to come back to at the end of the day.'

There were a million other twenty-five-year-olds wandering around London's streets trying to look edgy in vintage or American Apparel, with a permanent hangover and a Topshop store card – I needed someone and somewhere to mark me out as distinct. I needed a home that wrapped its arms around me when I walked in through the front door. I totally convinced myself that once we had got our own place, our relationship would be catapulted to an untouchable level. We wouldn't be common or garden variety 'sharers' any more, bickering over shelf space in the bathroom. We would be an authentic cohabiting, co-eating, co-sleeping couple. Solid and sound, like a nugget of gold. And the longer Simon resisted, the more of a challenge it became. I would never have admitted this to ninety-nine per cent of people.

'Look at this place, though,' he said, pointing to the slagheap of clothes I called my wardrobe, the books slumped over the carpet, my work papers thrown across the bed, a cloudy vase holding a dried-up bunch of once white roses.

'I mean, Christ, have you ever thought about tidying up in here?' he said, frowning.

This was one thing I didn't like about Simon. He had a way of making me feel like a wayward schoolchild about really inane things. My cheeks burned. Admittedly housework was not my forte, but this place had never felt like a home, so what was the point in trying? When we'd first moved in, I'd made a frenzied attempt at personalizing the place, but it felt so temporary, so half-hearted, I couldn't be bothered. Besides, tidying took levels of self-discipline that I didn't possess. I was never going to be the kind of girlfriend who polished doorknobs or ironed socks. I slowly pushed a fur-lined coffee cup under the bed with my toe.

'But it will be different,' I said later when we were sharing vegetarian tacos with Hanna in the living room (comprising one battered sofa, one chair and a TV on the floor). In my head I said: When Hanna's not here, decorating the, albeit scant, furniture with her beautiful long limbs, white-blonde hair and roll-up cigarettes smoked with easy elegance, I can have you to myself and we can get on with it.

'Different how?' Simon said, glancing at Hanna, who was painting her toenails blood-red, scrunching up her tiny freckled nose in concentration. Her skirt fell to her hips, displaying a long caramel leg and a trim of white lace from her size eight underwear. On her ankle she wore a red and green friendship bracelet, and in her nose, a diamond stud. I suddenly felt drab and cumbersome in comparison. My knickers were of the laceless variety, my legs not so long, brown or slim. Nothing of me, not even my earlobes, was pierced. Of course, these things shouldn't have bothered me – Hanna was my friend – but they did. When she moved, men watched; when she talked, men listened. I hated myself for it, but I couldn't deny I felt jealous of her. She was just so pretty and blonde and feathery and fairy-tale perfect. Living with Hanna was like having a unicorn in your front room.

'I'm not sure I'm ready for roast pork with all the trimmings and trips to Furniture Village,' Simon said.

He was half smiling, half serious. I told myself he was trying to be funny. But I was determined to convince him it was the right thing to do.

'You know I'm strictly a city girl!' I said, looking at him as if to say, *Don't you know anything about me?*

While Simon drank a bottle of beer and rubbed his big feet together, I sat behind a copy of *Cosmopolitan*, absorbing myself in an article about how to be an FFF: fun, fearless female. It was an arduous read: the rules seemed inflexible. I felt exhausted.

'It's not that I don't love you,' Simon said absentmindedly. His eyes were fixed on an episode of *Buffy the Vampire Slayer*, and I wasn't sure who he was talking to. Me? Sarah Michelle Gellar?

'It's just frightening, the commitment of a new place,' he continued. 'It's a big step, you know? We're living together here, but we have our own space to be ourselves. I can chill out in my own room, do a sit-up without being disturbed. Do you understand what I'm saying?'

I stayed silent. I thought about my own room, tiny and cluttered, with a small window overlooking the local Costcutter bins. There was an uninspiring brown carpet, brown curtains and a small set of brown drawers. Blu-Tack was forbidden, so I'd leaned my pictures against the wall and draped a wire of star-shaped fairy lights over my mirror – my nod towards interior design. Was I myself in there? No, I left remnants of myself in there, my discarded possessions and my dead skin, that was all. I couldn't wait to get out of it and move into a proper flat, but why was I trying so hard to convince Simon of my worth as a live-in partner?

Simon looked at me, waiting for a response.

'Erm,' I said calmly. 'I'm just trying to remember the last

time I did a sit-up. Five years ago, I think. And that was under duress.'

I had never really liked to exercise in the frantic, obsessive way Simon did. While he hurled himself at rowing machines, cross-trainers or weights, I preferred to avoid them entirely. I didn't swim either. I hated deep water. So the only exercise I took was walking and I walked everywhere. I even walked in my dreams – Simon told me I frantically kicked my legs in my sleep. And I often woke up feeling exhausted for absolutely no reason besides the red wine I'd polished off while horizontal on the sofa the previous night, waiting for him to come back from clambering up a climbing wall.

'So you don't understand what I mean, then?' he said. 'About the space issue? What if we argue, Juliet? We'll have nowhere to go and sulk.'

Hanna slapped Simon's foot and said, 'Grow up.' She was wearing her blonde hair in plaits, pinned to her pretty heart-shaped head. She looked at me. 'You've been together, what, over four years now?' she said, cornflower-blue eyes sparkling as she spoke. 'When you have a row, you kiss and make up.'

Hanna's grasp of English pronunciation sometimes failed her. She pronounced 'row' as in rowboat. Simon grinned. I knew he found it endearing.

'Do we have to "row"?' he said, mimicking Hanna. 'Before we kiss?'

'I don't have a canoe,' I said.

He grabbed me and nuzzled his face into my neck. I fell into him and knocked over my wine glass. I loved the feel of his big arms around me.

'Get a room,' Hanna said.

'Or a flat?' I said.

It wasn't clear whether Simon had heard.

Simon, Hanna and I had met at Nottingham University. He was doing a PGCE to become a PE teacher, I was studying History of Art and Hanna was a Drama student. We lived in the same hall of residence – G Block – on Nottingham's leafy campus and bonded in the safety of the communal lounge. While the moon shone then faded, we talked, drinking Strongbow cider, until the morning mist licked the windows.

I had worried before going to university that it would be full of terrifying students who already had their lives mapped out. But it wasn't like that at all. There were all sorts: druggies, Goths, academics, sports freaks and a few not unlike me – smiling eagerly at everyone, not knowing which pigeon-hole to fly into. I just did my best to prove to people – and myself – that I was a reasonably stable, friendly person, in spite of everything that had happened in the past. I concentrated on sharing interesting but insignificant bits of information about my life. I didn't once bring up my family. How could I? Instead, I told them how I'd grown up in Cornwall, loved junk shops and eating peanut butter straight from the jar, and that I ordered my DVDs by degrees of sadness. I told them how my hair, currently shoulder-length and curly dark brown, had once been up to here (I lifted my hand to the top of my ear, pulled a face) and peroxide blonde. I said I didn't believe in true love and love at first sight, that it could only be lust, couldn't it? I told them I was terrified of water and despised people who didn't give a damn about people less fortunate than them. I kept it brief and superficial and they bought it.

'And this happened,' I said, pulling up my sleeve and showing them the scar that ran from elbow to wrist, 'when I fell through a glass door, aged nine and a half.'

The memory of the blood springing from my skin, coagulating into tiny scarlet seeds, was as clear as day.

'Poor Juliet,' said Simon, so warmly that, impulsively, I hugged him.

It wasn't until the end of the second year, when the three of us had moved into houses with friends we'd made on our separate degree courses, that Simon and I became an item. There were no fireworks or starting gun to mark the beginning of our love affair. Rather, it crept up on us like the tide, or wrinkles. When I asked Simon why he was attracted to me, he kissed my nose and said: 'Because I can't quite work you out.' He said I was enigmatic. I was keen to appear mysterious – for something to distinguish me from astonishing beauties like Hanna – so I played up to Simon's appraisal. I bought incense. I applied thick eyeliner, read Anaïs Nin and Richard Brautigan novels in the cafeteria, customized clothes I bought in charity shops, wore net skirts and listened to The Velvet Underground with my window wide open and the volume turned up. I tried absinthe and didn't tell him how horribly sick I was afterwards.

'I want to unravel you, Juliet,' he said in a Frankenstein voice (I let it go that once) before we kissed for the first time. And when we did kiss and hold each other close, I felt relieved and surprised. Relieved that at last the unsaid 'thing' between us had been said, and surprised at how lovely physical contact with a fellow human being was. It had been so long since I'd held anyone close that once I held Simon I didn't want to let go. Unlike Hanna, who had male students begging to date her, bulging out of their Lee jeans in desperation to catch a glimpse of her ankle, I'd remained single. Hanna had tried to set me up with her various rejects, but, hoping to cling on to a modicum of self-respect, I refused. Then Simon came along and laid his interested cards on the table. And we were happy, I thought. We never discussed marriage or babies, but I convinced myself I was finally on to a winning streak, that the past was the past and that wonderful things were on the horizon. The prospect of moving to London and into a flatshare with Hanna was exciting. It was the cheaper option while we got our careers 'established' in London. That's how we spoke, as if our fabulous jobs were a given. Now Hanna was returning to Sweden and Simon and I were earning enough to afford a bigger flat in a more salubrious area. I wanted to move – this flat had so many layers of wallpaper, we joked it was like a padded cell, and the carpets were not so much threadbare as floorboards. Opposite the train station, the glassware and windows trembled as commuter trains rumbled past day and night. There was a leak in the bathroom and a notice slapped on the gas fire saying: WARNING – UNSAFE, DO NOT USE. Our Christmas tree, from five months earlier, still lay outside the front door, a pale brown skeleton. I made no effort there whatsoever. In fact, with a dried-up teabag here and a pink nail-polish spillage there, I actively sabotaged the place.

'OK, Jules, I'll do it, let's get a place together,' Simon said now, poking me in the back with his big toe. 'As long as my Star Wars figurines can be on the mantelpiece.'

Hanna looked over at me and raised her eyebrows into arrows. Her expression said: Do you really want to move in with this big, hairy child?

I realized I was trembling and on the verge of tears. I swallowed hard and focused on my dream: us lying on a sheepskin rug, spooning chocolate fondue into each other's mouths, elbows resting on stylish cushions I had handmade from vintage scarves, roaring with laughter, a light golden glow enveloping us. Yes, I know it was a hopelessly romantic notion, but otherwise we were just a man and a woman existing in a flat. I wanted much more than simply to exist in a flat. I wanted to fly to the moon. And no one was going to stop me now.

'OK,' I said, giving Simon a private smile. 'It's a deal.'

Hanna left the room and my eyes flicked back to the FFF article. It said: 'Do you live life to the max?' and 'If not, why not?'

Our new flat was beautiful. On the first floor of a Victorian conversion, it was huge. The outside had been painted the colour of clotted cream and an enormous pink rose bush clung like an eyebrow above the front door. The neighbouring house, dilapidated and boarded up, was menacing in contrast. It smelled like dead cats, or how I imagined they would smell. But I shut my eyes and nose to the peripherals. Nothing could ruin today, nothing at all. I wanted it to be perfect and I anxiously scrutinized Simon's expression, desperate for him to fall in love with our future home. Inside the flat, it was a blank canvas: clean, bright and white, except for the living room, which had been painted swimming-pool blue. Even though it was boiling hot outside, the rooms were cool. There were sash windows from floor to ceiling in the bedroom, steps up to a bathroom and – my favourite – a small shared conservatory, plush with pots of ferns left by the previous tenant. I was so excited to see the place again that I stared at each room until my eyeballs ached. Simon beamed at me and held my hand. His eyes were as shiny as new shoes. At that moment, I was one hundred per cent sure we'd done the right thing.

'Shall we explore?' he said with childlike excitement. I grinned back at him – this was Simon at his best. Some nights I lay awake worrying that it was Simon the Kid I loved the most. His childhood stories enchanted me. When he was five, he'd thrown a brick through his parents' living room window to free a trapped butterfly. At seven, he'd taken his two dogs and kitten for a ride on the canal, on a rubber dinghy, only to be rescued by the emergency services and featured on the evening news. He reminded me of Huckleberry Finn, and I loved that about him. Occasionally, when talking about teaching, he came over all serious and earnest. When he sat discussing targets and Ofsted reports in a monotone, I thought to myself: You make me feel as bored as a scarecrow in a potato field. I longed for the butterfly, the bricks, the rubber dinghy. But I didn't want to think about that now. This was the first day of the rest of our lives. Today was The Beginning.

'Home, sweet home,' I said as we carried in our boxes as quickly as was humanly possible, unpacked my mannequin, the bedlinen, a bedside lamp and the kitchen equipment.

We'd ordered more furniture online from IKEA, but that would arrive in a couple of days. Just putting our knives and forks into the drawers made me unfeasibly happy. This was our home. Our love nest.

'Oh, Simon,' I said, running my hand along the granite worktop in the kitchen. 'I'm so happy. I completely love this place. Do you?'

He surveyed the kitchen cupboards, stared up at the ceiling and the tiled floor. He opened and closed the fridge.

'Uh-huh,' he said.

That evening, as the heavens opened over London, we ate greasy fish and chips sitting cross-legged on the floor and guzzled a bottle of Prosecco. I noticed Simon was swallowing his chips whole, like a seal. As we talked I felt strangely jumpy, my stomach a combustible mix of excitement and nerves. At midnight, our legs heavy with tiredness, we decided we'd do the rest of the unpacking the next day.

'This is our first little home,' I said, flinging my arms around Simon's neck. I waited for Simon to say something meaningful, to mark out this moment as special, to whoop, anything. He said nothing. I waited a while longer, then broke the silence myself.

'This might sound silly, but I'll say it anyway,' I said, suddenly serious. 'I've been waiting my whole life for this – to have a real home. I've dreamed about it. Really, actually dreamed about it. Now it's here and I can't wait to get started. I'm going to try to make it perfect, Simon. You, me, this place. I want it to be perfect.'

I paused for breath. He scratched his chin. I heard a tap dripping from somewhere in the flat.

'I know your parents' place has been your home for ever,' I said quietly. 'But I want this place to be *our* home.'

For a split second, I desperately wanted to tell Simon everything. The whole truth and nothing but the truth. My throat felt dry.

'If I tell you something . . .' I said, then I faltered.

'What?' he said anxiously.

I sighed, waving my hand. 'I just want you to understand that having this home with you is very important and I'm going to make it all perfect and you really happy.'

The words rushed out of my mouth and I was surprised at the force of them. It was the closest I'd ever come to telling Simon the truth – that meeting him had allowed me to believe that I could forget about everything that had gone before and be genuinely happy.

'It doesn't have to be perfect,' Simon said, smiling warily. 'I'm not interested in a hearts and flowers home, you know. Just relax, will you?'

He fell silent and I felt suddenly deflated. Couldn't he just let me, for this moment, believe that it could be perfect? That if I really tried, I could make someone happy?

'No, of course I know it doesn't,' I said curtly. 'I'm just trying to show you how much all this means. That's all. It's not about hearts and flowers. What do you think I am? Let's have a drink.'

I poured us another glass of Prosecco, and we stood awkwardly in silence. Since we'd met at college, we'd hardly ever been *alone* alone. And even though this was what I'd wanted for a long time, I felt self-conscious and anxious. With no noises coming from other housemates, I felt acutely aware of a deep silence that hung in the rooms like sea mist. I turned on the radio and tried to change the subject. I chattered and chirruped about improvements we could make to the place: we could scour markets for lovely old furniture, seek out treasures from junk shops. Simon looked at me blankly. The cynic in me was mocking, asking what did I think I was doing? My voice sounded strangely thin and high. I had an awful growing feeling of disappointment, of anti-climax, but I pushed it away. Perhaps if I hadn't been so determined for everything to be so perfect, I would have told Simon how I really felt. I would have told him the truth. Instead, I smiled a weak smile and kissed his cheek.

'I have my grandma Violet's old book here somewhere,' I said half-heartedly, stepping over boxes, rubbing my forehead. 'I used to read it when I was young, a manual about, um, you know, how to make a house a home, if you see what I mean. How to be a Little Miss Homemaker . . .'

I tripped over a carrier bag full of coat hangers, spilling my glass of wine on the carpet. We laughed at exactly the same time. It was a relief to laugh.

'Come here, Little Miss Homemaker,' Simon said, grabbing my hand. He led me into the bedroom, untied my wraparound dress, removed my laceless underwear, pulled me on to the bed and kissed my lips. I was relieved at the intimacy. I listened to the sound of the rain.

And that's when he called me Hanna.

Chapter Two

To reduce clutter, homemakers should cut down on knickknacks. One important piece looks better and cuts down on moving many aside for dusting.

Ladies' Home Journal Art of Homemaking,
Virginia T. Habeeb, 1973

Leaving Simon in bed, I phoned Hanna from the bathroom. My fingers shook as I punched in her number. She answered immediately with a breezy, 'Hey, Juliet! You OK? Jesus, it's so late. Why are you calling?'

My stomach lurched at the sound of her voice. Rain streaked across the bathroom window and I pressed my nose up against the glass.

'Juliet?' she said again. 'What's up?'

I swallowed hard and forced the words out.

'Hanna,' I said, holding the phone so hard against my ear it burned. 'Have you ever slept with Simon?'

I tried to keep breathing. I stayed pressed up against the

frosted glass window, watching the outline of a woman running from a taxi to her door, a newspaper over her head. I bit my lip so hard I tasted blood.

'Come on, Hanna,' I pleaded, trembling now. 'Tell me the truth. Have you?'

I thought about the first time I'd seen Hanna at university. She had been wearing a leopard-print dress and red cardigan, her hair a bolt of white gold. I had been awestruck by her uniqueness. On that superficial level, I was drawn to her and wanted to be her friend. God knows what Simon had thought.

'Oh, Juliet, it meant nothing,' she said meekly. 'And it was only once. Remember when you went to stay with Joy that night in March? We shared a bottle of whisky and he literally *stuck his tongue down my throat*. I know I shouldn't have gone along with it, but I guess I was too drunk. I've wanted to tell you for months. But you seemed so happy. I didn't know how. It meant nothing, Juliet, honestly. You know I'd hate to hurt you. Please believe me.'

I closed my eyes. I remembered the night I had gone to visit my great-aunt Joy, who lived in Bow. I'd decided to stay over because we were going to the cinema to see some arty film she'd raved about, and could only get tickets to the late showing. I thought about the following morning, when I got back home. Everything had seemed perfectly normal. Hanna had slept late and Simon was sprinting across Greenwich Park with his pedometer, his geometric-patterned duvet cover neatly spread over his bed.

'How could you?' was all I managed to say before I let out a horrible, choking sob. On the backs of my eyelids were pictures of Simon and Hanna naked together, of his tongue (suddenly reptilian and forked) stuck down Hanna's throat. Of this flat, our new home, condemned and demolished to dust. I felt strangely exposed, embarrassed, because they had known something I hadn't for months. Had they been laughing at me?

'I know this is awful for you, but I didn't plan it to happen,' she said. 'Please, Juliet. It was Simon. He leapt on me like a hound on heat, not the other way round.'

I flinched at her words. Already I was conjuring up hideous X-rated images of them together.

'Oh God,' I sniffed. 'I thought Simon was in love with me. I believed it. You let me believe it. That's why I moved in with him. Why didn't you stop me?'

I thought about Simon's silences earlier that evening. Was he standing in our new flat listening to me talk about the cutlery drawer, all the time longing to be with Hanna? I flushed boiling red and dug my nails into my cheek.

'Oh, Juliet, you were so determined to have your little home together,' she pleaded. 'Please, Juliet? I'm so sorry. I don't want to row.'

She said 'row' as in rowboat. Again.

'It's row!' I said furiously. 'Like, "how now brown cow"!'

I heard sirens blast past her. I hung up and sat on the edge of the bath, bleary-eyed. I sobbed miserable, stomach-wrenching sobs. I felt like the most wretched person alive. Then I heard Simon coughing outside the door. Oh, Simon. I ran the taps and splashed my face in icy cold water. The pipes groaned at me.

'Juliet?' he said, knocking gingerly. 'What are you doing in there?'

I looked at my reflection, at the wheels of red skin circling my eyes. OK, so I wasn't Hanna, but I wasn't unattractive. People often said I looked 'old-fashioned', which sounded like the name of a racehorse, but I think it was intended as a compliment. My curly hair framed a heart-shaped face constellated with freckles. My eyes were brown, lashes black, thick and long. My nose was small and neat, my lips full and very pale pink. I was never going to be Kate Moss, but I had boobs and hips that Simon claimed to love. I had a sinking realization that I was going to be sad for weeks, doing the wretched, miserable things that The Heartbroken do. The whole purpose of moving into the flat was to be happy, to have a joyous future together. That had been my plan. Now what? I fleetingly wondered if I could forgive Simon, but then pushed the thought away. Even if I forgave him, I'd never be able to forget. The pictures of them together were indelible. Thumping my fist on the sink, I chastised myself for letting myself get into this situation. How could I have been so brainless as to become dependent on Simon to make me happy? I should've known that people let you down. More than anyone, I should've known that. The cynic in me chuckled, 'I told you so, fool. I told you it would never work, but you refused to listen. See now?'

'Come out, Juliet,' I heard him say through the door. 'Come back to bed. Please.'

I put my hand on the door handle and pushed, not knowing what to do or say. But as I walked into the bedroom and looked at Simon's face, I knew there was no future.

'You can move out immediately,' I told Simon shakily, wrenching a blanket and a pillow from an open box and clutching them to my chest. 'Go to your parents' house and pick up your stuff when I'm at work tomorrow. I don't want to . . .'

I held up my hands, looking for more words, but, defeated, let them fall back down to my sides. Simon looked at me as if I had just fallen out of space.

'What's happened?' he said, sitting on the mattress. 'You're tired. Come back to bed with me.'

His voice was soft and his cheeks slightly pink. He was too good-looking. But I couldn't start it all off like this. I could not build our nest on a broken branch.

'Hanna's happened,' I said, staring at a spot above Simon's head. I couldn't look him in the eye. 'I should have bloody known. I feel like such a fool! Hanna's what happened. To you.'

I was trembling with fury now, aching with it. I longed for him to tell me it was all a big, fat mistake. That I'd had a nightmare. That Hanna was a fantasist. That he'd put hallucinogenic drugs in my chips. Anything.

'Fuck,' he said, thudding his head down on the pillow and putting his hands over his face.

'Exactly that,' I said. 'That's exactly why you have to go. You've been fucking fucking her, you fuck-head!'

No other words came to mind.

'Fuck,' he said again.

I shook my head in disbelief. He didn't have to reiterate. I didn't appreciate him rubbing it in. On my way out of the bedroom, I picked up his Jabba the Hutt figurine and snapped off its stupid little tail.

'Easy, Juliet!' Simon said, following. 'Just listen to what I have to say, will you?'

I lifted my head up, but said nothing. Tears streamed down my face and I gestured at Simon to pass me a tissue. He handed me the box.

'I don't care what you have to say,' I said, wiping my eyes. 'You betrayed me. You *stuck your tongue down Hanna's throat*!'

Simon sighed enormously. Ridiculously, I had the unhinged urge to giggle. I felt like I was having a surreal, out-of-body experience, like a puppet someone else was controlling.

'This is such a female thing,' he said dully. 'Jumping to conclusions. What's that book – *Men Are From Mars, Women Are From Venus*? Why don't you just hear me out.'

I stood up and pointed towards the door. 'The conclusion is that you fucked my friend and let me believe you loved me, Mars Boy. Now GO!' I screamed. 'OUT!'

Mars Boy? Where did that come from? I vaguely wondered if the neighbours could hear the new hysterical resident screaming upstairs. I imagined them pointing to the ceiling, shaking heads and raising eyebrows.

'OK!' Simon said. 'I get it! You hate me, but listen, it was a stupid, stupid mistake. I don't want to lose you over this ridiculous thing...'

I was shaking violently now, so I tried to concentrate on something else while Simon dressed and shoved some things into his bag. I picked up my grandma Violet's homemaking bible and blindly flicked through the pages of smiling ladies brandishing dusters. A bundle of hand drawings and *Home-maker* magazine cuttings slipped from the book and fluttered to the floor. My eyes rested on a headline: 'How to Breathe New Life into an Old Curtain Pole'. I sighed.

'Juliet,' Simon said in his soft voice. 'Please. We're above this, aren't we? Above having a screaming match about a stupid drunken night I can barely recall. Let me stay. I really, really don't want to go back home to my parents' house.'

I took a deep breath. Simon's home, a four-storey palace in Hampstead, was incredible. It would hardly be a chore to return there. It was the kind of home magazines borrowed for photo shoots. The carpets were five inches thick, the furniture was all antique, there was an Aga in the kitchen that discreet staff maintained. Plus his mum and dad were wonderful, kind-hearted, generous people who loved their four children impossibly much. They made the Waltons look like the Wests. I imagined the pure delight on his mum's face when Simon knocked on the door needing a place to stay. She'd have him tucked up in bed with a hot-water bottle in seconds.

'Go away,' I said, pointing to the door. And after some sighing, he did. He went. I held my breath as I listened to his footsteps fade and then moved to the window to watch him walk down Lovelace Avenue. Simon glanced up and I pressed my palms flat on the glass, two little white flags. I broke out into fresh tears.

I stood there by the window wondering what to do now the life I'd longed for was over. My rosy spectacles had been stamped on and crushed to dust. I sank to my knees and leaned my head against the window for a long time. No longer did I see spectacular views of London, or a beautiful tree-lined street, or a buttery sunrise. As the first smear of dawn arrived, I saw a mangy fox standing in a puddle, peeing up a wall. I saw a wonky 'To let' sign stuck in the front garden of our building and a discarded bag of chips bloodied with tomato sauce tossed over the pavement. I listened to the desperate hum of the fridge and felt hot with panic.

'What will I do now?' I said to the walls.

There was no reply. I'd have to get used to that.

Chapter Three

Our personal annoyance will make us more than
usually careless around the house. Do you take out
your wrath on inanimate objects – do you ever bang
doors and slam dishes or punish innocent household
equipment?

America's Homemaking Book,
Marguerite Dodd, 1957

Unlike Simon's family, my clan had nothing in common with
the Waltons. My parents had met at college in St Ives in
Cornwall twenty-six years ago. My dad, Charles Rice, was a
lecturer in Art, and Ava his kohl-eyed, flame-haired flirtatious
student. Charles was thirty-five and married when he first
saw eighteen-year-old Ava. Then, she was the kind of pin-up
pretty that stopped men in their tracks. Charles described
Ava's face as a painter's palette: apple-green eyes, ink-black
lashes, cherry-pink lips and a burst of burnished orange as
a fringe. Their meeting was explosive and scandalous. It cost

Charles his marriage and his job, and Ava her place at college. As my dad often told me, they were so consumed by each other, they didn't care much for what was lost, only what was found.

Despite their seventeen-year age gap, I think they were happy for a while. I have photographs to prove it – one that I especially like of them running along a sandy beach with out-stretched arms like aeroplanes, huge smiles on their faces. But after I was born, when Ava was still only nineteen, their relationship floundered. While Charles worked hard to afford the rent, Ava grew bored of devoting every hour of day and night to a colicky baby. She spent more and more time away from my dad and me, disappearing to some party or other. Neither she nor Dad was especially interested in domesticity, so with a truant mother and a bewildered father, the first few years of my life were chaotic.

'I'm working like a slave,' Ava would say, yanking bed sheets off the washing line, shaking them out with such force I'd fear for my eyes. 'I would much rather be out in the dunes, sky-watching, wouldn't you?'

'Yes,' I nodded. The sky seemed far less complicated than the ground. I hated living in such disorder. Nothing was where it should be. Ava, who insisted I call her by her real name, could never find me matching socks, or an ironed pinafore, or my hairbrush, or the motivation to make a packed lunch. Her haphazard approach to home life embarrassed me. When I was seven years old and my friends came over to play, I made sorry excuses about my 'artistic' mother who was too busy being creative to help us bake fairy cakes. My little friends would nod knowingly, then flee back to their reward charts and Barbie bedspreads. While their parents didn't seem to mind cooking for their family, Ava despised it. I can still picture the scene now. Bloody lamb chops flung out on to the table, Ava brandishing the meat cleaver in mid-air, blade glinting in the sun, her body stiff with resentment. Those poor lamb chops.

But still, our house had a grain of charm. I remember the smell of it – wood-burner smoke and incense mingled with dust as thick as ash. The property was dark – the bedroom walls upstairs had been painted such a deep shade of mushroom, I couldn't see my kirby grips. And when on a sunny day you looked in from the outside through the small Georgian windows, even with your nose pressed right up against the glass, all you could see was blackness, which made it a perfect hideout. My bedroom was above my parents' room, and if I lay with my ear pressed to the carpet, I could sometimes hear their arguments. I did that a lot, hoping to find out what was wrong and try to make it right. What I saw in Dad was a man hopelessly in love, and in Ava a woman who didn't want to be my mother or a wife. She would attempt maternal love: when we went for picnics by the sea, she would chase me into the waves, fling seashells into buckets, buy silence with sherbet lollipops, but it was clearly an effort. When I played in front of her, she didn't look at me like a daughter, more like she was watching an orangutan in a wildlife documentary. Irrationally, I worried that it was because I didn't look much like her, that the dark freckles that covered my skin somehow made me ugly to Ava, who had alabaster skin paler than snowdrops. I even tried to scrub my freckles off once with a scouring pad I stole from the kitchen sink.

By the time I was eight years old, things had got so bad between Ava and Dad and she was spending so much of her time away from our home that she might as well have been living another life entirely. Months later I discovered that she *was* living another life entirely, and I started to hate her. I hated her more than anything else in the world. I devoted myself to making my father happy, shielding him from the truth that Ava was a bad apple with a rotten core until one day I couldn't do it any longer. That was the day he drowned.

After my dad died, Ava went to Australia for a holiday that lasted the rest of my life. She came back occasionally to tick me off her 'To Do' list, but I was raised by my grandmother Violet, Ava's mother, who lived in a village on the Cornish coast a few miles from St Ives. Though I missed my dad more than there are words to express, it was a relief to be with Violet. She welcomed me with open arms and lived a structured, simple existence that I was pleased to fall in line with. Every day mirrored the last. She rose with the birds, worked as a dressmaker (our house was always full of local women with bits of fabric pinned to their bras) for long days and spent the evenings teaching me to knit, crochet and sew. By the age of ten, I was an expert. They were ideal hobbies for a grief-stricken girl. I could stare at Butterick patterns, needles and backstitch until my eyes hurt. I could go for hours without looking up, avoid facing the absence of my parents, who had apparently vanished in a puff of smoke. Violet was very patient with me. When I locked myself in my bedroom to cry, she would sit outside the door and talk to me through the keyhole. She helped me put up photographs of my dad and never said a word about his enormous dressing gown that I clutched in bed every night. And when I wondered why Ava had abandoned me, she would take me in her arms and hold me tight.

A widow, Violet was incredibly house proud, verging on obsessive. It was her *thing*. She took great pleasure in detail – matching curtains and cushions, arranging freshly clipped roses in glass vases, serving delicate home-made fairy cakes on blue and white china plates. I loved everything about her house – the dark beams, the smell of beeswax, the 1950s style Belfast sink in the kitchen, the grandfather clock, the glass cabinet lined with tiny silver snuffboxes, the copper kettles and shelves stacked with homemaking books. But she was by no means a Stepford Wife. She surprised me with her dark streak. When Violet's RAF-pilot husband Aaron died, aged twenty-six, after his plane crashed on a routine flight, the plane's fuel system was found to be at fault. Joy told me that after receiving a condolence letter from his commanding officer, Violet wrote back in capital letters, RETURN TO SENDER. AARON WAS 26 WHEN HE DIED. FUCK YOU! I'd never heard her swear – let alone at the military.

I loved Violet so much, and when she'd died of a heart attack a summer ago, I'd been horrified that she'd died alone. She'd been a mother to me and I missed her very much. I still had her ashes in a casket that I intended to scatter when I was ready. In her will, Violet had left me her cottage, which was now on the market. Most of her possessions were in storage, and all I had with me in London were her ashes and her favourite homemaking book, *Homemaking Hints for a Happier*

Home. Oh, the irony. With her handwritten comments scribbled across margins – sometimes reading like diary entries – it was my only surviving link to her. Picking it up now, more of Violet's dressmaking patterns fluttered out of the pages. I bundled them up and noticed a letter folded round a picture of a baby swaddled in a white blanket, wearing a pink knitted hat. The baby had a shock of black hair sticking out from under the hat. I'd had fair hair, so it wasn't me. Who was it, then? Putting the photograph down, I unfolded the letter with the photo and instantly recognized Ava's spindly blue handwriting.

> *Dear Mum,*
> *Enclosed is a picture of Rosie. I hope you will keep this photograph safe for me – it is the only one. I know you do not approve, but I firmly believe the right thing to do is to give*

And there it stopped. I flicked quickly through the book, looking for more pages to the letter, but couldn't find anything. I read the letter again and frowned. It was dated the year my dad had died and had been sent from an address in Sydney, Australia, where Ava went before she began travelling the world. Who was Rosie? I gulped. *What* did Ava firmly believe? I didn't understand – and with everything that was going on, I didn't have the energy to think about it. But why had Violet left it in the pages of her homemaking book? I felt oddly muddled and unsettled; an enormous black question mark unfurled in my brain.

Then my mobile rang, making me jump. I dropped the

letter in surprise, my heart pounding. I picked the phone up, half expecting it to be Simon. Perhaps he hadn't slept either. Perhaps he wanted to beg me for forgiveness. Perhaps the whole thing had been a bad dream. But it wasn't Simon. It was my boss, Philip Jackson. I blinked in confusion.

'Sorry to call you so early,' he said, 'but can you come in for nine a.m.? I'd like to see you before my meetings begin. That gives you fifty minutes. Can you make it?'

I didn't give a damn about meetings. I hadn't even been to bed. I wanted to lie under the duvet for a few days or call my best friend Imogen to tell her everything. But Philip had a way of making me behave like an obedient twelve year old. I thought of him in his immaculate pale linen suit and platinum cufflinks, already pacing his office, high on caffeine, phone pinned to his ear.

'Yes,' I said automatically. 'I'll be there.'

I hung up and looked at my watch. I had forty-five minutes before I was due at work. That gave me five minutes to get showered and dressed, ten minutes to walk to the station and half an hour to travel. I was going to be late.

Shoving the letter back inside the book, I automatically got into the shower and turned on the hot water. My mind whirred. Simon had slept with Hanna, left me here alone in this flat. I didn't have a clue what to do. How would I ever afford the rent? I'd have to move out, probably into a shared house again. Out of the shower, I quickly towelled myself dry, pulled on a crumpled blue tea-dress, smudged on blusher and a dash of mascara, dragged a comb through my wet curls, grabbed my bag and walked out into the May sunshine.

Placing one foot in front of the other, I concentrated on the pavement slabs. It was hot out in Lovelace Avenue, one of those London streets that felt gentrified despite being in a distinctly average suburb. If everything had been as it should have been, I would have enjoyed this, peering into our neighbours' windows. I would have stopped at Mimosa, the French coffee shop on the corner, to order a coffee and a croissant. Instead, I felt sick to the stomach and, despite the heat, visibly shivered. I couldn't stop thinking about Simon and Hanna. Every couple on the street holding hands was Hanna and Simon. At the railway station, every couple's parting kiss belonged to Hanna and Simon. I felt desolate, imagining what people would say to me in consolation, their heads held sympathetically to the side – 'You'll find someone else, you're so young. Men are bastards.'

Fuck that. I didn't want anyone else. I wanted my old life back. But that had gone now, hadn't it? I visualized air fizzing helplessly out of a punctured balloon. Whoosh! Gone!

Stepping on to the train, squashing myself into a writhing mass of sweaty commuters, I held my breath. For the first time in a long time, I felt completely unravelled. I couldn't do a thing about it. It was terrifying.

Chapter Four

It's quite likely that you'll peter out, you know, after a
few hours slogging away.

The I Hate to Housekeep Book,
Peg Bracken, 1962

In my head, I didn't travel by tube with my nose wedged in a
stranger's unwashed armpit. I cycled into work, a wicker
basket attached to the front of my classic Raleigh. In my head,
I was painting the walls of my new flat in Lovelace Avenue
chilli-pepper red, while Simon was restoring an antique chair
we'd found in a skip. I wasn't standing outside my office, a
majestic building in St James's, in tears.

I looked up at the familiar red flag suspended above the
entrance and forced myself to go in. I racked my brains for
lingering glances or hushed conversations I must have missed
between Simon and Hanna. There must have been clues. But
I hadn't paid attention, had I? I couldn't believe I hadn't even
got a whiff of the affair going on under my nose. I should have

taken more notice of the acid churning I'd had in my gut. I'd thought it was excitement, anticipation. But perhaps it had been a warning.

I absent-mindedly flashed my credit card to the uniformed guard. He nodded and smiled. I'd made mistakes I must never make again. Now I knew: never take your eye off the ball. Never take your eye off your man's balls. Never trust a soul. Not even your own, because your instincts can be way off.

Pushing open the door to my office, I saw that my colleagues were in already, noses to the grindstone, gritting their teeth. I resisted the temptation to run in the opposite direction and lose myself in the hubbub of Londoners outside. I fixed a smile on my lips.

'Meeting, Juliet,' said Philip before I'd even put my bag down. 'When you're ready?'

'Coming,' I said, shoving it on my chair and whipping off my cardigan. 'Just let me get my notebook.'

Whenever I talk about my job to my friends, they 'ooh' and 'aah' in envy. I work for Rosendale's auction house, at their headquarters, as a press officer in the Popular Culture department, which features iconic twentieth- and twenty-first-century items from film, rock 'n' roll, celebrity and entertainment. Madonna's conical bras, nude shots of Kate Moss, John Lennon's songbooks and diamond necklaces belonging to 1940s Hollywood stars were all in a day's work. It was a good job, yes, but dealing with demanding journalists all day could be exhausting. Ten minutes couldn't pass without one of the press office team covertly gesturing the 'wanker' sign while on the telephone to a journalist. At the moment we were working on the 'Celebrity Sale of the Century', an auction being held in aid of the Terrence Higgins Trust. The items Rosendale's had up for sale were mind-blowing – the entire estate of pin-up Bettie Page, clothes from Jimi Hendrix's wardrobe and, the icing on the cake, newly discovered items belonging to Marilyn Monroe. It was my job to drum up interest in the press about the auction. Not that I'd have to do much drumming – the British press adored Marilyn.

'Are you all right, Juliet?' Philip said. 'Your eyes look red.'

Philip was my boss, the Director of Communications. He was handsome in a way that made him difficult to look at. Most people's cheeks coloured when they met him for the first time. He had wavy hair the colour of hazelnuts, bold blue eyes that drank you in when you looked into them, and a plum-dipped voice rich and deep enough to present on Radio 4. His favourite word was 'fantastic', even when things definitely weren't. He looked like a man who sailed a yacht at the week-end, with one hand on the rudder, the other wrapped round a cocktail. But he was actually a father of three and a notorious flirt. Rumour had it that his penis was pierced, but I didn't buy it. He wasn't the type.

'Oh yes,' I said. 'Fine. Tired. I've been moving house – burning the candle at both ends. I need an early night. Tired, yes. Sorry.'

My bottom lip trembled, so I bit it and forced a smile. There was no way I could cry in this office: these people didn't do tears in public. They did stress management, back-slapping and teeth whitening, hilarious anecdotes and big, sweeping hand gestures. Tears were reserved for the psychiatrist's couch, or the locked cubicles in the Ladies'.

'Too many late nights,' I continued. 'That's all. I'll buy some eye drops. Optrex are pretty good, aren't they?'

I felt my colleagues' eyes on me. It was awful. I should have just told the truth. I should have stood on the desk and made an announcement: Simon slept with my friend while I was selecting luxury bedlinen from Graham and Green, and I think I'm going to shrivel and die – ta-dah!

Philip stood there for a long moment, then filled a plastic cup from the water cooler and handed it to me. He shook his head sadly and put a hand on my shoulder. It was the first time he'd ever touched me. I thought, Philip's hand is so hot my blood is boiling. I wondered if he was transmitting some kind of message.

'The schmuck that made you feel like this deserves pay-back,' he said, then lifted his fists into the air like a boxer. 'If you want me to sort him out, I will.'

I forced the corners of my mouth up into a smile. Tears stung my eyes. I felt as if I was dissolving under his gaze. For a split second I thought, Is Philip flirting with me?

'Come on, let's go in,' he said, signalling towards his office with a jerk of his head. 'There's something we need to discuss.'

In Philip's office, I sat on the squeaky leather chair opposite him and smoothed down my dress. Philip's aftershave – lemon and bergamot – filled my nostrils. I knew it was Givenchy, because the office had clubbed together and bought him a bottle for his birthday. I glanced up at the gold-framed photographs of his angelic blonde children on the walls, beaming down on us like the cast of *Swiss Family Robinson*.

'I'll get to the point,' Philip said, snapping the lid on and off his fountain pen. 'I'm worried about you.'

I gulped. Philip was worried about me? For one dreadful moment I thought I was going to get the sack. Was it true that IT read all employees' personal emails? I thought about all the messages I'd sent to my friends, all the loved-up emails to Simon in recent months. God, there were some embarrassing ones in there. If so, I might as well go and flush my head down the toilet right now.

'Wh – why?' I asked, forcing a smile on to my face. 'Is there a problem with my work? You know I love my job, but perhaps I've been distracted lately with moving house and everything—'

Philip exhaled and let out a low laugh, like a horse blowing out air.

'On the contrary,' he said. 'You are a brilliant press officer. What I meant was that I'm worried you're not challenged enough in your daily tasks. Ellen seems to cream off the best jobs for herself, leaving you with the more boring cold calling, press releases et cetera. Personally I can't bear boredom!'

He pulled a face and waited for me to respond. It was true, Ellen did get the exciting stuff, like going out for long lunches with journalists, attending photo shoots or organizing launches around Rosendale's sales, while, on a bad day, I could probably boil my job description down to 'envelope stuffer'.

'Me neither!' I said, matching his exclamation, though I felt like lying on the floor and staying there. 'What I mean is, I'm not bored, but yes, I would like to do more. Any challenges you think I could take on, throw them my way!'

Philip stood up and walked to the window of his office, where he looked out at the city.

'I knew it,' he said, before turning to face me. 'Ellen's taking the tastiest cuts for herself. But luckily for you, I have the perfect project for you to stick your teeth into. Channel 4 want to make a behind-the-scenes documentary on Rosendale's Charity Sale of the Century. A producer is coming in to meet me later in the week, but I know they want a Rosendale's representative to help present the programme. I immediately thought of you: young, fresh, dynamic, attractive. You would be perfect.'

I heard the words 'present' and 'dynamic' at the same time as returning to a memory of Simon leaving the flat last night. I'd completely zoned out, but Philip was looking at me expectantly, his eyebrows almost disappearing into his hairline. I realized I was meant to be looking excited.

'Fantastic!' I said, forcing a grin on to my face, then, as an image of Hanna and Simon naked in bed suddenly flashed into my mind, I felt an overwhelming need to be sick.

'Do you mind if I – ' I said, standing up. Then, pointing to the door, I clamped my hand over my mouth and darted out of Philip's office and into the Ladies' toilet.

Thankfully, no one else was in there. I just reached the toilet in time to retch and sob. After a minute, I washed my face and drank water from the tap. I told myself to get a grip. When I came back to my desk, Philip was locked in his office, talking to someone on the phone. I sent Philip an apologetic email, telling him how much I'd love to be involved (even though I wasn't absolutely sure what I was signing myself up for), then messaged Imogen.

Simon's jumped ship. Everything we've ever said about
Hanna is true. She is irresistible to all men, even mine.
Can you meet tonight?

She replied in seconds.

I am flabbergasted. I'm so, so sorry. 6pm, usual place?

After the longest day in history, I walked to our 'usual' place,
a small vodka bar in Old Street. Imogen and I had spent many
nights there getting accidentally drunk, dancing together like
mad things on the tiny dance floor. I was early, so hooked my
bag over a bar stool and ordered a vanilla vodka and ginger
ale. I felt horribly self-conscious, but forced myself into
smiling at the barman, who I'd seen here before.

'For medicinal purposes,' he said, placing a shot-glass of
clear liquid next to my tumbler of vodka and ginger.

'Oh no,' I said, half smiling. 'Is it that obvious?'

'You look like I feel,' he said. 'Which is shite.'

I smiled wanly, drank the tequila shot down in one and
scanned the room: there was only one other man afflicted
with sitting alone. He glanced up at me and gave me a sly grin.
I glared at him and picked up a beer mat, pretending to be
engrossed in its shamrock design. I reminded myself to bring
a book next time; something uninterruptable – perhaps
Tolstoy or a dictionary.

'Juliet?' said Imogen from behind me. 'You look so sad.'

In her blue and white polka-dot dress and high heels, she

was an Edward Hopper creation. Her hair was poppy-red and her eyes big brown buttons. She was gorgeously curvy and alluringly pale, as if she was made out of fondant icing. She held out her arms, hugged me and asked the barman for two of the best cocktails he knew. I pulled out a stool for Imogen and told her everything.

'Simon was unbelievably bad for you,' she said earnestly, jet-black earrings in the shape of lightning bolts swinging as she spoke. 'He was two-dimensional, self-obsessed, unromantic, and has proved to be a typical bloke whose brain is in his pants. Honestly, Juliet, you are so, so, so much better off without him. You're funny and warm and lovely. You don't realize it yet, but one day you'll be relieved that you're not with him.'

'I don't know,' I said, sighing. 'I feel so betrayed and . . . humiliated by them both. And our flat, what am I going to do about that? This has been my goal, to get somewhere decent to live with Simon. This was "The Beginning", and he's let me down. It's a massive nightmare. I can't believe I let myself get into this situation. I should have known this would happen.'

I fished for a tissue from my bag. I was on my second packet of tissues in twelve hours.

'Oh, Juliet, they've treated you like crap,' she said. 'But they're going to feel terrible now. How will they live with themselves? Simon is such a loser to do this. I'd like to twist his balls off. And you – I swear you'll be OK in time. Men will swarm, bees to honey, when you're ready for them. You know, you could have anyone in here.'

I looked at the men standing nearest to us: a spotty, balding suit, a fat, white-haired man who looked like a pillow with the feathers coming out, and a gay couple gyrating to the music.

'Why aren't I excited by that prospect?' I asked Imogen.

'OK, OK,' she said, following my gaze. 'But compared with Simon, these men might be saints. Plus, he was quite boring. He kept his receipts, didn't he? That says it all, if you ask me.'

'He only kept them to make sure he wasn't being ripped off,' I started. 'But I know what you're saying.'

'He's the most boring man on earth,' she said resolutely.

I listened and nodded and drank more vanilla vodka and ginger ale and wondered why she had waited until now to tell me how awful Simon was. Already it was happening, that thing that good friends do – the mantra they chant in the face of heartbreak. I'd done it myself many times. I was grateful to her. I loved Imogen – she was an unapologetic person, unlike *me*, who apologized profusely when people bumped into me. 'Sorry' was my default setting.

'Sorry, Imogen,' I said. 'I've sat here ranting on about Simon as if there's nothing else going on in the world. I want to know how you are. How are your wedding preparations going? Not long now!'

I tried to inject excitement into my voice, but Imogen's face clouded over. I thought I saw fear in her eyes. She emptied her glass and ordered another.

'Don't worry about that now,' she said, dismissively. 'Juliet, I want you to know there's no one to touch you. Look at you – you're the catch of the century. You're the coolest girl I know, and letting you go is the biggest mistake Simon will ever make.'

She made me sound like I was his employee.

'Could I make an official complaint against him?' I asked.

I drank far too much, burst into tears (again!) on a Japanese man having a smoke outside the bar, then forgot where I lived. Imogen had to phone Simon for the address of our new flat so she could take me there and put me to bed with a bucket and a towel next to my head. Before I passed into oblivion, I noticed my grandmother's hardback book, its gold-edged pages jutting out from one of the packing boxes: *Homemaking Hints for a Happier Home*. I hauled it out and put it on the bed, then wept a few more tears into my pillow.

I was the coolest girl.

Chapter Five

When embarking on your domestic tasks, always do so
on a relatively full stomach, otherwise you will become
lethargic, irritable and tempted to do absolutely nothing.

Homemaking Hints for a Happier Home, 1959

'Eating a spoonful of Marmite is supposed to work, as long as
you hold your nose,' Imogen said when I called her the next
morning, suffering with the Worst Hangover Ever. 'Or rehy-
dration salts, or something so hot and spicy it makes you cry.'

Lying in bed, I stared up at the ceiling, waiting for the spots
in front of my eyes to swim away.

'I'm already crying,' I whimpered. 'I think maybe I'll just
wait here in bed until I die. Why did I drink so much?'

With my free hand I lifted up the edge of the curtain near
the bed and squinted in the morning sunlight.

'Because that bastard Simon let you down,' she said.
'Every heartbroken person goes out and gets pissed. It's part
of the healing process. But you need to eat now. We didn't

even have any peanuts last night. Haven't you got to go to work?'

I let the curtain fall and slowly rolled over on to my front, hiccupping alcohol. I buried my head in the pillow and remembered Philip's new-found enthusiasm about my participation in the press office. I couldn't disappoint him on day one.

'Yes,' I said. 'I'll have to go in, otherwise it'll look really bad and I'll probably lose my job as well as my boyfriend. I'll make myself a sandwich or something. Thanks, Imogen, for getting me home last night.'

Cautiously, I lifted myself up into a sitting position, where I stared at my grandmother Violet's book, taunting me from the bottom of the bed. Forget about *Hints for a Happier Home*, I needed *Hints for Hangover Hell*.

'Remember,' Imogen said. 'Eat something hot. I swear it works for me. Speak to you later, OK? You're going to be fine soon.'

We hung up and I staggered through to the kitchen, climbing over packing boxes and great bundles of bubblewrap. Sweating pure alcohol, I leaned up against the sideboard, drank a big glass of water, then made myself the hottest sandwich I could with some dubious ingredients I'd brought over from the Greenwich house: pickled chillies, horseradish sauce, mustard and a sprinkling of tabasco. I ate it quickly, feeling water – or tears – streaming out of my eyes and nose, the back of my throat burning. I was crying now, but I couldn't blame the sandwich. I blamed Simon. If everything had gone to plan, we'd be experiencing the heavenly early days of cohabiting, feeding each other chocolate mousse or playfully throwing cushions at one another or lying on the bed together holding hands and talking about the future.

'Get to work,' I told myself, checking my watch. I knew that if I carried on with normal living routines, like getting dressed and eating and going to work, I would be at less risk of going under and turning into a completely crazy person.

With a few dodgy moments on the tube, when I felt my face turning a grapey shade of green, I managed to get to work. I bought two giant BLT sandwiches from Pret A Manger, a ham and cheese croissant, a large cup of coffee, orange juice, crisps and a slice of fudge cake, all fuel in the fight against feeling horrific. At least, feeling this bad, I had to focus all my concentration on not passing out, so couldn't think of Simon and Hanna quite so clearly.

'Philip tells me he's given you a project to work on,' Ellen said when I reached my desk.

'I can't believe I actually got here,' I said, amazed.

'You want a medal?' Ellen said, frowning. 'So, what's the project about, then?'

Ellen was so thin and spiky I suspected she was just a bundle of sewing pins under her clothes. I was not in the mood for her, or anyone, today. I wondered how quickly she'd fall to the floor if I flicked her with a tea-towel. I looked around for one, but alas, no tea-towels.

'Channel 4,' I said, sinking into my chair. 'Behind-the-scenes documentary or something.'

Ellen turned her nose up and sniffed, hopefully in disapproval at the documentary and not at the whiff of alcohol emanating from my pores.

'That sounds hopelessly vague and I doubt it will ever

happen,' she said, turning her attention to my Pret bag. 'What's all this food for? There's a zillion calories in there. Do you have an eating disorder?'

I shook my head and, as she walked away, opened up one of the BLT sandwiches, shoving it into my mouth.

'No,' I muttered. 'But you have a personality disorder.'

For most of that morning, I ploughed through my food mountain and stared blankly at my computer screen, rereading old emails from Simon or Hanna, looking for clues and finding nothing. How could they have both been so calculated about keeping their affair secret? If it had been the other way around, there's no way I wouldn't have confessed in an emotional outburst. But Simon and Hanna – they'd given away absolutely nothing. What else were people I loved hiding from me? I shuddered. The world was a dangerous place.

'Juliet,' Philip said from behind me just after lunch. 'I have Dylan from Channel 4 here, waiting in my office. Could you come in?'

I turned to face Philip, quickly licking my teeth, hoping I didn't have food stuck in between them, and pulled an anxious face.

'Don't worry,' Philip said with a wolfish grin. 'There's two of us and one of him.'

I stood up and on wobbly, exhausted, hung-over legs, trailed him into his office, where Dylan, the TV guy, sat. He stared at me, an astonished expression on his face.

'Hello . . .' I said, reaching out to shake Dylan's hand. Then I stopped because he was suppressing a laugh.

'Oh dear,' he said in a soft, Scottish accent, staring at my face. 'You and me both.'

Just like mine, Dylan's face was completely covered in freckles. Self-consciously, I lifted my hands to my cheeks.

'I used to put lemon juice on mine to bleach them away when I was a kid,' he said. 'Didn't work, and anyway, my mother told me they were angel kisses, so I quit the lemon juice.'

In spite of my mood, I smiled.

'It's actually very fashionable to have a sprinkling of freckles this season, according to *Vogue*,' I said with a quick smile. 'At least you don't have this curse as well.'

I pointed to the hedge of curls on my head. My girlfriends envied my ringlets, but I'd previously forked out hundreds of pounds in Vidal Sassoon getting them straightened.

Philip cleared his throat and poured glasses of water for all of us.

'How can *Vogue* say freckles are "in"?' Philip said, smiling his broad, cool smile that made me think of icebergs. 'You either have them or you don't, surely? Anyway, let's make a start, shall we? Fantastic.'

As Dylan began to talk about the behind-the-scenes documentary he wanted to make in the run-up to the Sale of the Century at Rosendale's, I stole another look at him. His hair, flopping forward as he reached for a pen from his bag, was longish and almost black, apart from a tiny snowy patch at the back near his ear, as if a white feather had landed there. His eyes were orangey hazel, his eyebrows straight and dark. He had a strong nose, full dark pink lips, and a dimple on the left side of his mouth, but not on the right. From the fine lines around his eyes, I guessed he was around my age – a couple of years older, perhaps. He was interestingly attractive. No doubt he had a Hanna lookalike clinging to his ankles.

'So you'll be happy to be on TV, Juliet?' Philip asked, grinning at me. 'I know I would be grateful to you, and you are the most obvious media star among us. You have the face for it.'

I swallowed hard. A face for TV? I couldn't think of anything my face was less suitable for right now, with its propensity to crease into tears at any moment. What had I signed myself up for?

'I'm no Davina McCall,' I said. 'Or that woman on *The Antiques Roadshow*. Fiona Bruce, is it? I've never actually stood in front of a camera before, and I blush easily—'

Philip coughed. He was frowning at me, widening his eyes and shaking his head almost indecipherably. Not for the first time, I wished I'd phoned in sick. Sensing my discomfort, Dylan stepped in. He pushed up the sleeves of his checked shirt, revealing freckly forearms.

'I can understand your hesitation,' he said. 'But by the sounds of things, you'd be perfect in front of the camera, really you would. I'd rather use a Rosendale's employee because you'll know what you're talking about.'

Would I? I still wasn't sure exactly what anyone was talking about, but both men were staring at me intently. I didn't really care about it at all. I just wanted to escape from that office as fast as I could and get back to my food, so I nodded enthusiastically.

'Is that a yes?' Dylan said.

My eyes flicked up to meet his, and I realized again how unusually attractive he was. He smiled what seemed to me to be a rather smug smile. I glared at him – arrogant pig.

'Yes,' I said, forcing brightness.

Dylan lifted his finger and pointed to his teeth while looking at me, indicating I had something stuck in mine.

'Lettuce?' he said. 'We'll have to watch out for that when we film.'

Philip and Dylan laughed heartily as I scraped the lettuce from my teeth. I blushed furiously and glared at Philip. Two of us, huh? I felt like a ballerina getting a bad lift from her partner: lifted to a great height on centre-stage, then dropped like a sack of dead meat. Boys – they were all the same. Lifted you up only to dump you down so low you were slam-dunking into a deep dark pit. What was the point of bothering with them? I vowed never to go near one, ever again, for as long as I lived.

Chapter Six

Curtains are to a house, what a dress is to a woman.

Sure & Simple Homemaking,
Jill Blake, 1975

When my dad died, I feared I would be punished for his death. I thought I'd go to prison or to hell or be struck down by a bolt of lightning if anyone found out the truth. To alleviate my awful guilt, I worked harder than ever before to endear myself to people. I became a passionate Brownie, earning badges from agility to crime prevention. In the playground I gave away Cola Cubes to anyone who happened upon me. I danced fervently round the maypole and put extra tinned peaches in Harvest Festival gift boxes. At the weekends, I did housework for Violet or scoured her craft books for home-made gift ideas: bags of peppermint creams, papier mâché jugs, hand-sewn tea cosies, jewellery made from shells and ribbons. The old people in our village were my main benefi-ciaries and had me pinned as their home-grown creative wunderkind. I was extra generous to them – they would be next to go to Heaven and could tell my dad I was trying really hard to be a good person.

When, years later, I moved to London, I realized that craft, my childhood pastime and therapy of sorts, was hip. I joined an alternative craft group in Brixton called the Home Help Group, which I was still going to, where girls got together and mainlined on gorgeous fabric, trimmings and buttons. As with many revivalist activities in London, it was all done with an ironic smile, though I secretly took it all very seriously. I loved it.

The first project we worked on was 'cloth beanbag animals' made from Liberty print fabric. It took me three long weeks to make mine, but when I excitedly took my creation home to give to Simon, a token of my devotion, he put down his dumb-bells, stared at me as if I was an alien, and laughed so hard I saw his tonsils.

'Is this a joke?' he spluttered, holding it up to the light. 'Is it supposed to be road-kill? It's like something a nine year old would make!'

He threw back his head, closed his eyes and guffawed. I stared at him and said nothing.

'Oh my God, I can't stop laughing,' he wheezed, resting his hands on his knees to catch his breath. 'So – oh, I can't breathe – seriously, Juliet, what is this thing?'

I picked up my green beanbag creation and held him close to my chest. I fingered the black eyes made out of tiny beads.

'A frog,' I said. 'It's a frog.'

'No shit,' he said. 'That's a frog?'

As Simon cracked up again, I burned with angry

embarrassment. But rather than tell him how angry I felt, how furious I was, I said nothing at all. I laughed as if I didn't care, then hid in the bathroom and cried into a flannel. I know he saw the disappointment and humiliation in my eyes. He drank it in, like a pint of water. It's strange, but I know he felt refreshed.

I remembered that hateful feeling now, when, two weeks after he'd gone, I was standing in my living room dialling Simon's number for the millionth time. Though I detested myself for it, I ran through a pathetic excuse for a message in my mind, before it clicked on to his stating-the-bloody-obvious voicemail; 'I'm not able to take your call right now. Leave a message!'

'We need to talk about the rent for this flat,' I said angrily. 'And will you pick up the phone for once?'

Clutching my mobile, I flopped down on to the sofa and sighed. I'd hoped that I'd be feeling stronger than this. I'd done all the dreary things people do when they're unhappy. I'd refused to eat. I'd had a pedicure. Turned up drunk at Simon's parents' house in the middle of the night to confront him (he wasn't in!), written him lengthy emails asking, *Why?* Bought a ridiculous yellow prom dress from Topshop that I'd never wear, high heels and expensive face cream from Selfridges.

At Rosendale's I'd pretended I was coping fine. I had been preparing for the days of filming Dylan wanted to do and was grateful for the distraction. Every night I missed Simon and was only able to sleep after a generous squirt of Bach's Rescue Remedy. Now it was the weekend again and the days stretched out like a runway, with no aeroplane to board. I phoned his number again, running through another message in my head.

'Oh, Simon,' I said. 'Would it kill you to ring me back?'

I threw the phone at the wall and looked around the flat. God, the flat! Far from the idyllic home for Simon and me I'd planned, inspired by cuttings from *Country Living* magazine, it was hell. Boxes stood waiting to be unpacked, the walls were bare, the windows curtainless. I heard Violet's voice in my head: 'Juliet, your windows are naked! What message are you giving the world?'

In no way was it the home I'd dreamed of. I'd been here two weeks and hadn't even bought milk. Without Simon, my yearnings to fill the air with the smell of baking had evaporated. I hadn't even bothered putting a chair in the kitchen – I was making do with a box we'd packed the glassware into. The place was in chaos.

I picked up a photograph of Simon and me taken last Christmas, him hugging me close to his chest. My yellow paper hat had slipped over my eyes and he had gold tinsel draped round his neck. I leaned it up against a wine bottle on the living-room table. I stood back and stared at us. Tears welled in my eyes. Yes, we were different personalities, but I had loved him. His serious face made me melt – even his obsession with exercise was endearing. I'd wanted to build a future with Simon, to love him. But now I realized that wasn't enough. He wanted someone I could never be.

'There are plenty more fish in the sea,' Philip had said at work. 'It's a cliché, but it's absolutely true. That's why it's a cliché, because it's true.'

I'd rolled my eyes. It was a stupid saying. Yes, there might be more fish, but what if the next one you caught was a piranha or a man-eating shark? I knew Philip was right, though, if horribly unoriginal. There was only one thing for me to do – get over Simon and move on.

Ripping the packing tape from a box I hadn't yet touched, I peered in and spotted the casket holding my grandmother Violet's ashes, wrapped up in foam. I lifted it out, peeled off the foam and rested it on the table next to the photograph. I thought back to her funeral last May. Simon had been supportive, helping me choose her burial outfit for the undertaker (I had to choose everything, right down to her stockings) and gripping my hand as we walked through the crematorium. Thinking of that softened my heart towards him. I picked up my phone from the floor and dialled his number for a third time that morning.

'Er, Simon,' I said shakily. 'Oh, I've been thinking about . . . Actually forget that, it's nothing, nothing at all.'

I shook my head in disbelief and ran my hands though my curls. My forehead was clammy with the deranged anxiety of the recently dumped. I put Violet's ashes on a shelf and noticed the pile of patterns that had slipped out of her homemaking book before Simon left.

I picked them up from the floor, laid them on the table and smoothed them out with my palm. There were *Vogue* patterns for sweetheart aprons, cushion covers, headscarves and tea-cosies, all retro, Forties and Fifties style. I picked up an apron pattern and looked at the diagram. The waist was cinched in with pleats, the top heart-shaped with heart-shaped pockets and a wonderful frilly tie at the back, with a headscarf to match.

I remembered her making them as Christmas presents for favoured customers. Maybe I should make one? Now that I had all this free time on my hands, I needed new projects – to distract me from phoning Simon or spooning peanut butter into my mouth, if nothing else. With her *Homemaking Hints for a Happier Home* book under my arm, I found a slice of bread without mould, made buttered toast and climbed back into bed.

I opened the first page of the book to black and white photographs of perfectly groomed smiling women doing their domestic chores. I couldn't decide whether their smiles were through gritted teeth, amphetamine inspired, or genuinely terrifically happy. I flicked through the pages and thought of Violet. She had loved this book, with its advice on candle wax removal and how to look after your husband's shoes. She had grown up in an era when dusting your toaster and making pounds of jam were of utmost importance. A time before the women's libbers took a match to their lingerie drawer and made it acceptable for us girls to lie in bed all day doing nothing. There was something comforting about the book – it fitted perfectly with my desire to have a homely home, though I felt mildly guilty for reading it. I'd been educated to think homemaking was a betrayal of feminism, but I didn't understand how sneering at women who chose to work at home, whether at childrearing or homemaking, was in keeping with the concept of sisterhood. Shouldn't women support each other's choices, whatever they might be? I didn't get much further with that thought because there was a knock at the door.

'Who's there?' I said nervously.

'Juliet?' called Simon's voice from the corridor. 'I need to talk.'

I jolted upright, shocked at how much just the sound of his voice could make me feel. My stomach filled with cement.

'Shit . . . oh no,' I said. I wiped the toast crumbs off my chest and reached for my Afro comb. Then I stopped. Why should I brush my hair? It had taken Simon an entire fortnight to come here. What did that say about how much he cared?

'Juliet?' Simon called again now. I put the comb down.

And in those difficult days, Simon hadn't called, emailed or made any attempt whatsoever to contact me. Every time the reception buzzer had sounded at work, I'd convinced myself it would be him, clutching a bouquet of sweet peas by way of apology. But despite my expectant gaze and crossed fingers, it was always the courier.

'Only me,' the courier had started saying through the intercom after days of seeing the disappointment on my face. He'd even given me a consolatory Wagon Wheel.

'Please, Juliet?' Simon said again. 'Open the door.'

I didn't reply. I looked at my reflection in the mirror leaning against the fireplace and saw a blotchy red face staring back. I'd cried a lot of tears in these two weeks, and the skin round my eyes was pomegranate pink. I had no make-up on, my hair was scraped high into a ponytail with a fluorescent yellow band, and I was wearing an M&S teddy-bear dressing gown I'd been given for Christmas one hundred years ago. On the floor were a plate of half-eaten dry crackers, various socks and a couple of empty wine bottles. My clothes were in a voluminous heap on the bedroom floor, my books in leaning towers against the wall. And what about the kitchen? An environmental health hazard. He couldn't see me like this. Sweeping down a mahogany spiral staircase in my Topshop prom dress, lit by the light of a crystal chandelier, perhaps. But not like this.

'Juliet,' he said. 'I know you're in there. Let me in.'

I heard him flip up the letterbox. To keep out of his eyeline, I lay flat on the carpet, like a soldier on the floor of the jungle.

'You have to see me one day,' he said.

'Do I?' I mumbled.

'I heard that,' he said. 'And yes, you do.'

This was typical Simon. He loved to give out instructions. He'd probably order me to do ten star-jumps next.

'No,' I said. 'I don't.'

Then I listened to his big footsteps clomp down the stairs, out into Lovelace Avenue and get lost in London. I thought: clomping footsteps – the sound of my sorrow. Oh, stop, I told myself. I was tiring of being miserable. I stayed on the floor for a while longer, just in case he came back to have the last word. I was still clutching Violet's book and I thought back to when I was fourteen and flicking through it one Sunday, while she polished the brass candlesticks. It was raining in torrents and I had been bored stiff.

'Why do you bother with all this?' I had asked, snapping the book shut and gesturing towards the brass. 'It's so boring. Haven't you got anything better to do?'

Violet had opened her mouth to speak then closed it again. Her face had turned a shade paler behind her make-up. Then she had cried into the cloth she was holding, her shoulders heaving up and down. I had never seen her cry.

'I'm sorry,' I said quietly, feeling like the meanest person ever to have existed. 'Let me help you,' I said, hovering near her chair.

Violet said nothing, only passed me another cloth, and we sat there together rubbing the brass, the rain beating against the windows, until it shone like sunshine. After that I always made sure to remark upon the brass, the dust-free corners, the rugs, the immaculate curtains, the polished floor.

Now, after pouring myself a vodka (I'd give it up soon), I opened the kitchen window. The early summer sun was hot and bright, the air was thick with roses, sweet, like caramel, with a bitter twist of car exhaust. I listened to planes zoom overhead, sirens blare and the neighbour's children shouting in the garden. I drank. Then there was another knock at the door.

'Juliet,' Simon said. 'I know you're in there and I know you won't let me in because you're probably wearing your teddy-bear dressing gown. But I have to tell you this. Come on, you've phoned me ten million times, haven't you? You must want to see me!'

The vodka made me brave.

'I'm all ears, Simon,' I said, taking another gulp of my drink. 'And I'm wearing fishnet stockings and high heels, thank you very much.'

Simon laughed gently. That familiar, lovely sound was enough to make me put my hand on the door handle. I very nearly opened it.

'I can't tell you while I'm standing out here on the stairs,' he said quietly. 'But Juliet, there's something you should know. Something important. Please.'

I tightened the belt on my dressing gown, pulled the yellow bobble from my hair, dragged the comb through my curls (I know), and swallowed the last of my drink. I glanced around the flat – an abomination. I took a deep breath and unbolted the door.

Chapter Seven

Of course this depends on one's particular lifestyle, but it would seem that most of us spend close to 50% of our at-home working hours in the kitchen. In her lifetime the average homemaker will wash and dry more than 1,500,000 pieces of silverware, dishes, pots and pans.

Ladies' Home Journal Art of Homemaking,
Virginia T. Habeeb, 1973

Imogen screamed at the top of her lungs. Heart thumping, I darted into the living room to find her standing on my blue leather armchair. She was jabbing her finger at an Office shoebox filled with photographs in the middle of the floor.

'Mouse!' she screeched. 'Behind there!'

'Are you positive?' I said, jumping up beside her. 'Where?'

We watched the box for a few moments, half expecting it to get up and walk away. Nothing happened.

'It was enormous!' she said, demonstrating a foot-long mouse with her hands. 'It went into that box.'

'Oh, hell,' I said. 'What will I do?'

It was Sunday morning, the day after Simon had called with his 'news'. Imogen had arrived with a box of fat strawberries, a pot of cream and a bottle of champagne. Standing at the door, holding out her offering, face flushed from the sun, red hair ablaze, red shoes to match, she looked uncommonly beautiful. I felt horribly pale in comparison and self-consciously covered the patches of eczema on my wrists. The skin on my arms has always acted as an emotional barometer. When I'm happy, my wrists are porcelain. When I'm stressed out, they are bright-red itchy weals. I smiled a weak smile and ushered her in. Her perfume, a lovely Jo Malone fragrance, filled my nostrils.

'You get the glasses,' she said, gesturing to the champagne. 'We need to sort you out.'

And while I was in the kitchen, to pick glasses out of the debris, she saw the foot-long mouse.

'You'll have to get a man in,' she said. 'One of those mousebuster people.'

'Oh God,' I said. 'Then I'll be finding little mouse corpses everywhere.'

We both pulled a face. This kind of thing, just like the unpacked flat-pack IKEA furniture, still unmade, was something Simon would have dealt with. I hated the fact that I felt so useless without him and vowed to change. The least I could do was learn to wire a plug. I'd never admit it to any other living creature, but I seriously didn't know how.

'I'll do it myself,' I said. 'I'll find every little hole in the flat and block them with corks.'

Imogen gave me an admiring glance. She stepped down

from the sofa and sat down, curling her legs up beside her. Picking up Violet's homemaking book, she pulled a face.

'You obviously haven't been reading this,' she said lightly.

'I have, actually,' I smiled. 'Did you know you get candle wax off a tabletop with lighter fluid? Granny knows best!'

Still staring at the carpet, scanning for mice, she ignored me and patted the cushion next to her. I sat down.

'Listen, Juliet, I think it's time you emerged from under your rock here where you're living with the mouse family and reading those grandma books,' she said. 'I think you should do something, like have a housewarming party. It'll give you something to focus on. You've got to stop moping.'

I knew she was horrified at the state of the flat but was too good a friend to say so. I opened the box of strawberries, offered her one and ate one myself. I stood up and pulled open the blind. Sunshine gleamed through the window and fell in stripes across the room. I winced at the light.

'It's only been a few days,' I said. 'I thought you said it takes half the length of your relationship to get over an ex? So I've got two years to go.'

'Did I say that?' she said, frowning. 'Sounds like bollocks to me. I know it's really hard, but you're not allowed to think about Simon any more. You've got to have a party and celebrate your single status.'

'I can't, Imogen, look at me!' I said, gesturing to the flat, then at my dressing gown and slipper socks, as though they were chains. 'My flat is a pit . . .'

I choked on tears before I finished my sentence and slumped back on to the sofa.

'It's just so . . . quiet here now,' I sighed. 'I know you think

I'm strong, and I am strong, I've always had to be, but I really let myself get hung up on this fantasy of having a home with the man I loved. How could I have been so stupid? I knew that I was taking a risk.'

Imogen shook her head and held my hand.

'You wanted it to be right and you gave him a chance but he failed you,' Imogen said calmly. 'It didn't work out, but that's not to say you'll never have a successful relationship again. You probably have another sixty years on the planet and there are a lot of other people out there, you know. Men and women whose paths you haven't yet crossed and probably won't cross if you don't ever leave your flat. It's time to move on and kick-start the next phase of your life. You can't let Simon finish you off.'

'Yes,' I said. 'I know you're right. But I honestly thought we loved each other, you know. Properly loved each other . . .'

My sentence dissolved. My internal cynic clucked. I took a deep breath and smiled, apologetically, at Imogen.

'Think about it rationally,' she said. 'How can someone who hurt you so badly be your soul mate? He wasn't right for you, full stop. Let me get you a drink.'

Imogen tiptoed through the boxes, then banged around in the kitchen, muttering to herself while stacking plates crusty with takeaway in the dishwasher. Something smashed and she swore. She was right. If he could do something so blatantly insensitive, how could he be right for me? I was going to have to harden my heart to Simon, I knew that, but it wasn't easy.

Imogen appeared at the door of the living room holding up a brown mixing bowl of congealed white lumps. A wooden spoon stuck out of it like a spade in a sandpit.

'Are you growing something?' she asked, half smiling.

'I tried to bake a fruit cake,' I said. 'But halfway through I realized I had no sugar or fruit. I meant to throw it out but I couldn't find the bin bags. I've turned into a slob, haven't I? You must be getting fed up with me. I'll get back on track, I promise.'

'OK, my alarm bells are ringing,' Imogen said. 'Should you really be doing that with your evenings when you have London on your doorstep? I wouldn't waste the flour, personally.'

She picked up a black dustbin sack and threw the mixing bowl and spoon into it.

'Saves washing up!' she said, brushing her hands together then handing me a cup of champagne. 'Of course I'm not fed up with you. Drink this, brush your hair and put your lipstick on, then we'll slag off that bastard-face, Simon, and bitch-face, Hanna, and email out invitations.'

I stood there biting my lip and murmured my protest. But Imogen didn't listen. She knew me too well to listen. I loved her for that. Dipping into my bag, Imogen sifted through God-knows-what and eventually found my lipstick. She handed it to me, and for the first time in days I applied a smidgen.

'Better?' she asked. I nodded a small nod.

'So, your party,' she said. 'Think of it as a divorce party – that's what they do in the States.'

'A divorce party?' I said, cringeing. 'That's miserable.'

'No,' Imogen said, smiling radiantly. 'It's the start of something new. One door closing and another opening. Oh, and Juliet, I want to ask you something about my ridiculous wedding. There's only ten weeks to go . . .'

She screwed up her face, disgruntled. Imogen was engaged

to marry her boyfriend of nine years, Jonathan, an account-
ant, who I secretly disliked. I tried hard to like him, for
Imogen's sake, I really did. She said he was admirably ambitious, hilariously funny and generous-hearted. But I didn't
see any of that. What did I see? I saw that he was clumsy with
Imogen's heart – he just didn't seem to 'get' her. And he had
unnerving eyes, like little black holes you could put your fingers through and there'd be nothing there but soil. Since I'd
known Imogen they'd continually broken up and got back
together. As far as I could tell, they barely saw one another.
He was often away on business and Imogen worked late most
days. And now, the bride-to-be, she glazed over whenever she
started talking about marriage. The one time we'd been shopping for wedding dresses, we'd ended up in a traditional
Greek restaurant in Soho getting wildly drunk on ouzo. I
smiled at the memory of Imogen standing on a table, her skirt
hitched up, hurling plates at the floor and flirting with the
waiters.

'I still haven't bought a dress,' Imogen said, folding her
arms. 'My mother wants me in a meringue, Jonathan's mother
wants veil and train, and—'

'What do *you* want?' I interjected. 'You know it's what you
want that matters.'

Imogen sighed and threw her hands up in the air.

'I want to go on holiday with you, lie on a beach and cleanse
my mind of weddings,' she said. 'But if you'll help me, we
could go to that awful bridal shop in Piccadilly and get it over
and done with.'

I smiled. 'Of course I will, but you don't sound very
enthusiastic,' I said. 'Are you having second thoughts?'

Imogen sighed deeply, tipped her head back and looked at the ceiling.

'No,' she said unconvincingly. 'I think I'm just worn out from work. I work like a slave! I have this new boss, Cath. She's an amazing woman, but she makes me work late. That's why we need a party – you have to have a party. Cheer us all up.'

I didn't want Imogen to marry a man she didn't love, but I'd hinted at it so many times, I felt I couldn't say any more to her without being blatantly rude. She had once confided in me that their sex life was disastrous, but whenever I mentioned it subsequently, she went quiet on me. Besides, what did I know about relationships? An image of yesterday, when I unbolted the door and let Simon back into the flat, washed over me. For a moment it was almost as if nothing bad had happened between us. Right out of the blue we'd had sex on the sofa and he'd told me how much he loved me and that he was sorry. Then he'd leapt up, pulled up his trousers so hard it must have hurt, and said, 'I can't do this.'

'You already have,' I said, in answer to which he'd burst into tears and left without telling me what he came to say.

'What do you say?' Imogen said now.

I looked at her, glowing in my living room like a lovely, expensive lamp. She clearly wanted to think about something other than her wedding. I also knew she really wanted to cheer me up. It would make her feel better if I felt better. I took a deep breath.

'You're right,' I grinned. 'We need a party.'

Imogen's face shone. She jumped up and down on the spot with her fists tightly clenched. Her happiness was dazzling.

She was my best friend. I wanted her to shine. I jumped up and down too.

After Imogen left, I panicked. There was still a quarter of the weekend to get through. On impulse, I decided to make an apron up from one of Violet's patterns. It couldn't be difficult – I remembered her making them in no time at all. I located my sewing machine and dug out an easy *Vogue* pattern for a gorgeous heart-shaped apron with frills all over it – the sort that would cost a fortune in those kitsch boutiques in Covent Garden – and a matching headscarf. I rummaged around in boxes and found a polka-dot print I could use, plus some ribbons I'd had for years, and made a start. As I worked, cutting the fabric on the grain, pinning and sewing seams, I thought about Imogen. Had I any right to tell her I thought Jonathan was wrong for her? I just didn't buy them getting married. But what could I say without being openly offensive?

As I concentrated on making my apron, hours sloped by. I drank coffee after coffee laced with vanilla syrup and lost myself in the whirr of my sewing machine. When I was done, I held it up against myself in front of the mirror and pulled on the headscarf. It was surprisingly good, though the coffee had given me a red face, a fluttery heart and demonic eyes.

Just then, the phone rang and I jumped, still attached to my apron. I thought it might be Imogen, having detected my doubt and needing to share hers. But it was Simon. My heart did a handbrake turn in my chest. My stomach turned over.

'What are you doing?' he said.

'Making an apron,' I said. 'What are you doing?'

'An apron?' he said with a small laugh. 'Jesus, Juliet, what's got into you? Are you insane?'

He said 'insane' so dramatically that for a moment I wondered if I was.

'What did you phone me for?' I said, annoyed. 'To harass me?'

'We need to meet,' he said, edgy and impatient like he'd also gone OTT on caffeine. In spite of myself, I warmed at the prospect of seeing him again.

'Do we, Simon?' I said. 'Is this your way of saying sorry? I hope an apology is in the offing? The least I deserve is an apology, please.'

Offing? Did I really say that? He ignored my comment and told me to meet him at the café in Hyde Park.

'I just want to tell you what I wanted to tell you yesterday,' he said. 'Before you took all your clothes off.'

I thought I heard amusement in his voice. What a git.

'In an hour?' I said challengingly. 'I'll be there.'

I put down the phone and fretted. My heart raced noisily in my chest.

I chose to wear a red dress and red sandals and left the flat and locked the door before I had an opportunity to change my mind or decide I needed a haircut or to floss. Walking quickly towards the train, I worried. What was Simon going to say exactly? Was he going to tell me how he lunged at Hanna? Why I wasn't good enough for him any more? That he had got bored of us? I sat on the train with my eyes closed, trying to calm down. It was impossible, so I opened my eyes and stared at the woman opposite instead. Reading the news in the *Observer*, she looked reassuringly miserable.

At Hyde Park, I saw Simon sitting on a white plastic chair outside the bustling café before he saw me. The way he sat, leaning forward with his hands together, looking at the floor as if in prayer, made me suddenly sad. My heart ached for him for a moment and I was reminded anew of what we'd just lost, because we had both lost something. Not just me, nor just him. I was standing there, staring, when he looked up and waved. It was an odd wave, like the way you summon a waiter. I bought myself a coffee, sat opposite him and waited. I was shaking like a leaf, but I didn't want him to see how nervous I was. Be calm, I told myself.

'I thought we should meet on neutral territory,' he said as if we were heads of state discussing nuclear weaponry.

'Hello, Simon,' I said awkwardly, as if he was someone I didn't know. I noticed he was wearing a blue jumper I'd never seen him wear before. Had he been flexing his credit card in FCUK while I was turning grey with misery?

'So,' he said sadly. 'How's the apron?'

I snorted.

'Insane!' I said, not liking the tone of my voice. 'What sort of question is that anyway, Simon? Are you wearing a new jumper?'

'What kind of question is that?' he barked. 'Yes, it is new. French Connection.'

'I knew it,' I said, as if I'd somehow scored a point.

He ran his hands through his hair. I wished he wouldn't. Normally I would run my hands through his hair. He used to like it when I did that – massaging his temples and scalp. I wondered who he was, really. If I'd ever really known him. Suddenly I felt numb, like I didn't care any more.

'Want a ride on one of the swans?' I said, deadpan, pointing at the queue of children waiting near the Serpentine. We both looked over at the pedalo swans and I swear we had the same thought: swans are monogamous creatures and mate for life. We'd said it to each other before in romantic strolls through this park, when I thought we were 'for always'. Now the swans were alien. The Queen was welcome to them, roasted and served up with sprouts.

'Juliet,' he sighed. 'I might as well come right out and say it.'

He looked at me with an expression that said he wanted me to understand that this was extremely painful for him. I nodded and raised my eyebrows. Surely, this was going to be the apology I'd been waiting for? I remembered the way he'd kissed me on the sofa only yesterday, gripping my shoulders hard as if I were a rope ladder on the side of a burning building. I stared at him, waiting for him to speak, for what felt like eternity. Even now he made me wait for his words.

'It's about Hanna,' he started. And before he went any further I noticed that poking out from just under his sleeve was the red and green friendship bracelet Hanna had always worn on her ankle. Was he wearing that the other day? My stomach did a somersault. My scalp started to tighten, my throat constricted. He might as well have stuck a butcher's knife straight into my heart and twisted it round and round.

'Hanna and I,' he repeated meekly. 'We're probably getting together. I'm sorry, Juliet, you're a wonderful girl and I know this hurts, but I'm the kind of guy who has to keep moving. I'm too young to settle down for good. When you said that thing about the second bedroom being the perfect size for a nursery, I just freaked out.'

'But we agreed you'd have your rowing machine in there,' I said pathetically. 'I just said it without think—'

'I'm sorry,' he interrupted. 'It's been a tough decision.'

It's been a tough decision. Like I'd failed a job interview. I scrabbled in my mind for something to say. How had he managed to turn it round like this?

He looked up at me to see how and where his words had landed. Anger flashed into my eyes like cherries on a fruit machine. I remembered the way he had held me on the sofa – like he genuinely cared. I couldn't find any words, so impulsively I picked up his glass of orange juice and threw it into his face. Childish, perhaps, but I have to admit it felt bloody good. As Simon spluttered and coughed and wiped his precious new jumper with paper napkins, people at the other tables were pointing, whispering.

'Jesus, woman!' he spat. 'Are you mad?'

'Just a little bit, Simon,' I said, my voice croaky. 'I've not even looked at another man since we got together. You've been having another relationship and now you're dumping me! Yes, I'm bloody mad. Furious.'

I was shaking with rage. I'd never felt this angry before. I thought my head would explode with it. And there was my cup on the table, half full of coffee, just calling up at me. I couldn't resist it. With a trembling hand, I threw that at him too. Several women gave me admiring glances, a nod of approval, a flash of a smile. Violet's dark heart beat in my chest.

Chapter Eight

Always have a lot of souvenirs around from far off places, even if you've just sent for them from a mail order house. It will give the impression of being a world traveler who hasn't been home long enough to have thoroughly cleaned the house.

Phyllis Diller's Housekeeping Hints, 1966

'If you're going to have a party,' Aunt Joy said when I went to her flat that evening, 'you've got to do it properly, like we did in the Seventies.'

We were sitting on Joy's balcony, at the back of her Bow flat. After meeting Simon I had gone forlornly home to Lovelace Avenue, but couldn't stay there alone. The flat seemed deafeningly quiet and I saw imperfections that bothered me – cracks in the walls, mildew on the windowpanes, doors leading to depressingly empty rooms. I had lain on the bed, hoping for sleep to take me away from everything, but every time I closed my eyes, I saw you-know-who with you-know-who. I felt so cheated. Eventually I called Violet's sister, my aunt Joy, and told her everything.

'Come over immediately,' she said dramatically. 'Your poor heart.'

It was lazy and extravagant, but I decided to get a cab to Joy's house. I jumped out at the deli near her house and bought a pretty apricot tart and a bottle of rosé, which I had almost polished off on my own. Also with us was Jack, a theatre lighting man Joy had wanted me to meet. I wasn't ready, in any shape or form, for anyone to play Cupid, but Joy was hard to refuse. Besides, his being there stopped me thinking about my terrible afternoon with Simon quite as much as had I been at home. I was learning the power of distraction.

'We used to throw our car or house keys into a bowl on the table back then,' Joy laughed, before breaking into a hacking cough. 'And whoever's set we picked up, we'd get naked with. I once drove all the way from London to Rochester in the nude with some rampant Italian chap. It was such a scream.'

She took a sip of her drink, a drag on her cigarette and tilted her face up to the sun. Her hair, grey but dyed cherry red, was gathered in combs on the top of her head, and her glasses hung round her neck on a thin silver chain and rested on her white blouse. Her lips, painted orange, matched the scarf thrown over her shoulders. One of her hands rested on the arm of my chair, and occasionally she patted me, making sure I hadn't dissolved into a pool of tears. I thought about the photographs I had of Joy and Violet standing together as children. Anyone could see that she and her sister Violet were cut from the same stone, but the years between them had turned them into very different people. Violet had been a Fifties woman in her twenties, and Joy was a Seventies girl even in the Nineties.

'That sounds better than any party I've been to,' said Jack, smiling at me. 'How about you, Juliet?'

Jack was dark haired and dark skinned but light eyed. He had an open face and little pink lips, like strawberry shoelaces, which he had a habit of biting with his top teeth. His hands, suntanned, were linked together behind his head, which made his chest seem as wide as a motorway.

'I get excited about going to parties,' I said, pleased to be having a normal conversation. 'But most of the time I stand there thinking I should be enjoying myself more than I am, or worrying about being left on my own with no one to talk to. Or already remembering it in anecdotes, like it's the next day and I'm telling someone about it. Do you know what I mean?'

Jack nodded and rubbed his stubble. I felt like that about a lot of life. Even here, on Joy's balcony, I was aware that one day I'd look back at this day and remember it quite differently from how it actually was. I tried to take an accurate mental snapshot.

'You remind me of Violet,' Joy said. 'She could never enjoy the moment for what it was. She analysed everything to death. Lighten up, Juliet. You're young and beautiful and one day you'll look back at yourself as you are now and wish you'd enjoyed being young and beautiful more! Take it from me. I know.'

Jack murmured his agreement and offered me a bowl of olives. He told me that he was a 'what if' man. 'Whatever decision I make, I agonize over what I didn't do. I'm a "what if the grass is greener" man.'

Joy spat out her olive stone into her hand. 'Sometimes it is so much greener,' she said. 'That's what I've learned.' She looked at me. 'Oh, I'm sorry, Juliet,' she said. 'I wasn't talking about Simon and Hanna . . .'

'That's OK,' I said bravely. 'I know you didn't mean that.'

We shared a sorry smile and Jack, oblivious, launched into a story about his childhood on a dairy farm in Sussex. He told us his best friend was a cow. 'So was my flatmate,' I said. Jack asked me about my job, and as I spoke I felt him watching me: not just my mouth but every bit of me. I tried to ignore him and poured all of us another drink. I put my feet up on a pot of pink geraniums. I looked up at the sky: eggshell blue, clear and vast. If it wasn't for the sounds of London around us, we could have been anywhere in the world under that beautiful sky. I half expected Pegasus to fly across the clouds.

'Isn't anyone going to ask about my new play?' Joy asked, pulling a sulky face. 'You know how much I love to talk about myself.'

I forgot to mention how much Joy likes the sound of her own voice. Perhaps, as an actor, it's a prerequisite. And fortunately for Joy, she was fascinating. Now, she made us laugh with stories about the first night of *Antony and Cleopatra* at Shakespeare's Globe. She was a natural actress – even then it seemed as if she was practising a role. As I lost myself in Joy's world, I realized I had forgotten Simon momentarily and was enjoying myself.

'Your life is like a novel,' I said to Joy.

'I hope there will be a steamy sequel,' she said. Jack winked at me. I stared into the bottom of my glass.

Later, after we'd finished two bottles of wine, Joy asked me to go inside and help her prepare some baguettes. Jack stayed on the balcony, smoking. He stood and stared out, like a lighthouse keeper.

In Joy's kitchen I studied the room: it was full of clutter, just like the rest of her flat, which felt more like a curiosity shop than a house. She didn't share her sister Violet's obsession with housewifery at all. One of the rooms, a box room, was so full of junk you couldn't even open the door. Stuck on the walls were pictures of all her actor friends, reviews cut out from newspapers and autographed programmes. Hanging up high were copper pots and pans, and the surfaces were peppered with jars of marinated treats. Her lampshade was a metal strip trimmed with dangling knives, forks and spoons. It was a kitchen with no rules or regulations. A place where butter, or shy people, wouldn't last long. I breathed in. The kitchen smelled of spice and was reassuringly homely. Joy opened a jar of sun-dried tomatoes and arranged them on a flowery plate with chorizo, two slices of which she folded in half and tucked in her mouth.

'You know your mum's coming over next month?' she said lightly. 'Has she been in touch?'

I folded my arms over my chest. The air between us was suddenly awkward. The thought of Ava coming back from Kenya to see me made me feel sick with dread.

'Yes,' I said dully.

Joy looked up at me and frowned.

'You're not looking forward to it much, then?' she asked.

I exhaled loudly.

'Not much, no,' I said. 'I see her once a year and every time we meet we end up having a silent stand-off. You know what it's like. There's too much to say, so we say nothing.'

Previously, Joy and Ava had gone for years without speaking. They'd had some falling-out I didn't know the details of, but now that they'd made up, Joy wanted us all to play happy families. I couldn't do that. My relationship with my mother was pretty much a lost cause. I sniffed to signal I didn't approve. Joy held her hands up in the air.

'I'm not interfering,' she said, 'but you two should really make it up. If you don't, you will definitely regret it. Take it from me, I know. The years will just slip by, and before you know it, it'll be too late to do anything about it.'

I hated this topic of conversation more than anything else. I never knew what to say, I never knew how to feel; I just didn't want to talk about it. It was easier that way – to ignore it. Joy looked up at my sullen face and smiled sympathetically. Watching her as she concentrated on unwrapping cheeses, I suddenly remembered the photograph of baby Rosie with half a letter from Ava.

'Oh, I meant to ask,' I said. 'I found this page of a letter Ava wrote to Violet from Sydney, the year my dad died, with a picture of a baby girl called Rosie. It's been bugging me a bit. Do you know who Rosie is?'

Joy's body stiffened, and for a second she looked taken aback. The muscles in her face seemed to flicker. She looked at me with a mixture of irritation and anxiety, I thought. With the cheese knife in her hand, she shook her head.

'No, no . . .' she said. 'I haven't got a clue. Perhaps it was a friend of hers or something. She went to stay with friends in Sydney, didn't she?'

'Yes, I think so,' I said. 'I don't know. Maybe I can ask her when we meet up next month.'

I poured myself a glass of water and gulped it down. Joy's face paled for a moment, then she rocked up on to her tiptoes to open the kitchen window, carefully moving a line of old-fashioned miniature medicine bottles, and flapped a leaflet in front of her face, like a fan.

'Jack brought this,' she said, handing me an inch of Camembert. 'What do you think?'

I let the cheese melt in my mouth. I was relieved to be talking about cheese.

'Lovely,' I said. 'And Jack is extremely handsome.'

'As boyfriend material?' she said. I swallowed the cheese. Jack was attractive, only a little bit older than me. He had strong-looking arms and a lovely northern accent. I imagined him in my bed, whispering into my ear, his hands on my back – perhaps he was just the tonic I needed. Perhaps he could help me forget Simon.

'Isn't it a bit soon?' I whispered, leaning in towards her. 'After Simon, I mean?'

Joy jerked her head up from the chopping board and looked at me, astonished.

'I mean boyfriend material for me!' she said, slapping her hand down on the worktop. 'I'm sleeping with him, Juliet!'

We laughed so hard I nearly burst a lung. Jack popped his

head around the kitchen door. I could smell the cigarette smoke on him.

'The party is always in the kitchen,' he said, resting his hands on Joy's hips and kissing her neck. 'That's where the pretty girls always are.'

Joy's eyelids fluttered when he nibbled her right ear. Her skin bloomed pink. She wasn't acting now, only being herself. She took his hand in hers and grinned at me. Suddenly I experienced that age-old adage, 'three's a crowd'. I checked my watch. It was nearly midnight.

'I think it's time I left you two lovebirds alone, before I turn into a pumpkin or gooseberry or something,' I said. 'I'll get a cab.'

'You'll have a replacement lovebird again all too soon,' Joy said, kissing me goodbye. 'Leave it up to Fate. Trust me, it's destiny, it's written in the stars.'

I smiled and laughed, but felt flat as the Fens. I had never taken much notice of 'Fate' or 'Destiny' – believing in them was a way out of taking responsibility, wasn't it? I said goodbye and walked outside to hail a passing cab. London's sky was dark purple now. I stared up at the sky. I peeled my eyes for coming stars – to see what was written. But just as I'd thought, I could see nothing at all. There was only space. Empty black space.

Chapter Nine

Make the evening his: Never complain if he goes out all
night, does not take you out to dinner or to other places
of entertainment; instead, try to understand his world
of strain and pressure, his need to relax.

Housekeeping Monthly, May 1955

'Just the girl I need,' said a soft Scottish accent from beside my
desk.

I turned to face Dylan, who was smiling a big, one-sided,
dimpled smile. This was the first time I'd seen him up close
since the meeting with Philip. I knew he'd been in to
Rosendale's a couple of times already to film shots of the
sales rooms in South Kensington, but he hadn't yet needed
me. I quickly scanned his face: cheekbones as sharp as knives,
orangey brown eyes, and that dash of white in his black hair,
like a dollop of paint.

'House hunting?' he asked, tilting his chin at my computer
screen. 'I like that one. Georgian, is it?'

'Oh, no, I . . .' I started, quickly locating a Word document on my desktop to click in an attempt to cover the property website I was on, where I was searching for Violet's cottage (I couldn't get over it being 'For Sale'). But my Word document was a half-written rant to Simon, typed in a seemingly monster-like font.

'I'm researching,' I said resolutely, standing up to block out my computer instead. 'Right, what did you want to do first?'

He yawned, apologized and rubbed his eyes. He appeared more pasty and dishevelled than I'd remembered, as if he'd been out all night running with the pack, probably in some trendy Hoxton club.

'Anywhere I can get coffee before we start?' he asked. 'I think I need a double shot. I don't feel my normal mercurial self today.'

Mercurial? So Dylan had a brain, too. Interesting.

'Downstairs and along King Street a couple of metres,' I said. 'There's a Caffè Nero.'

'What can I get you?' he asked. 'I'll be two minutes, maybe three.'

He was smiling again – a knockout smile. I just had to smile in return.

'Skinny cappuccino,' I said. 'Thank you.'

I'd never ordered a skinny cappuccino in my life. I loved coffee, but I liked it doused with vanilla syrup, or chocolate and full-cream milk, and I never had it after three p.m. because the caffeine kept me up all night. The office manager, Lisa, who I sat next to, frowned at me, but I shook my head and shrugged. Clearly Dylan made me desperately nervous. I sighed – I knew it was going to be hard to behave normally around him.

When Dylan returned, carefully carrying a tray with two very full cups of coffee on, like a cake with burning candles, we drank them (sipped, in my case) before we moved to one of the showrooms, where the items for the Rosendale's Charity Sale of the Century were currently being stored.

'OK,' said Dylan. 'I've got two hours before I have to go. Can we film Max Carle's gnome art and then Bono's hand-written lyrics, please? Perhaps if you could introduce them and talk about how much they expect to go for? Then we'll move on to Marilyn's effects.'

Max Carle's conceptual art was expected to collect thousands in the auction. I watched Dylan's eyes sweep over rows of garden gnomes that had been remodelled by Max, an emerging pop artist from Glasgow, to be representative of Britain's 'undesirables'. One was holding a knife and a broken bottle, another was half-naked and peeing up a wall, and another was a skinhead 'giving the finger'.

'I don't think much of this,' he said, picking up a gnome with a demonic expression and a razor in his hand. 'Rather a cynical view of society, don't you think?'

'I think it's quite clever,' I said.

'I see,' he said, with fake sincerity. 'Are you into all of this, then?'

'Some of it,' I said. 'Conceptual art is in the eye of the beholder, isn't it? Someone might pay a fortune for those gnomes, another might not pay a penny. I like to think about the motivation of the artist. What drove Max Carle to make that? Black humour? Frustration? Anger? He's come up against great criticism. People have complained it's in bad taste, but I think anything that makes people think is good, don't you?'

'Hmm,' said Dylan. 'I'm not so sure I need disfigured garden gnomes to make me understand society's dark side. It's pretty obvious when you pick up a newspaper. Personally, I think it's too easy to be cynical in art and literature. It's the same with music. How many songwriters release miserable dirges? Too many. This is some cool guy who thinks he's making a comment on society, but I think it's pretty cheap.'

'Then we'll have to agree to disagree,' I said succinctly.

This was a debate I got into in the pub, with pissed people who thought that, as I worked for Rosendale's, I could answer for the entire arts world. Dylan chuckled and began unpacking his camera equipment.

'So, what are you like, then?' he said, adjusting the lighting in the room. 'Apart from being smart? What are you really like?'

That was the kind of question I asked myself in the dead of the night and didn't know the answer to. I blushed.

'What do you mean?' I said, letting my hands fall to my hips with a slap. 'I'm like this, I suppose.'

Dylan shook his head.

'I'm not sure,' he said. 'That first meeting we had with Philip. You were utterly distracted, staring into the distance, arms folded, big, sad eyes, slightly vague . . .'

Dylan was looking at me so intently, I wondered if he could see straight through me: right through to my heart booming in my chest. I suddenly had the weird sensation that I could tell him anything and he wouldn't judge.

'Come on,' he said. 'Make this job more interesting for me. It can be so laborious, filming the same item fifteen times with a silent press officer in tow. Plus this is my last job in Britain for a few months. I want to remember it.'

He yawned again and I felt annoyed. Was he just pretending to be interested? I decided to ignore him.

'Last job in Britain?' I said. 'Where are you going?'

'California,' he said. 'To make a documentary about my one passion in life – surfing.'

I shuddered. I hated the sea with every bone in my body.

'You're coming back though, aren't you?' I found myself asking.

'I guess so,' he said, pushing his hair behind his ear. 'Obligations at home. Though my studio flat is hardly a place I'd call home. It's barely big enough for me and my surf-board – I'm not joking.'

I frowned. Dylan living in a tiny studio flat didn't fit with my impression or assumption of him. Other TV directors and producers I knew earned over seventy thousand a year and lived in slick loft conversions in Islington.

'So, back to you,' he said. 'What's this place like to work for? Are there horrendous office politics, even here? I hate office politics, they make me want to curl up and die. Is that why you were so distracted in that meeting with Philip?'

I sat down on a hard-backed chair and wrapped my arms around my waist. I was horrified to feel tears welling up in my eyes. I swallowed hard to stop them, dug my nails into my palms, but I couldn't hold them in.

'No, I'm having – ' I stopped and gulped. The tears were coming now, sliding silently over my cheeks and neck, slick like oil. I couldn't make them stop.

Dylan walked over to me, handed me a tissue, put his arm

over my shoulder for a moment then took it away. He smelt lovely, of warm summer days, cut grass and tree bark.

'Shit,' he said. 'That wasn't meant to happen. I'm so sorry if I've upset you. I thought you were going to tell me your boss was an idiot. I shouldn't have said anything, I'm sorry.'

I wiped my eyes and sniffed. I was burning with embarrassment and shame.

'No, no,' I said, hiccupping with emotion. 'It's just I . . . I've been . . . I split with my boyfriend . . . and I'm trying really hard to . . . I don't want to think about him any more. It was such a shock . . . I don't want to talk about . . . I'm supposed to be having this party, but . . . oh . . . God, how embarrassing . . . I'll be fine, just give me a minute.'

Dylan gave me a quick hug. I recovered myself and sighed, puffing out my cheeks. I felt ludicrous.

'The guy's a prize idiot,' he said kindly. 'I'm terrible for the foot in mouth thing. I'll shut up. Why don't we go and get a drink afterwards? A glass of ale always makes me feel better.'

'A drink?' I said. 'With a strange man who just made me cry on a garden gnome's head?'

'Blame the gnome,' he said, with a winning smile.

After I'd composed myself and apologized ten million times, I showed Dylan the lot expected to raise the most money: Marilyn Monroe's vanity case. The items inside the case – a diamond necklace, a silver silk dress, a silver pair of shoes, a compact mirror, a fountain pen and a journal – were so valuable they were kept in a locked, alarmed cabinet night and day. I had to wear gloves to handle them while a bored-looking security guard waited at the door, probably longing for a heist. Having Marilyn Monroe's vanity case was the scoop of the year – a previous auction of her effects in New York in 1999 had raised thirteen million dollars, and had set a world auction record of $1,267,500 for the dress she wore to sing 'Happy Birthday' to President John F. Kennedy at Madison Square Garden, New York, in 1962. This case had appeared out of the blue, donated by April Flaxman, an old friend of Marilyn's and now a hotel owner in Cornwall. April was also happy to be interviewed by Dylan, which would make his documentary much more interesting.

'You're a natural in front of the camera,' Dylan said after he'd filmed me listing Marilyn's lot. 'Ever thought of being a TV presenter?'

'No way,' I said. 'I couldn't think of anything worse than being watched by millions of people. Imagine the viewers, sitting in their living rooms, only opening their mouths to slag off your hair or dress or talk about how fat you are. Awful!'

'I wouldn't like it either,' he said. 'I prefer anonymity, and anyway, I hate watching TV programmes.'

'That makes no sense,' I said. 'That's what you do for a living.'

'Yes, I know,' he said. 'But in my job I'm always watching and never actually doing. I'm a parasite. What I really want to do is surf, especially on a hot day like this. I could spend my entire life on the beach. There is nothing more thrilling than the sea.'

I shuddered and felt strangely disappointed. The last time I'd been to the sea, a few years ago on a day trip to Brighton with Hanna, I'd only gone in as far as my knees when I'd had a panic attack, gulping for air like a beached fish.

'Pub then?' he said. It was four-thirty.

I imagined my colleagues' critical eyes on me as I picked up my bag.

'Um, I'm not sure . . .' I wavered.

'You can pretend I'm interviewing you,' he said. 'In fact I will interview you – you make an interesting subject. Please come.'

'What if I've got plans?' I said.

Dylan gave me one of those smiles and I couldn't help smiling back.

'I know the perfect place,' he said. 'I'll grab us a cab.'

'You've twisted my arm,' I said.

'Step into the world of Gaston Berlemont, Francis Bacon and the Bernard Brothers,' he said, opening the door of the French House on Dean Street, Soho. 'My favourite watering hole.'

I'd seen this place from the outside but had never actually been in. If this was Dylan's favourite bar, I knew we'd be friends.

'I know that because I read a *Time Out* review,' he said. 'Not because I'm a French House scholar. So, what can I get you? They don't serve beer in pint glasses here, nor is there music or any mobile phones. All part of the charm, don't you think? I'm not a celebrity spotter, but isn't that Prince Edward over there? What would you like? Wine? Beer? Cider?'

I was opening and closing my mouth like a fish because Dylan hadn't stopped talking. My eyes flicked around the bar, a small, intimate, old-fashioned space decorated with fabulous black and white photographs. Drinkers, an eccentric collection of young and old arty types, leaned up against the bar, knee-deep in conversation. A woman with bright red lipstick and a Wrens-style dress was serving.

'I feel like we've stepped on to a 1940s film set,' I told Dylan. 'Yes, cider sounds great.'

While Dylan ordered, I found a tiny wooden table for us to sit at. Behind me the wall was half mirrored and half covered in old newspaper cuttings. He placed a glass in front of me and I thanked him.

'Cheers,' Dylan said, clinking glasses with mine.

'Cheers,' I said.

'No,' he said. 'You didn't do it right. You have to clink glasses and look me in the eye at the same time, otherwise it doesn't count. Again? You know, in the olden days, alcohol was thought to have bad spirits in it. People clinked glasses to get rid of the spirits, so let's clink to getting rid of that bloke of yours.'

I lifted my glass.

'Good idea,' I said. 'Cheers.'

I looked him in the eye and we swapped smiles. I instructed myself not to blush.

'So, are you okay then?' Dylan asked. 'I know how shit heartbreak is. You can't sleep or eat or concentrate. It's the pits.'

I nodded and wondered what kind of woman had broken Dylan's heart. A beauty, I bet. 'I'll be all right,' I said, trying and failing to sound strong. 'I'll have to be.'

There was a few seconds' silence before I spoke again.

'Do you have a girlfriend?' I asked, surprising myself as well as him.

'Er...' he said, slightly taken aback. 'Well, actually, yes. I have an on–off relationship with this French girl, Sylvie. She picks me up and drops me like a hot potato, depending on who else is around.'

He shrugged and tucked his hair behind his ears.

'Meaning what other blokes are around?' I interrupted. He shook his head.

'Women,' he said. 'She refuses to commit. She likes being "free" herself, just so long as I'm available when she wants me. But if I so much as look at another girl, she freaks out and wants us to be a proper item again. She's impossible to have a relationship with. Very fiery and irrational. But she's French and gorgeous, so hard to resist!'

He laughed darkly and narrowed his eyes.

'I'm a sucker for long legs, a sexy accent and a wild streak,' he continued, looking at me. 'She surprises me, you know? There's nothing dull about her. Plus she loves the surf too, lets me go off all over the world for weeks on end without whining. Other girls have hated that I'd rather be in the sea on a Sunday than lying in bed eating croissants and dissecting our relationship. When I'm away working, she sees other people, I know she does, but it kind of suits us both for the time being.'

He chewed a fingernail and looked down at his shoes, red Converse All Stars that looked about a hundred years old.

'Kind of suits you both?' I said. 'For the time being?'

Dylan screwed up his face and widened his eyes.

'Am I working on the wrong programme?' he said jokily. 'Is this *Trisha* and not Rosendale's at all?'

'Sorry,' I laughed. 'I'm just intrigued. I feel like I know you or something. Maybe it's the freckles. Maybe we're long-lost relations.'

Dylan pulled a face.

'I hope not,' he said. 'That would be too weird. I would like to think we—'

His sentence was interrupted by the shrill bell of his mobile phone. He whipped it from his pocket and pointed to the door, which he walked out of – mobile phones were strictly forbidden in the French House. He returned about thirty seconds later.

'Fucking hell, I'm an idiot,' he said nonsensically, pulling on his jacket. 'I'm really sorry, but I've got to go.'

I looked at the almost full drinks on the table.

'You haven't finished your drink,' I started. 'Didn't you say you wanted to get some food . . .'

But when I looked up again, I just caught sight of the heel of a red Converse going out of the door. He was gone.

I sat still for a few moments, blazing with irritation that he'd just left me like that. Weren't we in the middle of a conversation? Hadn't I been mid-sentence? Now I wouldn't even have the chance to tell him I was pissed off. Who wanted to be left in a bar by a bloke ten minutes after he'd invited you in? Had Sylvie demanded he come home? Probably.

Already I was forming a picture of Sylvie in my mind – a raven-haired tempestuous beauty throwing onions at Dylan's head. I imagined them in the world's wildest oceans, surfing the waves, and shuddered. The thought of Dylan's passionate private life with his French goddess left me feeling oddly deflated and as plain as a sliced white loaf.

An old sensation swept into my heart. It was a mixture of homesickness, anxiety and fear. I took a deep breath and instructed myself to be brave. I fumbled in my bag for my copy of *Country Living* (a guilty pleasure), read an article about transforming an old door into a nearly new headboard (where do you find old doors?), and drank the rest of my cider, pretending I did this sort of thing all the time. I thought: I must look as if I don't need anyone or anything. If I pretend to be cool and tough, I'll begin to believe it. Then, as I left the bar, a middle-aged man bumped into me, tipping half a glass of red wine down my dress.

'Oh, I'm so sorry,' I said, though it wasn't my fault at all. I blushed wildly and felt tears spring into my eyes.

Out in the street, I sighed an enormous sigh. Cool and tough? Who was I kidding?

Chapter Ten

The best way not to entertain any kind of household
pest is to avoid inviting them in the first place.

Ladies' Home Journal Art of Homemaking,
Virginia T. Habeeb, 1973

It was the day of the housewarming/divorce party. I had
hardly slept. Heaving myself out of bed, I groaned. After getting back home from work at about ten o'clock the previous
evening, I'd spent the night staring at the long shadows on the
ceiling, wondering how I could cancel the party. I had drawn
a complete blank. It was tonight and I hadn't done a thing in
preparation except squirt floor cleaner on the bathroom tiles
and then accidentally knock my head on the sink so hard that
I felt faint.

My flat resembled a junk yard. Somewhere in the depths of
my befuddled mind, I'd imagined turning the rooms into
homely posits of shabby chic before the party. I'd have bright
cushions on the sofa, maybe a throw slung casually over its

back, pretty but cheap crockery bought from charity shops and used as bowls for nibbles, bouquets of dried herbs hung up in the kitchen, or at the very least a mirror or two put up in the living room to give a better sense of space. But what had I done? Nothing. In the one evening I'd had free, I'd made another of Violet's aprons out of two metres of Alexander Henry butterfly-print fabric I'd found in Oxfam for £5. I'd made a headscarf to match, and both had turned out surprisingly well. I'd put them both on and looked comfortingly retro. But the living room was now covered in threads and scraps of material. And every time I'd tried to tidy, I'd made no progress whatsoever. I'd pick something up and put it down somewhere else, only filling up another surface.

I made a mental list of what I needed to do: buy party food, plenty of booze, iron my dress, select music. Splashing my face with water and brushing my teeth – the sink needed cleaning too – I had a strange feeling of doom. Was I ready to have all my friends in my flat? I'd invited everyone I knew to ensure it was busy – my closest friends at work and the rest. I'd even mentioned it to Philip, but I don't think he'd even heard. There was nothing worse than a half empty party. But was I really ready to pretend I was over Simon and open my inner sanctum up to scrutiny? If your home is an expression of self, my guests would have me down as a 1950s lunatic.

Opening the blind in the bedroom, sunlight poured in, exposing dust *everywhere*. Did I even own a feather duster? It was tough, but I had to try to be positive. Forty, possibly more, people would be here later. The thought made me feel slightly hysterical. I had to make an effort. It was all down to me now. Me alone.

Unpacking a small box in the bedroom, I quickly sifted through old photographs, utility bills, biros, old make-up (why had I kept a tube of virtually empty Maybelline mascara?) and a handful of cockleshells Simon and I had collected on a day trip to Brighton. Feeling ruthless, I threw them all into the dustbin. I flicked through the photographs and stopped at one of Dad and me taken on a snow-covered hill. Sun made the snow gleam impossibly white. Our faces were lit with smiles. I held it still and stared. Dad was always there, woven into the fabric of my thoughts, but when I saw a picture like this, the memory of his death shocked me all over again. In the picture I was grinning, looking at Dad, who was laughing hard, with one leg out at a strange angle as if he had fallen over while running towards me. I stared at it for a long while, letting the familiar ache of guilt slide over me, then propped it up against my bedside lamp. I had no memory of that day, but knew that now I'd seen the picture, it would become as real as if I did remember. Death was like that. Dad had become a collection of photographs and everything real, like the astonishing depth of his voice, or the worry beads he carried in his pocket, or the gentlemanly manners he cared so much about, had faded. My palms sweated as I remembered the day he'd drowned. I thought of him at the bottom of the sea, swallowing litres of saltwater until the saltwater swallowed him.

'Don't think about that now,' I told myself. 'Not today.'

I sighed and wiped my eyes with the back of my hand. I had to be strong. No more tears, no more emotional outbursts, no more gloom.

'Right,' I said, flinching at the sound of my own voice. I hadn't got used to talking to myself yet. 'Get on with it.'

I caught the bus to the high street and bought rainbow Chinese lanterns from a local Chinese supermarket. From the florist I bought bunches of poppies, and from a smiling shop assistant at the Non-Stop Party Shop (could there be a better place to work?) a disco-ball. I spent a small fortune in the deli on skewered chicken, flatbreads, Moroccan pepper dips and falafel. I bought champagne and rose syrup to make rose cocktails from the recipe in Violet's *Hints for a Happier Home* book that had been written on a scrap of paper in peacock blue ink. She'd added: *These are fabulous, try them* along the top.

After staggering home, nearly cutting off the circulation in my hands with heavy plastic carrier bags, I did the best tidy-up job I could manage and arranged the flowers in water jugs. I studied the recipe and made the cocktails: mix 1 teaspoon of rose liqueur with 4 dessertspoons of rose syrup, pour 1 teaspoon of this into the bottom of each champagne flute, open a bottle of champagne and fill the flutes, then decorate each one with a fresh rose petal. I tasted one and smiled – Violet was right, they were fantastic. Cocktail in hand, I tried on ten dresses, then chose to wear a black and white polka-dot dress that I hoped made me look carefree, not miserable and heart-broken. I drank quickly to quell my nerves and felt slightly bleak. What I really wanted to do was curl into a ball, sit in the wardrobe and wait for morning.

Then, just before seven o'clock, something happened. I'm not sure what made me do this right before the party, but I picked up Violet's book, *Homemaking Hints for a Happier Home*, and fanned open the pages. Among various magazine cuttings and patterns slotted into the leaves, I think I must have had a sixth sense that I would find the missing page of Ava's letter hidden inside, all folded up. When I did, I unfolded it and sat on my bed, leaning up against the pillows. I picked up the first page with the photograph of baby Rosie from my bedside table and read both pages.

Dear Mum,

Enclosed is a picture of Rosie. I hope you will keep this photograph safe for me – it is the only one I have. I know you do not approve, but I firmly believe it is the right thing to put Rosie up for adoption. Getting pregnant with Stephen was a terrible accident, a mistake that proved too much for some to bear, I know that. I have to live with that knowledge for the rest of my life. But at least now I am trying to do the right thing. This way, with new parents, Rosie will have a chance, just as Juliet now has a chance at a normal life, living with you. I don't expect you to understand me, or for Joy or Juliet to ever forgive me. Indeed, how can I ever forgive myself for the mess I've caused? All I can say is that it's clear to me I was never meant to be a mother. I don't have what it takes. I have already booked a round-the-world ticket, which I will start using in February. Until then, I'm working in a café in Sydney. If you want to be in touch, write to me at the hostel address above. Please tell Juliet I love her and that it's not her fault.

Ava

My heart pounded and thumped in my chest. Swinging my legs off the bed, I stared at the letter. The airmail paper was thin and the ink was blurred in small drops from what might have been tears. Sweat prickled on my brow and I clenched my jaw. I read the words through again, more slowly, mouthing them. I tried to absorb the meaning. My hands were shaking violently. Did things like this really happen? So Ava had another daughter? I had a half-sister? And my dad knew about her pregnancy? I screwed up the letter and threw it across the room. Standing up now, I paced the bedroom with my hands clasped together. I stared at the scrunched-up ball on the floor, picked it up and smoothed it out, and read it once again.

'My God,' I whispered. 'I cannot believe nobody told me this!'

The doorbell sounded. Rubbing my temples, I felt breathless with panic. I couldn't face anyone now, but I had to. People were coming for a party, for God's sake. I tried to stand and stumbled over in my heels. What kind of fucked-up, detestable person would lie to her own daughter about having another baby? My own mother. And clearly Violet knew too, and possibly Joy. What about me? Why wasn't I allowed in on the secret? My stomach twisted and my eyes stung.

The doorbell sounded again. I gulped back tears. With the letter still in my hand, I walked to the door, took a deep breath and looked through the spy-hole. I saw white-blonde hair. I saw a freckled nose, pierced with a diamond stud. I saw a bunch of sweet peas and a bottle of Gordon's gin. I saw Hanna.

Chapter Eleven

When you entertain, don't hesitate to ask different types of people, because that makes an interesting party. But don't invite people who will be at such odds that it causes real conflict.

Ladies' Home Journal Art of Homemaking,
Virginia T. Habeeb, 1973

'I know what you're thinking,' said Hanna, her voice quivering. 'That I shouldn't be here ... but just give me a minute.'

She moved towards me, holding out the posy of pink and purple sweet peas and the bottle of gin. I leaned against the wall, clutching the letter, feeling unfettered horror. How could Ava have done such a thing? Somewhere out in the world I had a half-sister. We could have looked after each other.

Hanna edged into the flat, eyeing me suspiciously.

'Are you OK, Juliet?' she asked quietly. 'You look as white as a sheet.'

I shook my head and opened my mouth to speak, but nothing came out. I suddenly remembered a photograph of a pale but beautiful Ava holding me as a baby, her hair falling over her shoulders. Had she been completely miserable behind that proud smile?

'I can't believe I've made you feel this bad,' Hanna said. 'I'd heard you were coping brilliantly. That's why I came over. To apologize and to say goodbye. But you're a wreck!'

Hanna was staring at me with huge, concerned eyes. She thought she'd done this to me. I almost laughed.

'Say something, please?' she said. 'Let me get you a drink.'

Hanna shook her white-blonde head and pushed past me into the flat. Ava's words played out in my head. *Tell Juliet I love her and that it's not her fault.*

'Here you go,' said Hanna, handing me a drink. 'Juliet, please speak. I'm sorry.'

As much as I hated Hanna, I could see I was scaring her. I was scaring myself. I had to get a grip. I had to put the letter out of my head. Hanna was here. Hanna, the girl who had stolen my future, was standing inches from me.

'OK,' I mumbled. 'What did you want to say?'

Hanna's shoulders dropped in relief that I wasn't in some kind of heartbroken wordless coma. She arranged herself on the sofa and leant back in the seat, one long brown leg bent under her, the other dangling, her arms stretched out along the back. She reminded me of creeping ivy. Wearing a grey mini pinafore dress and blue Mary Jane shoes, Hanna had dressed up. Normally she wore skinny jeans, a tunic and flip-flops. Beside her, on a small wooden table, red candlesticks burned and dripped into my new heart-shaped candleholders.

She stuck her little finger into the molten wax and didn't flinch an inch. Brazen.

'I'm going back to Sweden for a few weeks,' she said. 'And I want to make peace with you first. It's important we make peace, Juliet.'

She said this loudly, as if it were an order. I opened my mouth to speak, but any speech I had mentally prepared for this situation evaporated. I was consumed entirely by the contents of Ava's letter. I didn't care what Hanna had to say.

'Simon's not coming with me,' Hanna said. 'We're not together. Despite the fact that he threw himself at me again, he's not my type at all, you know? It was all a silly mistake.'

Her eyes flicked up at me and she smiled broadly. I think she thought this statement would bond us, as if I had realized exactly the same thing. Inside I was screaming '*Go away!*', but nothing came out.

'No offence,' she said when I didn't answer. 'Can I get another drink?'

I nodded briefly, but only wanted her to go. I needed to go into the bathroom and plunge my hot face into cold water. I needed to read the letter again. I needed to decide whether to set fire to it or flush it down the toilet. I had to make a plan.

'Gorgeous flat,' she called over her shoulder. 'Did you make this?' She held up my apron.

I nodded.

'Do you still go to that "Home Help" thing you used to go to then?' she asked. 'I was always really jealous that you were good at making things. Remember that frog you made Simon, though? Ha! That was funny.'

I sat on my hands, not knowing how to behave.

'I shouldn't say this,' she said, 'but I kind of miss us all living together. Life doesn't make sense now, especially with none of us speaking to each other any more.'

Sudden anger surged through me. About Simon and Hanna, about the letter. I steadied my breath.

'But I thought you were a happy couple now,' I said calmly when she came back into the room. 'That's what Simon said when I met him in the park.'

Hanna shook her head and tittered.

'That's what he wanted,' she said, putting her head to one side. 'But I didn't want it, and he doesn't know what he wants, anyway, does he? He's a confused boy. You're better off without him, you know.'

I exhaled loudly. I couldn't stand to hear that phrase one more time. I ground my teeth loudly.

'What will you do in Sweden?' I said. 'Apart from sleep with your friends' boyfriends?'

She ignored me.

'Maybe I'll travel round my own country,' she said. 'I can't seem to settle, you know . . . since Adele died.'

Hanna rubbed a finger round the top of her glass. She had barely spoken about Adele since those first few weeks at university. Adele was Hanna's sister, who had died at six years old. She'd shown me a picture of her, a white snowflake of a girl dressed in a green pinafore and white shoes. I'd never forgotten what she'd said about her dad, that he would drive the car out into the country lanes near their home and just scream and shout as he drove. Hanna could hear him from their garden. Then, when he came back, he was quiet again. My anger momentarily slipped away.

'I'm sorry about Adele,' I said, softening. 'Really I am.'

It's funny, because since I'd found out about Simon and Hanna, she had become an almost mythical creature in my head, intimidating in her beauty and charm and worldliness. I didn't think of her as simply attractive any more, I thought of her as utterly irresistible, devastatingly beautiful, magnetic. I saw her everywhere: it was her face on the poster advertising campaigns in the tube, her eyes staring out from the pictures in the newspaper. I imagined how much better life would be if I had her white-blonde hair or her long tanned legs. Embarrassingly I thought, If only I had her figure, Simon wouldn't have betrayed me. Does every betrayed person think that in their most private thoughts?

Now, though, seeing her there in front of me again, she seemed more normal than the Hanna I'd conjured up in my mind. She was undeniably pretty, but apart from that, I reminded myself that she was a wannabe actress who'd barely had any work at all. She was Hanna, the Swedish girl, who had lost her little sister Adele. Yes, Hanna had slept with Simon, but she was not an untouchable goddess. And now that I had read Ava's letter to Violet, she seemed incredibly insignificant.

'Will you forgive me?' Hanna said, gathering in her long arms and legs and sitting forward to face me. 'For what I did that terrible night?'

I had to admire her balls for coming here and saying this.

'Was it terrible?' I said, finding my voice now. 'I always thought Simon was pretty good between the sheets.'

Silence. Then the doorbell went. I'd left the door open and I heard people walking straight in.

'Hello?' I called, standing to meet the group.

'Hostess! Hurry up and get us a drink, will you?' Imogen's husband-to-be Jonathan shouted from the hallway.

Imogen, wearing a stunning silver dress, her wavy hair like red velvet, whacked him on the arm. Jonathan, as thin as a stick in his mod suit, laughed uproariously, then lunged at me and kissed me on the forehead.

'Hello, Jonathan,' I said, smiling wanly at Imogen. 'Come in.'

Imogen, Jonathan and a couple of their friends were breathing out pure alcohol. If I lit a match they'd go up in flames. Imogen ran her fingers through her hair and smiled apologetically.

'What the hell is she doing here?' she said, noticing Hanna in the living room, putting on a record. Music jerked into life.

'Apologizing,' I said quickly. 'She's going back to Sweden. Imogen, look, can we talk? I've just found out something dreadful.'

My words were stilted. I felt like I'd been punched. Imogen pulled a worried face then nodded, handing me a bottle of bubbly.

'Jesus. She could have picked a better night. What a bitch,' said Imogen, then, waving her arm at Jonathan and co., said, 'Sorry about this lot. They've been in the pub since four. Now, what did you want to say?'

Leaving Jonathan and the others to stumble towards the drink, I led Imogen into the bedroom, quickly closed the door and stood leaning with my back against it.

'She's not pregnant, is she?' Imogen asked quietly, searching my face with her eyes.

'Who? Hanna?' I said, frowning. 'No, no. It's this I'm talking about. This letter.'

I handed her the letter and sank down on to the floor, crossing my arms around my middle. The skirt of my dress ballooned over the floorboards. She quickly read, then sat heavily on the bed.

'Fuck,' she said, suddenly pale. 'What a thing to find out. I can't believe they never told you. What about Violet? Why didn't she tell you?'

I shrugged, stood up and paced up and down beside the bed. Music blared from the living room.

'Maybe this was her way of telling me?' I said. 'I'm so *furious*! Why have they treated me like a little girl who can't cope with the truth? What is it about the truth that frightens everyone so much? And I've spent my whole life thinking that it was all my fault, that—'

I stopped talking and started crying into my hands.

'Oh, come here,' Imogen said, hugging me. 'I think you need to talk to your mum. Isn't she coming over soon?'

The doorbell sounded again, a glass smashed and raucous laughter erupted from just outside the bedroom. We both looked towards the door. My heart raced. Imogen patted my shoulder.

'Look, Juliet,' she said, folding up the letter and handing it to me. 'You can't think about this now. Nothing's going to change overnight. You have to try to enjoy this party, or get through it, anyway. Let's go out there and get drunk. Fuck everyone and everything. We're here now. Just think for the moment, for now. We'll decide what to do about this tomorrow.'

I loved the way Imogen said 'we' as if we were in it together. She always did that. Out of nowhere, I remembered a fancy dress party we went to as Charlie's Angels, handbags swinging from our elbows, hair lacquered solid. A drunk bloke had pinned me against a wall and tried to put his hand up my skirt, but Imogen had hit him over the head with her handbag. We'd dined out on it for weeks.

'OK,' I said shakily. 'Let's do it. Thanks, Imogen. You look gorgeous, by the way.'

Imogen shook her head dramatically.

'I've plastered on the make-up,' she said. 'I'm covering up a multitude of sins. Something's happened, something big.'

She put her hand on the door handle and pushed.

'What?' I said. 'What's happened?'

'I'll tell you later,' she said. 'You have enough on your plate right now.'

My legs felt like jelly, but I made it back into the living room. Suddenly it was packed with people making noise, apparently enjoying themselves. Did I know them all? There was only one way I could get through the night. I'd have to get blind drunk. I needed to be out of my head. I wanted to forget it all. So I drank champagne cocktails like they were going out of fashion. I kept busy. I spun this way and that, offering plates of nibbles, filling up glasses, drinking. I felt like I was riding a never-ending carousel. Then Hanna tapped me on the shoulder and told me she was leaving. I tried to focus on her face. My head was spinning.

'Look, I hope you and Simon can work it out,' she said. 'I meant nothing to him, nothing at all.'

Her words seemed to hang over her head like a cartoon speech bubble. I laughed out loud. The idea of getting back with someone who had betrayed me so spectacularly was ludicrous, even if a part of me desperately wanted to. I showed her to the door.

'Go home, Hanna,' I said. She reached out for my hand, one last attempt at making amends, a handshake to remember our friendship by. She was standing very close to me now, close enough for me to smell her coconut shampoo. I stared at her head and decided her hair was too white. I could see the pink of her scalp. I imagined her travelling home on the plane, reliving this party, worrying that she hadn't achieved what she wanted to.

'I'm sorry,' she said, taking my hand and holding it there for a second. 'I don't think you—'

'Time to go, Hanna,' I said. 'Have a nice life.'

I opened the door to let her out and leaned heavily against the wall. God, I was drunk. I thought, one minute a person is your friend, the next there is nothing there. Like a ribbon at the end of a race, it is torn down and trampled into the mud. The same can go for your family. One minute you think you're an only child, the next you're not. I felt a knot of panic tighten in my stomach and reached for another drink.

An hour later, I was so drunk I could barely breathe. The carpet was sponge, the walls at all angles. Lurching into the kitchen, I opened the window, made myself an exceptionally strong coffee, drank two pints of water and held ice cubes on my forehead. I sat still for fifteen minutes and began to sober up, very slightly. A thought blew into my head – did Rosie look like me?

'Juliiiiiiiiieeeeeeeeett!' I heard Imogen shrieking as I edged my way back into the living room. 'Did you make this?'

She was holding up my apron. The polka-dot one with the heart-shaped pockets and frilly trim.

'Yes,' I nodded. My head was now pounding. I felt slightly irritated. 'So what?'

She pulled it over her head, modelling it. Someone wolf-whistled.

'It is fabulous,' she said. 'Honestly, they're properly good. You could sell these. You could sell these to my boutiques. They would make fantastic gifts. Really, I am seriously impressed. You're a dark horse, aren't you? Have you made more?'

'Yes,' I mumbled. 'No. Not really. I made a matching headscarf and tea-cosy. They're daft. No one would want to buy one.'

'I would,' said Jen, one of the girls from the press office.

'Me too,' said Helen, Jen's flatmate. 'Will you make me one? I'll commission you.'

'Yes,' I said, moving over to the window. I had no intention of making anything for anyone. Their attention was embarrassing and misplaced. They clearly felt sorry for me.

I opened the living room window and leaned out, breathing deeply to steady myself. I was still incredibly drunk. I wondered if I should have told my neighbours about this party. They would be cursing me right now, especially the family next door with the newborn baby. I'd have to apologize. Then a black cab pulled up outside, the engine purring. The door opened and a person emerged. I'd never seen this person from above before; I'd only ever looked up at him. But there was no mistaking that hairstyle and those broad shoulders and the tan and that plum-soaked London accent thanking the driver. It was Philip. I couldn't believe he'd actually turned up. I felt instantly more sober. I leaned back from the window and banged it shut. Philip. Oh blimey, Philip.

'Jesus Christ,' he said when I opened the door. 'You look even lovelier in your natural environment. Like a snow leopard on a Tibetan mountain.'

'Hardly,' I said as he kissed me on both cheeks. His skin had a sweet smell: kind of like crunchy praline, almost vanilla. Leaning in to him briefly, I felt the heat from his skin from under his dark blue linen shirt. Music and conversation blared behind me.

'A housewarming gift,' he said, handing me a rolled-up red doormat with DOORMAT written across it.

'Thanks,' I said, trying to shoot him a knowing look. 'Are you trying to tell me something?'

I put the mat on the floor and swept my shoes across it in a self-conscious demonstration.

'Don't be paranoid!' he laughed. 'I thought it was funny.'

I grinned to show him I'd got the joke.

'So where is your wife?' I said. 'I mean, is she able to come too?'

I shouldn't have asked this question, but because I'd heard rumours at work that they were on the rocks, it was somewhere in my mind. I was hardly thinking straight, anyway. Philip took off his jacket, rubbed his jaw and narrowed his eyes. He lowered his voice and scanned the party over my shoulder. People were dancing furiously now, and the floor was vibrating with the drumbeat. In the distance I was aware of a baby crying.

'I thought you knew that we're not together any more,' he said. 'We're mid-separation, in fact. Our marriage is in the process of ending. We're engaged to be divorced.'

He half laughed and I pulled a face. Engaged to be divorced.

I was beginning to hate thinking about relationships. Everywhere you looked they were imploding. Anyone who believed in true love was delusional.

'I'm sorry,' I said. 'I wish I hadn't asked. Would you like a drink? I've had a few too many, to be honest.'

He pushed his hands deep into his pockets and cleared his throat.

'Yes, indeed I would,' he said. 'A very large drink would be gratefully received.'

Holding a large vodka and tonic, Philip walked into the living room and commandeered a group of my friends. He was like that – unafraid of new people or new situations. Or that's how he appeared, anyway: driven and determined, always in control. While talking, his eyes flitted to me. Occasionally he smiled. In between snippets of conversation, I listened to his voice booming over the record and thought how everything about Philip was big. Voice, personality, shoulders, wallet. Penis? I bit my bottom lip. Did I really just have that thought? It was the alcohol, the music, the numerous lives between my four walls making me suddenly have bizarre thoughts. But sleeping with Philip? The thought had never occurred to me before. And why should it have done? Philip was married. He was my boss. I'd always been with Simon. It was a ludicrous, crazy thought and I pushed it back into the dark depths it had emerged from. I poured myself another pint of water.

'Juliet,' Imogen said suddenly, pulling at my arm. 'Come over here.'

Imogen pulled me down on to the edge of the sofa. Our hips pushed up against each other as we squeezed on to one cushion.

'He's furious with me,' Imogen hissed under the music, pointing at Jonathan. 'Look at him.'

I saw Jonathan leaning on the wall by the front door, tapping away on his mobile phone, his mouth set in a straight hard ruler of a line.

'Shit,' Imogen said. 'I've really done it this time.'

'Done what?' I said, but Imogen stood up to follow Jonathan as he opened the front door to leave. I started after her, but then felt a hand on my lower back. I turned to see who it was. Philip. He looked like he wanted to ask me a question.

'Did you want me?' I asked.

The skin around his eyes creased into miniature smiles. What was he? Thirty-five? Thirty-six? I tried hard to imagine him as a father, carrying his little girl on his shoulders, reading his son a bedtime story. I couldn't see him in that role at all. Philip was one of those one hundred per cent testosterone men. When he wasn't working, he'd be chopping down trees or wrestling.

'I couldn't possibly answer that, Juliet,' he said. His smile was like a fishing line. I was vulnerable and drunk. I felt it enter my body and hook the edge of my heart and tug at it.

'Follow me for a minute, will you?' he said, his hand still on the small of my back. I followed him into the kitchen. He was quiet as people came in to fill up their glasses. Then, when we were alone, he leant against the sideboard and took a deep breath. I wished we weren't standing quite so close to the sink. It smelled horrible. A vague recollection of something I'd read in Violet's book about how to banish nasty odours flashed into my mind. What was happening to me?

'Remember your first day at Rosendale's?' he asked. He smiled.

I'd never seen Philip this close before. He had a splatter of small moles on his face and neck, as if someone had ridden a bike through a puddle and splashed him with mud. His eyes were the colour of summer skies and his nose was regally straight, as if drawn with a set-square.

'That day, when I saw you walk into the office, I thought you were lovely. I know that, as your boss, I shouldn't say this, but fuck it, we're not at work now. I thought you were an absolute fox.'

My heart was pounding so hard I felt sure he could hear it above the music. Was he deliberately trying to embarrass me? Was this some kind of joke? I started to sweat and waved a 'Welcome to your New Home' card in front of my face like a fan.

'That's hilarious,' I said, reddening. 'Would you like another drink?' He smiled ruefully and touched my arm gently.

'You're embarrassed,' he said. 'Sorry.'

I thought about the times he'd ignored me at work. The days when he slammed into the office, swore at his email and didn't look up from his desk until home time. I thought about the day his wife had arrived at the office – a blonde, pretty woman with tiny chattering children hanging off her limbs like cow bells.

'No, I'm not,' I said. 'I'm just having a weird night. A very, very weird night.'

I thought about the letter but pushed it from my mind. To keep busy, I poured Philip a drink and concentrated on him.

He was unlike any other man I knew. He was incredibly ambitious, exciting, powerful, confident and as big as a horse.

'I knew you'd be brilliant with the filming,' he said. 'Dylan has told me you're a natural. I'm not surprised.'

I thought of Dylan. Obviously he wasn't coming. Since our drink in the French House we'd worked well together while filming, but he continually dashed off at five o'clock with an expression of grim determination on his face. I'd asked him where he was going, but he shook me off, telling me that it didn't matter, which I thought was pretty rude.

'Perhaps you'll change careers?' Philip said. 'You could be a TV presenter.'

Philip was flirting with me. I felt an unexpected thrill. But I was not going to flirt back. The man was married. He was my boss. I could not sink that low. He touched my waist. One look into his lascivious eyes told me exactly what he wanted.

'I'd better go and . . . check on the others,' I said. He looked alarmed, disappointed even, and shoved his hands under his armpits as if he were an octopus keeping his tentacles under control.

'Sure,' he said.

Imogen bounded over to me, took my hand and dragged me into the bathroom. She was very drunk, more so than me, swaying like a dandelion in the wind. She climbed into the bath and lay there, fully clothed, her silver shoes next to the silver taps. Her face was pale under her pink blusher.

'I see Philip wants to sleep with you,' she said, winking at me. 'Don't go there, Juliet. Disaster. He's married, isn't he?'

I locked the bathroom door and brushed my teeth.

'Getting divorced,' I said, spitting water into the sink. 'And

I'm not going there. Christ, give me some credit. I'm in the throes of a total life meltdown here. I'm not about to sleep with my boss to add to the gravity of it all.'

I filled a glass with water and handed it to her.

'Thanks,' she said, sipping from the glass. 'God, I feel sick.'

'You'll feel better if you drink all that water,' I said. I sat on the stool next to the bath. 'What's the problem with Jonathan tonight?'

Imogen covered her face with her hands. I picked up my body brush from a hook near the shower and poked her in the waist with it.

'Come on, Imogen,' I said gently. 'What's up? I want to know. I've just shown you a letter that throws my whole life up in the air!'

She looked up at me, her expression very serious. Her normally light, mossy-green eyes were as dark as the bottom of a wine bottle.

'I've been thinking, really thinking,' she said quietly, 'that maybe I'm not who I think I am.'

I'd never heard Imogen so serious. She was surprised herself and looked up at me with a half smile on her lips. I felt myself wanting to giggle.

'Who are you to say that?' I said. I couldn't help myself. And we both laughed uproariously. We laughed much harder than the joke warranted. It was absolute bliss, to laugh.

By four a.m. everyone had staggered away, singing in the street, leaving behind a party trail of glasses, ashtrays and discarded items of clothing. The rug in the living room was submerged under crushed breadsticks, peanuts, cigarette stubs tossed on plates and half-empty wine bottles. My heart dipped at the state of my flat. If it had seemed unhomely before, now the Apocalypse felt imminent. Where was the home I'd dreamed of, adorned with glowing lamps, Persian rugs and the comforting smell of warm Bakewell tart? Where was the sanctuary I'd thought I was moving into, with two people in love working to make it a home? Turned to shit, that's where it was.

Oh God. What now? My ears were ringing, my stomach churned. Now that the party was ending, I'd have to confront the contents of the letter. I'd have to make a plan. First, though, I had to get rid of Philip. He was noisily clanking cups and spoons in the kitchen, making coffee. I'd hardly spoken to him since his earlier flirtation. Hesitantly, I joined him in the kitchen and stared at our joint reflection in the window. I felt both exhausted and wired at the same time. My eyes were dark with smudged mascara. I considered telling him everything about my parents, about Simon and Hanna. But I sensed he didn't want to know all my problems.

'I look like a raccoon,' I said, looking at myself in the back of a spoon.

'I don't know any raccoons,' Philip said, 'so I can't comment. To me, you look more like an old-fashioned film star, with freckles.'

I wanted to laugh at that astoundingly generous comparison, but I managed to control myself.

'Look at London,' I said stupidly. 'Isn't it mystical at this time?'

Philip said nothing. Beyond the window, dawn was breaking over the city, the pale lavender sky contrasting against dark buildings. There was a faint hum of engines, trains rumbling with freight, a street cleaner sweeping the gutters. Suddenly tremendously tired, my body sagged. Philip put his hand on my shoulder, almost fatherly. My fears about the letter were in the forefront of my mind. I thought, If I open my mouth and start talking, I won't stop until I've said it all. I stayed quiet.

'Juliet,' Philip said, 'you should buy some fresh coffee. Ecuadorian is best. This instant is horrible. I wondered if I could possibly stay the night?'

I didn't move. I understood that he was inviting himself into my bed. Part of me wanted to fall into his arms right there in the kitchen. He would be warm, strong, masculine. He would throw me over his shoulder and take me away from it all. He would stroke my hair, tell me everything would get better. But he was married, and a father. I thought of the portraits of his kids hanging in his office, carefully strung from the picture rail. I hated him for being weak. I hated him for making me weak. I knew I didn't have the strength to resist.

'It's nearly morning now,' I said flatly, trying to be strong.

'And your point is?' Philip said, stiffening. I sensed he wasn't used to being rebuffed. He gave me a hard look, tucked a strand of hair behind my ear, then pulled me to him. I felt his breath, crunchy praline, on my mouth. He kissed me firmly, searching for my tongue with his. I listened to a bird wolf-whistle in the gardens outside. A horribly raw desire flooded through me. Disaster, I thought. I kissed him back.

Later, after we had had sex, Philip lay on top of the white sheets with his arms and legs outstretched like an enormous starfish. Guilt washed over me in a clammy tidal wave. I teetered on the very edge of the bed, wondering how I could undo what I'd just done. While I fretted, he talked to me about the 'imprisonment' of his marriage.

'It's as if we're in a play called "The Marriage",' he said. 'And we're such accomplished actors that the audience keeps coming back for more.'

'But you must have been happy at one point,' I said. 'Can I have some sheet, please?'

He lifted his legs up and I pulled the sheet up to my neck.

'Perhaps,' he said. 'But I've learned that one person could never satisfy me completely. I'm too hungry.'

'That's awful!' I said. 'You make your wife sound like a roast dinner.'

He gave a quick smile and sniggered from the back of his throat, as if he was trying to cough something up.

'Can I have more juicy cuts and sauce please?' he said with a laugh.

It was then that I started to dislike him intensely.

'Well, I believe that one person can be enough,' I said. 'It's people's expectations of one another that are at fault. We all need to regulate our expectations, and then everyone would get on much better. What do you expect from your wife, for fuck's sake? A mother to your kids, a career woman, a house-keeper, a shag, a mate, a cook? What else? No woman can be all those things. No one wants to be all those things.'

'You're so young,' he said, so patronizingly that I wanted to elbow him in the face. 'I have put my all into marriage. I've been a role model husband, but now it's over. I'm so tired. You young things have so much energy. I need sleep.'

I knew he had probably talked his way into the beds of half the women in London. That wouldn't surprise me at all. What did surprise me was that I'd willingly slept with him while knowing I definitely shouldn't, while hating myself for it. I'd fooled myself into thinking it didn't matter. It was just a few minutes of escapism. It was just an extension of a hug and a kiss. In a lifetime of moments, this was just one inconsequential moment.

Who was I kidding?

Juliet, I thought. What the hell is going on?

My life was unrecognizable. Frightening, even. I couldn't think any more thoughts. As Philip fell asleep beside me, I squeezed my eyes shut. I said a jumbled made-up prayer to a non-existent God to please make it all go away. As the sun rose, I slipped into sleep and dreamed a confused dream about the body of Charles, my father, who art in Heaven, floating face down in the sea.

Chapter Twelve

Women have been known to boil their tea towels with a
lemon rind, to whiten them [but] a tea towel that's seen
long and honorable service has a right to a few scars and
blotches, as don't we all.

The I Hate to Housekeep Book,
Peg Bracken, 1962

I sat alone in the kitchen, drinking strong black coffee. Philip
was still snoring disconcertingly loudly in my bed. My skin
smelled of his bergamot aftershave, my chin was sore from
his stubble. His jacket was draped over the kitchen chair
and his leather wallet sat on the table, coins cascading out,
as if he had laid a bet at a casino. He'd been in the flat for less
than twelve hours, but it was like he owned the place. I sighed.
Never in my life had I felt this awful – I was drowning in
guilt and regret. Each time I thought of Philip in my bed, I
broke out in a horrible cold sweat.

But there was something else on my mind, something more

momentous even than sleeping with Philip. The letter. Wearing a sweatshirt and tracksuit trousers to show Philip I was now strictly off-limits, I pulled the letter out of the drawer, unfolded the paper and read it again, my fists clenched in my lap. Goose pimples popping up everywhere, I said the words in a loud whisper to make it more real. My mother had not only abandoned me, she had lied to me about why she was going away. I had a half-sister out there somewhere! It was the oddest, most implausible idea to get my head round – like walking on the ceiling or swimming through mud.

'Morning, beautiful,' Philip said from behind me. I gasped and pushed the letter away from me. Sunlight shone through the blinds and fell over my hands in white gold.

'Sorry,' he said. 'Did I startle you?'

Philip, naked except for a white tea-towel strategically placed, as if he was about to step into a sauna, walked over to the table and sat down next to me. He put his hand on my thigh. He pushed his other hand through his hair. Dark crescents underlined his eyes from lack of sleep. He yawned and stretched and grinned. He had the relaxed demeanour of someone who had cheated on his wife before, many times.

'No,' I forced out a laugh. 'I'm just very, very hung-over and I feel horrible.'

I didn't say how much I hated myself for what I'd done. Oh my God, Philip had a wife and children. I imagined them now, waking up in their plush home in Richmond, crying into their organic muesli, wondering where Daddy had gone. Never in a million years did I want to be a home-wrecker. I couldn't understand how I'd got here. I was no better than Simon and Hanna now, was I?

I shifted uncomfortably under Philip's gaze. Around us waited empty bottles, dirty plates and pink chunks of watermelon flesh someone had decided to saturate with vodka. I heard the faint sound of scratching in a cupboard. Home, sweet home.

'You have the booze blues,' he said. 'That's all. Aren't you a bit warm in all that clothing? It must be thirty degrees in here.'

I shook my head and folded my arms across my chest.

'I'm ashamed,' I started. 'I shouldn't have acted like that. I think I was temporarily insane or something. I was in a bad way and shouldn't have gone to bed . . . your wife, she must . . . '

Philip's face darkened. He bit his lower lip and waved his hand in the air as if his wife were a gnat he wanted to kill.

'My wife and I don't have a relationship,' he said. 'I told you that last night. Our marriage is ending . . . our marriage is, has been, complicated. Some marriages are more complicated than others, you know? You must understand that? It's an institution that hasn't worked out for us. You get me?'

I nodded slowly to show him I did. I thought about the DOORMAT he'd bought me and wondered if I should strap it to my head. How many times had I heard stories about men who, when they no longer had sex with their wife, sidled off into another woman's bed, claiming to have no 'relationship'. What about the children, the mortgage, the holidays, the daily phone calls, the legal bind? Did that not constitute a relationship?

'Look,' I said, rubbing my forehead. 'I'm sorry, but I'm just not comfortable with it. I really don't want to be the kind of person who sleeps with married men. It's just so, so cheap and nasty.'

Philip knelt down on the floor next to me. He held my head in his hands.

'I'm not a horrible cheating bastard,' he said. 'I swear to you, my wife and I live separate lives. We're splitting up, we're separated now, but it's complicated. She has a lot of issues. She's nuts. I wouldn't make a fool of you, Juliet. You're too young and gorgeous and delicate for that.'

I was about to insist that I wasn't delicate. But I felt exactly that. Ava's letter had devastated me. I couldn't tell Philip about it and I didn't want to. He would just think I was a crazy person with more 'issues' than his wife. I just wanted him to leave, so I could think.

'You'd better go,' I said, trying to smile while looking around the kitchen. 'I need to clear up my flat. This place is a nightmare – it's a complete tip.'

Philip ran his finger down my spine and cupped my breasts with his hands. He kissed my neck so gently, my body caved into his. I was disgusted with myself. Whatever he said about his wife, he was still married. But if I was going to be really honest, I was also comforted by the intimacy. While I was with Philip, while he wanted my body, I could be someone else. I didn't have to be Juliet Rice.

I told myself to remember his obnoxious comments last night, gathered my strength and pushed him gently away.

'Look,' I said, but then the words caught in my throat. I couldn't say anything else. I started to cry.

'Oh God, come here, Juliet,' he said. 'You'll make me cry too. It was the sex, wasn't it? It was truly amazing. I worried you might not like my little surprise, but my cock ring really is great, isn't it?'

I sobbed into his shoulder. I heard him sniffing along too. I thought about his penis ring, which I'd glimpsed mid-throes – a gold hoop through a pig's snout.

'Great,' I lied.

It was not my finest moment.

After Philip had left – I had to literally push him out of the door – I phoned Imogen and told her about everything, including the pig's snout. She gasped dramatically.

'Do you think the alarm goes off at security in airports?' she giggled. 'Why don't you come to meet me in town? Piccadilly Circus, statue of Eros, at one? We'll buy a wedding dress for me, then go and make a plan for both of us. I'm in trouble too. Jonathan's furious with me. Maybe we should run away like Thelma and Louise? Don't worry, Juliet, we'll sort it out.'

I dressed quickly and was relieved to shut the door on my flat. I couldn't face clearing up the party debris. I hoped when I was out it would magically evaporate. I hoped a home-making goddess would wave a wand and transform it into the comforting home I'd longed for. Perhaps when I returned she'd be there, plumping up the cushions I'd made, holding out a cold glass of white wine and a foot spa. Ha!

I sat on the top deck of the bus into town. It was microwave-hot up there. We were basting in our own sweat like roast chickens. Whenever I thought about Philip, I thought I might throw up with guilt, so I pushed him right out of my mind. Hopefully we could forget about it completely. In the office on Monday it would be as though nothing had happened. It was a drunken mistake, never to be repeated. His wife would never need to know, and anyway, they were breaking up. I could feel relatively guilt-free, couldn't I? A stupid one-night stand, that's all it was.

I stared out of the window. Every girl I saw passing on the pavement made me wonder the same irrational thought – Is that Rosie? I let out an enormous sigh. I was struggling to get my head round what the letter had said. I just hated the fact that people couldn't tell the truth. If I'd known the truth, perhaps I wouldn't have spent my whole life believing my disastrous family life was all my fault.

I folded my arms and leaned back in the seat. I desperately wanted to talk to Simon about Rosie, but I couldn't. I rang Joy instead and left a garbled message asking her to phone me back. Then I rang her again and told her it was urgent. Questions crept about my brain like teeming ants. I shivered at the fact that I might never have found the letter at all. Would that have been better?

As the bus rattled onwards, puffing out black exhaust, my mind drifted back to the day my dad died. I remembered screaming his name at the very top of my lungs as the black ocean swallowed him up like a scrap of driftwood. My screams had made the seagulls soar and screech and circle above me. I thought of Dad's lungs filling with seawater. I wondered how long it had taken for him to die.

'Piccadilly Circus', the bus's recorded message said. I looked out of the window and saw Imogen near the statue of Eros. She was smoking a cigarette with the God of Love! I jumped up and I pressed the STOP button.

Stop the bus, I want to get off. Stop the world, I want to get off.

Chapter Thirteen

For lipstick stains, rub petroleum jelly into stain, then
sponge with carbon tetra-chloride. If trace of colour
remains, sponge with alcohol.

America's Homemaking Book,
Marguerite Dodd, 1957

'Just look at this place,' Imogen whispered as we walked
through the main doors of Becoming Brides. 'Are we in High
Street heaven?'

The shop, a wedding emporium on Piccadilly, was filled
with white wedding paraphernalia in every form. White fabric
covered the walls, floor and ceiling. Ribbons, tiaras and feather
boas snowed down from the light fittings, and clothes rails
bulged with wedding dresses. Girls twisted and turned this
way and that, like ballerinas, in front of full-length mirrors,
watched by beaming staff dressed in white top hats and tails
(poor souls). Stuffed white doves perched on the counters and
the Wedding March played repeatedly through enormous

speakers. On screens jutting out of the walls, the Wedding Channel flickered. The shop was absolutely buzzing with brides-to-be, their mothers, sisters, aunts, nieces and copious other female relations. A few lone men hung around, shuffling from foot to foot, full of regret. I gazed around the shop, fearing snow blindness.

'I can't believe it,' Imogen said. 'It's so tacky. I didn't realize it would be quite so depressing. Maybe they do drive-thru weddings out the back. Let's get any old dress and get out so we can talk about real things.'

'You can't just get any old dress,' I said. 'This is your wedding day. Let's try to get into Bridezilla character here, shall we?'

'I hate weddings,' she said. 'You know I do.'

I held on to Imogen's shoulders and pointed up at a wedding ceremony playing out on the television on the wall.

'Imagine that's you,' I said, jerking my head towards the bride-to-be. 'Imagine Jonathan waiting for you at the altar. Everyone's smiling at you when you walk into the church, gasping at your beautiful dress.'

Imogen frowned and closed her eyes.

'Are you with me?' I said. 'I want you to put yourself there, outside the church. The horse and cart or white limousine or minicab or Harley-Davidson has dropped you off, you gather up your dress and—'

'Yes, yes,' she nodded. 'I get the picture.'

'OK, so you make your entrance, then Jonathan turns round and sees you gliding towards him in your fantasy dress. So what is that fantasy dress, Imogen? What do you really want to wear?'

'Black,' she said, deadpan.

I shook my head and gave her a look. A shop assistant hovering nearby began holding dresses up for Imogen to look at. She gave me a nervous smile. I saw panic in her eyes.

'What about this one?' I said, trying to ignore the assistant and pulling a simple strapless dress from the rails. 'Look, it's covered in tiny pearls, and this bodice thing is pretty . . .'

I flipped over the price tag and showed it to Imogen.

'Jesus,' she said, snatching it out of my hands and putting it back on the rail. 'Juliet, it's awful. I'd rather wear a body bag.'

'Bin bag, you mean,' I said. 'What about this one?'

Imogen put her hands up to her cheeks. The Wedding March was still playing in the background.

'Do you know what?' she said. 'I can't bear this. Let's go and hide in a coffee shop. We have too much to talk about to concentrate on all this taffeta. It's making me queasy.'

I put my hands on my hips. Every time we'd tried to buy her a dress she'd done this. I picked up an embroidered veil, handmade in Orkney by the people who didn't make oatcakes. It was £245. I handed it to her decisively.

'Look,' I said, 'just try something on. Then you can get more of an idea of what you like. Good idea?'

Imogen's eyes suddenly filled with tears. The Wedding March blared out of the speakers for the thousandth time. She held the veil up to her face and wept.

'Oh, Imogen,' I said quietly, peeling the veil from her hands. 'What's wrong? Let's get out of here. I didn't mean to upset you. What's making you cry?'

'Sorry,' she said. 'Christ, I never cry. Why am I crying when you've got the important stuff going on? Are you OK about that letter?'

'Yes, I'm OK,' I said. 'But I really don't know how I feel yet. I think it's still sinking in. I want to know what's upsetting you, though. Let's get out of here.'

She handed me the veil and I saw a streak of her red lipstick across the middle.

'Oh God, look,' I said, pointing to the stain. 'Quick, stuff it under that pile there.'

Imogen stuffed the veil into a stack of white things. Linking my arm through hers, I led her out of the shop and towards the safety of a patisserie two doors down. We walked there together in silence, then chose a seat right next to a gorgeous display of cloud-like meringues in pink and white. The smell of coffee and the hum of people chatting instantly made me feel better. Imogen perched on the edge of her chair, pulling her hair into a ponytail as she held the band in her teeth.

'Let's have something naughty,' I said. 'Then tell me what's on your mind.'

We ordered two strawberry tarts and two cappuccinos. The waiter, a French guy, called us 'English roses' and made a big fuss of serving us. I felt like a thorn beside Imogen's rosiness, but I smiled nonetheless.

'Don't encourage him,' Imogen hissed, glaring at him. 'What are you going to do about Philip? Work's going to be difficult now, you know.'

I'd known Imogen for years. I knew that you couldn't push her to tell you what was on her mind. She relented in her own time. When she was ready to tell me what was going on, she would. I was her warm-up act today.

'I know,' I said, digging my fork into the tart. 'I can't believe I actually slept with him. What am I doing with my life?'

Imogen smiled. She flicked her hair over her shoulder and sipped her cappuccino.

'You're just being normal,' she said. 'Everyone makes mistakes, don't they? I've made enough. Remember danger-man Dominic? He's in prison now for putting someone's face in a box of fireworks. Lovely.'

She looked around the café. She seemed restless.

'What about your flat?' she said. 'Can you afford to stay there now that Simon has gone?'

I thought about my flat, the party debris rotting in the heat, the smeared fingerprints over the living-room walls, the flagrant mice vandalizing my packet noodles.

'Not really,' I said. 'I need to either earn more money or move out, and I expect it will be the latter.'

I glanced out of the window and jumped in surprise. Staring through the glass at the cake display was Dylan, with a dark-haired, very pretty girl I assumed was Sylvie. My stomach flipped and I blushed. He noticed me and waved. We shared a look. I waved back with my fork, spraying myself with crème pâtissière and pastry crumbs. The girl I assumed to be Sylvie fixed me with a hard stare. She said something to Dylan and he shook his head. Then they walked quickly off. He glanced over his shoulder at me as he went and I felt an unexpected tremor of excitement. I waved my fork again and this time lost a strawberry.

'I've had an idea about that,' Imogen was saying, gesturing at me to wipe my face. 'I meant it when I said your aprons and headscarves were great. Why don't you think of a name to call yourself, get a label printed off and sew up some examples for me to show Cath at work? I'm sure she'd go for them. Also, what about your Home Help Group? Don't they do a market stall or something?'

I was still thinking about Dylan and Sylvie – I hadn't imagined her in jeans. For some reason, I'd imagined her in a dark blue silk dress – the kind that reflects the sky, like a pool of mercury.

'Hello?' Imogen said. 'Are you listening? I'm offering you the chance of making a few quid here and you're zoning out.'

'Are you joking, Imogen?' I said. 'They're never good enough to sell.'

Imogen put her hand against her chest.

'Hand on heart,' she said. 'They are one hundred per cent perfect for our boutique. With a little bit of fine-tuning, you've got yourself a nice little earner. You could shift them at Spitalfields Market too. You just need to get motivated. Good way to meet a bloke, not that you're interested right now.'

Our plates were empty and the waiter was hovering.

'What blokes buy aprons from markets?' I laughed. 'So, anyway, are you going to tell me what's going on or what?'

I vaguely knew what she was going to say: you didn't need to be a genius to work out that she didn't really want to marry Jonathan.

'Or what,' she said, giving me a quick smile.

'Come on, Imogen,' I said. 'I'm dying to know, or I'll die waiting to know at this rate.'

Imogen picked up her bag and fiddled with the zip nervously. She didn't look at me as she spoke.

'If I tell you something, will you promise not to hate me?' she said.

She located her pocket mirror and held it up to her eyes. I wondered if she realized how pretty she was.

'I could never hate you,' I told her, which was the truth. 'Tell me what it is.'

She put the mirror back in the bag and zipped it shut. Resting the bag on her knee and hugging it, she spoke quietly.

'My parents really desperately want this wedding,' she said. 'They've been saving up for it since I was born and even announced our engagement in the *Telegraph* last week.'

Imogen pulled a face. I imagined Imogen's mum, Patricia, proudly telling anyone she met that Imogen was finally, *finally*, at the ripe old age of twenty-five, getting married.

'But that doesn't matter if you're not happy,' I said. 'All I care about is whether you're happy with Jonathan – that's all that counts. Are you happy? Do you want to marry him? You don't have to do anything you don't want to. You know, a few years ago you said you didn't agree with marriage anyway.'

The waiter cleared our plates, humming to himself. He tossed a menu on the table, nearly slicing off my nose, presumably in case we wanted pudding after our puddings.

'Jonathan's parents are over the moon about it,' she continued. 'They've booked this amazing manor house hotel in Wiltshire for the reception. There are giant goldfish in an indoor pond and a swing hanging from a willow tree in the gardens. I've been with Jonathan for so many years, and I do want to marry him. I am definitely going to marry him, but . . .'

She stopped dead.

'But what?' I said.

Imogen closed her eyes. Her voice was a whisper, half lost

in the steamy whistle of the cappuccino machine. I strained to hear.

'Well,' she said, ever so softly. 'I still can't believe I did this, but, well. God, Juliet, you'll never believe this, but last Friday night I . . . I . . . um, I slept with a woman.'

My mouth fell open. This was major. This was life changing. How could I not have known this about my best friend? Suddenly my life seemed to be full of things I didn't know about. I widened my eyes.

'You slept with a woman?' I said. 'No! How could I not know this? Does Jonathan know? Is that why he was pissed off at my party?'

'He doesn't know the details,' she said, breaking into a flushed grin that she quickly retracted. 'He only knows that I was out all night. He doesn't know I spent the night with Cath.'

'Cath,' I said. 'The woman you work with at LOVE? The one with seven-inch high heels and hair down to her bum? She's gay?'

She nodded quickly. 'And do you know what, Juliet?' she asked.

I shook my head and waited.

'It was heavenly,' she said, placing her hands flat on the table. 'Like nothing else before. And it wasn't just about the sex, it was about the person, about Cath.'

'Oh, Imogen, this is big,' I said, signalling to the waiter for coffee refills. 'Tell me everything.'

Chapter Fourteen

You'll be amazed how cozy, cheerful and lived-in a new
house can look with a few decorating tricks. Compose a
'still life' of vegetables in the kitchen. You'll be surprised
how many big things go unnoticed!

> *Ladies' Home Journal Art of Homemaking,*
> Virginia T. Habeeb, 1973

On the bus home, I couldn't find a seat. I stood the whole
way, my nose pressed up to the window, fretting about
Imogen's revelation. OK, so she was having a fabulous fling
with a woman. Good on her. Maybe she was now lesbian or
bisexual, or maybe it was a one-off – most likely she didn't
need me to put her in a category. It didn't matter what she
was or wasn't. The thing that horrified me was that she was
still planning to marry Jonathan, giant goldfish et al. When,
in the café, I'd suggested she call the wedding off, Imogen had
stared at the red Formica table for a long time, then looked
up at me with big wet tears streaking down her cheeks.

'I can't not marry him, Juliet,' she said. 'You know I can't. My parents are over the moon about the wedding. We've been together for ever.'

She said for ever as if it was a death sentence. I thought how strange it was that, depending on a person's enunciation, words could completely change in meaning. I'd always loved the words 'for ever'. But clearly Imogen didn't, and there was no way I was going to let her marry someone she didn't love and who perhaps wasn't even the right gender. I knew I was going to have to do something – and soon. I imagined a scene where I hurled myself on to the flagstones of the church floor as she was about to take her vows, beating the ground with my fists and shouting 'No!' I hoped it wouldn't go that far. Whatever it took, I was determined for Imogen to be happy, and I just knew she wouldn't – couldn't – be happy with Jonathan.

Getting off the bus at the corner of Lovelace Avenue, I dragged my legs home. I was tired. Scrabbling around in my bag for my key for at least five minutes, I finally let myself into the main front door, immediately skidding on a pile of glossy junk mail. I longed for a hot bath and a cold glass of water. After that I'd decide what to do about the letter. Joy hadn't yet called back, so perhaps I'd have to bite the bullet and call Ava, currently in Kenya. Ultimately, she was the only person who would be able to tell me the truth, though the truth wasn't exactly her forte.

Sighing, I switched on the hall light, which was on a timer for one pointless nanosecond – not long enough to get halfway up the stairs. I was filled with dread about the mess that would greet me. All I could think about were the bed sheets, stinking of Philip's potent aftershave and crumpled after our vigorous activity. I cringed. I entirely regretted sleeping with him. Yes, he was handsome, but so was the London Eye. Philip was my boss. He was married. It was unthinkable, really. I had been stupid. I was obviously in a vulnerable place after Simon. Needy. I hated to think I was so desperately insecure that I would sleep with the first man who looked in my direction, but I had. Whatever Philip said about his marriage, I didn't want to take any part in wrecking it.

'What the—' I said when I reached the front door of my flat. It was swinging wide open on its hinges. My heart boomed in my chest. In all the years I'd lived in London, I'd never been burgled or mugged or robbed. Now I envisaged a gang of thieves brandishing knives, intent on my execution. I thought I heard a noise coming from inside the flat and a voice in my head told me to call the police, quickly, but instead I pushed the door open further with my fingertips and poked my head gingerly into the hallway.

'Hello?' I called. Did I really expect burglars to call out a greeting?

Then I noticed him. There, sitting on the sofa reading Violet's homemaking book, naked apart from my polkadot sweetheart apron, as if he were the subject of a life drawing class, was Philip.

'Philip!' I said, clutching my chest. 'You scared the bloody life out of me! How the hell did you get in? What are you doing?'

I dropped my bag on the floor. I gaped at the flat – it was spotless, more spotless than it had ever been. Unrecognizable. There was some new furniture. My IKEA table had been built and my lampshades properly hung. An arrangement of polished apples sat in a bowl on the table. It looked vaguely homely for the first time since I'd moved in.

'How did you get in?' I asked again, looking round at everything. 'Did you do all this?'

Philip was grinning from ear to ear. He ran his hand through his hair, which stuck up on his head as if someone had rubbed a balloon against it. He patted the seat beside him. I suddenly felt very freaked out. Was he certifiable?

'Philip, are you drunk?' I said, trying to sound normal. 'Why have you cleaned my flat?'

His eyes were misty and narrow like a mole's. A lazy smile sat on his lips and he started to laugh.

'Clean up?' he said. 'Me? Of course not! I got Teresa, my fabulous cleaner, to do me a favour while you were out. I borrowed your spare set of keys so I could give you a little surprise. I wanted to help you out, to show you I'm not a bastard and that I do actually have feelings for you. Do you think this apron suits me, by the way?'

I thought about the Philip I knew at work – he was nothing like this. He sealed deals and talked shop. He schmoozed journalists, dined art dealers and antique collectors. Never in a million years had I imagined him doing this. I noticed a bottle of vodka on the floor, half empty, and one of my plates forested with cigarette ends. He must have been here for hours. I couldn't decide whether he was drunk or totally insane. A shiver shot up my spine.

'Come here,' he said, stretching his arms up to me. 'Why do you look so worried? I'm not a psycho, you know.' He laughed heartily.

Tentatively I sat down next to him on the sofa. He leaned into me, his breath pure alcohol.

'Philip,' I said, searching for the right words. 'I . . . it's lovely of you to do this, to clean up and everything. But I think I said this morning that I don't feel comfortable with you being here, especially half naked, you know? And borrowing my keys – isn't that just a little bit OTT? I think you should go home to your family.'

I tried to make my voice sound light, but it wobbled all over the place. I longed for my old, simple life: watching Simon polishing his Star Wars figurines, listening to his skipping rope snap against the floorboards.

Philip put his hands behind his head and stared up at the ceiling.

'Come on, Juliet,' he said. 'I thought we were on the same wavelength. I just wanted to show you I cared. I thought you'd appreciate this.'

He gestured towards the table. The apples shone obediently.

'But, Philip,' I said, irritated, 'you're married. I don't want to be a mistress to you, or to anyone. I've only just broken up with Simon and that wasn't even my choice. I'm just not ready, and you're so much older, and married. I'll say it again: you're married!'

'Oh, I know I must seem strange,' he said. 'Jesus, I'm sorry, Juliet. It's just that . . . I'm not that much older.'

He was drunk and looked suddenly sad. My mind raced with reasons why he should leave this instant, but Philip carried on speaking, oblivious.

'Angela, my wife – she's so demanding,' Philip said,

turning to face me. 'She wants so much, she expects so much – it's difficult to deliver. You, you're different. You're unspoiled, uncomplicated. I can relax with you, tell you anything. You appreciate the small things in life, Angela doesn't. She's slowly sucking the life out of me . . .'

I shivered. The room went cold as if six ghosts had walked in. I didn't want Philip to confide in me.

'Won't you have a drink?' Philip said morosely, picking up the vodka bottle. 'To keep me company?'

My heart sank. I longed to tell him to leave, but he was my boss, which made it all ten times worse. I shook my head and stood up.

'I couldn't touch another drop,' I said exhaustedly. 'Er, I have to make some more aprons tonight, for Imogen's shop. I said I would. So, if you don't mind, I'd better get on with it. I'm sorry. Please, I think you should go.'

Philip's face darkened. He stood up and stormed through to the bedroom, taking off my apron as he went and flinging it on to the floor. He slammed the bedroom door behind him and stayed in there for ages. I hopped from foot to foot, wondering what he was doing. Hopefully he was dressing and not sprawling himself across my mattress or polishing his penis ring. I couldn't believe that Philip was naked in my flat. I imagined telling the other girls at work on Monday: they'd be gobsmacked.

'Never repeat a word of this to anyone,' he said, opening the bedroom door, fully dressed now, his hair under control.

'Of course not,' I said. 'Look, thanks for the cleaning. I appreciate that. Really, it's thoughtful of you. I'm just so worn out now.'

'I wish you'd give me a chance,' he said curtly before handing me back my keys. 'I'd love to take you to France. We have a farmhouse there. It's idyllic. You'd love it. But remember, not a word at work. I'm trusting you, Juliet, OK?'

I smiled eagerly to show that I was trustworthy. I longed for him to go so I could lie down. I needed time to think. I opened the door and stood by it, willing him to leave.

'See you Monday, then,' I said. I felt shaken, exhausted.

'So long,' he said dramatically, stroking my cheek and squeezing my arm. My skin itched with dislike.

I closed the door behind him, sighed loudly and stayed there with my head leaning against the wood until I heard the main door downstairs click shut. I moved to the window and watched Philip walk away down Lovelace Avenue. I realized I'd now seen him from every angle.

Could life get any more complicated? I thought, stretching out on the length of the sofa, my hands resting on my chest.

I glanced at the clock. It was just after seven. Needing distraction, I decided to make another apron. Imogen had inspired me. If I really could make extra cash, I should try. I pulled a box of material from under the bed, plugged in my sewing machine and, switching on the TV, picked a pattern out of Violet's homemaking book and began work.

I thoroughly enjoyed stitching on decorative ribbons in neat lines. Stitching had become a comfort of sorts. At ten o'clock, my apron complete, I positioned it on the sofa, stood back and admired it. I took a picture on my mobile phone and texted it to Imogen, then realized how hungry I was.

Shoving a pizza in the oven, I pulled on my yellow Marigolds to finish off the last few bits of washing-up Philip's cleaner hadn't done. Lazy wench. Ten minutes later, with my rubber gloves still on, I opened the oven and pulled out the rack holding the pizza.

'Shit... shit... no!' I said as my glove melted on to the hot rack. My finger was being singed through the rubber and I dropped the pizza on the floor, topping side down. Plunging my hand into the cold washing-up water, I sighed heavily. There were bits of pizza all over the floor and my rubber gloves were punctured with holes. I imagined Violet shaking her head at me in despair.

'You know, Juliet,' she would say sarcastically. 'Your idea of housework is to sweep the room with your eyes.'

Throwing the whole lot in the bin and opening a box of chocolates, I flopped down in front of the TV. My phone rang. It was a number I didn't recognize.

'Hello,' I said.

'It's Dylan,' Dylan said. 'How does this sound?'

My cheeks flushed with pleasure and surprise.

'What's that?' I said.

'Two days out of the office with me,' he said. 'To film April Flaxman, the Marilyn lady, down in Cornwall.'

A grin broke out on my face.

'Awful,' I said sarcastically. 'I can't think of anything worse.'

'I thought you'd say that,' he said with a laugh. 'But you've no choice. It's all agreed with Philip. Oh, how was your party?'

'Great,' I lied. 'Brilliant. I'm suffering now, though.'

I waited for his reason for not coming, but it never came.

'I'll pick you up on Thursday at six-thirty a.m., then,' he said. 'Oh, can you text me your address?'

'I can come to yours if you'd rather?' I said.

'I wouldn't if I were you,' he said. 'Tower Hamlets can be a scary place at dawn. My estate, anyway – a pal of mine made a documentary for *Dispatches* about how lawless it is a few months back and he said dawn was one of the worst times. He was very surprised to find me living there on the seventeenth floor. We're not all crack addicts.'

I put the phone down and frowned – why would Dylan live in such a rough estate? Surely he could afford something better on his salary? But what did it matter? I liked the sound of Dylan's voice, his soft Scottish accent. I felt a bolt of excitement at the prospect of being alone with him.

I walked through to the bedroom, changed the sheets, then sat on my bed and turned out the lights. The blinds were open and shadows fell dark and long across me. Gazing out of the window at the houses opposite, I tried to imagine what would be visible if the outside walls of those houses were pulled down, the interiors left intact. What unfurling dramas would I see? What deaths or births or joy or sorrow would there be? What were those people doing right now? I had a sudden breathless feeling of wonder. Even though my life was a confused mess, I thought: I'm just one of millions of people in London. We are all in it together.

It wasn't just me, alone in this city, alone in my so-called home, alone in my life.

Chapter Fifteen

To bake perfect fairy cakes, you need to create a happy space in the kitchen. Light candles, put on a pretty housecoat and play soft, soothing music to help you mix excellent batter.

Homemaking Hints for a Happier Home, 1959

Ava phoned me at work the next day from Kenya. Her calls made me think of another era: monochrome movies with a switchboard operator listening in. There was a time delay, a phenomenal crackle and an echo on the line, but I could hear by her tone that she was annoyed with me. I knew it was because I hadn't yet responded to her email about her visit to London.

'Did you get my email?' she asked. 'I sent it two weeks ago.'

'I'm sorry,' I said, scrolling needlessly through my emails until I located hers. 'I've just forgotten to write back.'

'I see,' she said. 'Right, well that makes me feel—'

'I know,' I said. 'I'm sorry.'

Hearing her voice made me desperate to ask about Rosie, but I couldn't imagine actually putting it into words. And part of me wanted to see her face when she found out I knew. Over the phone, she'd have more opportunity to lie.

'Well, I'd better go,' I said. 'I'll see you soon.'

'Oh, darling,' she said, her voice warmer now. 'Why does it always have to be like this?'

I wanted to scream at the top of my voice, '*YOU TELL ME, MOTHER. YOU'RE THE ONE WITH ALL THE SORDID SECRETS!*'

'I'm sorry,' I said calmly. 'I'm just horrendously busy.'

I looked at my desk, empty except for my coffee cup, and hated myself for lying.

'How's Simon?' she said.

'He slept with my flatmate,' I said matter-of-factly. 'I'd better hang up now.'

'Oh, Juliet, that's awful,' she said. 'I'm trying to talk to you. Why do you sound so cross?'

'I'm sorry, I can't hear you, the line's breaking up,' I said. 'Goodbye.'

I put the receiver down. My hand was shaking. I wondered if she might call me back, as she sometimes did, but after a few minutes I knew she wasn't going to. Oh God, our relationship was disastrous. It would take aeons on a psychiatrist's couch to improve it, but I thought there was very little point in even trying. With every year that passed, we became increasingly distant. Sometimes, when months passed without us speaking, I felt like she had died. But even though we had become so estranged, these phone calls always left a horrible sinking sensation in my gut. How could it have got this bad? How could she have let it get this bad?

Out of the corner of my eye, on Philip's secretary's desk, I spied an enormous box of cupcakes that had been sent into the office by a PR company. Most of my colleagues were as thin as pencils and wouldn't even sniff the air above them, but I was suddenly desperate for one. I chose a gigantic chocolate one with vanilla whipped icing and took it into a small spare office used for stationery and excess pieces of furniture where I could enjoy it alone, out of the gaze of the Size Zero Brigade. I closed the door and took a massive bite, letting the icing ooze all over my lips. Delicious. I started to forget about Ava and Philip. I took another bite, and another, until my mouth was stuffed full of sweet joy. My fingers, chin and lips were covered in sticky goo. Then the door swung open with such force it banged against the wall.

'Oh,' said Dylan, suddenly inches away from me, carrying a box. 'Did I disturb you?'

I didn't move. Dylan put the box down and grinned a lop-sided smile as if he was about to burst out laughing. I blushed flaming red and wiped at the icing on my face, only making it worse.

'Um, hello,' I muttered. 'I was just ... I'm ... I didn't know you were ... I'll get out of ... let me wash my hands.'

Dylan stifled a yawn. I noticed his eyes were red and his skin pale. Maybe he'd had a wild night swinging from the chandeliers with Sylvie.

'That looks pretty good,' he said. 'Wait here a minute.'

I sat in my chair, my fingers suspended in mid-air, icing drying around my mouth. Dylan returned holding two more cupcakes. He put them down in front of us and started eating his, letting the icing smear all over his face. I laughed.

149

'Go ahead,' he said, pointing to the one on the table. 'Have another.'

'I couldn't,' I said. 'What are you doing here, anyway?'

'Come on,' he said, breaking it in half. 'Share it with me, then. Wow, these are delicious. I'm just dumping some lighting equipment and finalizing details for our Cornwall trip. Oh, I forgot to mention, do you mind if Sylvie comes for the ride?'

My stomach slipped into my boots, but I shook my head and smiled blandly.

'No,' I said, my voice thick with icing and cake. 'Why would I? Of course not. That's fine with me, absolutely fine.'

He looked up at my face and touched my nose with his finger.

'Icing,' he said. 'On your nose. Here, let me. You really know how to enjoy yourself, don't you?'

My entire body was blushing. Could there be anything more embarrassing than this? He'd already seen me in Patisserie Valerie scoffing a strawberry tart. I sighed deeply and fished in my bag for a tissue.

'I'd better get back to my desk,' I said. 'I can't eat that one – you have it.'

As quick as a flash, he bent down, stuck his face in the frosted icing and looked up at me.

'Do I have anything on my nose?' he said. 'You would tell me, wouldn't you?'

'No, nothing,' I said, smiling. 'You're as clean as a whistle.'

I worried for at least an hour after that about what Dylan thought of me. He seemed to find me vaguely amusing, but did I want to be a joke? I would have preferred him to be dazzled by my elegance, intimidated by my glamour, silenced by my intelligence. But so far he'd seen me bolt out of a meeting, witnessed me bursting into tears about Simon and caught me secretly gorging on cupcakes in the cupboard. I was a lost cause, wasn't I?

Thankfully, Philip was out at a meeting in north London, so I spent the rest of the afternoon emailing people, including Imogen's sister, Zoe, who wanted to organize a hen night for Imogen. Her email subject was 'nipple tassels', and the message itself was peppered with dozens of double entendres. I knew it was all meant to be tongue-in-cheek, but even the suggestion of a hen night involving nipple tassels made my heart stop. However, I had to agree to help out. What else could I do? Tell her that Imogen had had a drastic change of heart?

After work, I walked towards the tube, wondering about my life and why it had become so confusing. A few months ago, I'd had it all planned out. Simon and I would move into our new flat and we would make a home with a capital H, complete with soft furnishings from Graham and Green or Liberty. And from the safety of that Home, we would conduct our happy lives as ideal partners – rum and raisin, salt and pepper, fish and chips. Then, I'd known where we were going. Now, 'we' had become 'I' and I was so lost I needed someone to give me directions. Outside the tube station, not wanting to go home, I decided to go to my Home Help Group meeting in Brixton. I had my aprons and headscarves in my bag – I'd take them along and get their thoughts on them. Plus I hadn't yet told any of my craft mates about Simon. I knew they'd be reassuringly outraged. And that he would join the hordes of boyfriend pincushions we'd made when any of the group got dumped. The tradition was to make a pincushion that looked like the bad boy in question, then we could all stick pins in him every time we met. Maybe we could create a service? Set up a website inviting people to send in a picture of their ex-lover which we could make into a pincushion? The modern day Voodoo doll.

Getting off the tube at Brixton in a blur of commuters, I walked towards the crossing and had just stopped at the kerb when someone grabbed my shoulder from behind.

'Hey!' I said, spinning round.

'Hey!' said Imogen's boyfriend Jonathan. 'Juliet, I saw you in the station and I need to talk to you.'

Jonathan looked dishevelled – as if he'd been sleeping in a skip. His normally tight mod clothes seemed to hang off him and he was out of breath.

'Have you lost weight?' I said. 'You look thin.'

Jonathan gave me a sad look. He chewed the inside of his cheek and said something about not being hungry any more. I asked him what the matter was and he asked me what the matter was with Imogen.

'Why don't you ask her?' I said, knowing I looked guilty. 'She's the one you should be asking. Not me.'

There on the street, between Iceland and Boots, in a few garbled sentences, he told me he knew that Imogen was having an affair but that he was prepared to forgive her. He said that if he didn't marry her he thought he would die, because without Imogen his life was a pointless void. I stopped myself from telling him I couldn't agree more.

'I beg you,' he said. 'I beg you to help her see sense.'

People were looking at us, so I removed Jonathan's tight

grip from my forearm and told him that I'd talk to Imogen, but I didn't know what difference that would make. Jonathan took his glasses off and wiped tears from his eyes. His skin was dry and flaking off all along his eyebrows. He looked so sad, so beaten. My heart went out to him.

'This is what love does to me,' he told me. 'Breaks me up into a million tiny pieces.'

I told him to go home and have a warm bath and something to eat.

'It doesn't feel like home,' he said. 'It's a war zone. I'm so tired, Juliet. So tired.'

I remembered something Violet had written in her flowery handwriting in a margin of her homemaking book: 'Home is where the heart is, but what happens when that heart breaks?'

'I know, Jonathan,' I said. 'I know what it's like, and I'm sorry.'

What could I say? Words were so inadequate. Jonathan apologized and then he thanked me and walked to the edge of the road. For a moment I worried he was going to walk right out in front of the traffic.

'Jonathan?' I called urgently. He turned and looked at me. There was a faraway look in his eyes.

'Be careful,' I said. 'I'll talk to her.'

He waved, and his jacket slipped off his shoulders a little bit. I don't know what it was about that moment, but it made me think of my dad and of Violet and of Simon, and it made me miss them all so much, I felt like falling down on the spot and never getting up. Those sudden moments of sadness always knocked the wind out of me. It felt like someone had taken a slingshot and hit the bottom of my heart with a piece of flint. I watched Jonathan stalk away, his head down. I waited for the feeling of heaviness to leave my brain. I wondered if you could ever out-run your thoughts and leave them behind in a pile of gravel on the pavement for someone else to sweep up. I ran and I ran.

I ran all the way to the Home Help Club at 13, Brixton Water Lane. The house was a Victorian four-storey, but divided into six or seven flats. Various conflicting styles of music were playing from the different flats. A scrub of land out front was dotted with orange plant pots and a rusty bike. I rang the bell and waited.

'Juliet?' said Amanda, the founder of the group and ultimate Queen of Craft. 'Good to see you. We're just debating what makes the best revenge.'

'Oh good,' I said. 'Maybe I can pick up some tips. Simon has dumped me. He slept with our flatmate. That's why I haven't been for a few weeks – I've been too miserable to leave my cave, which, incidentally, is the new flat I had just moved into with him.'

'The bastard!' she said, throwing her arms around me and pulling me close. 'That is outrageous! Come in and tell us what happened. We've a few bottles of wine on the go.'

There was a lump in my throat as I followed Amanda through a dark corridor into the living room, which was lit by old-fashioned standard lamps. It had a lovely, comforting 'lived-in' feel and, like my flat, was pretty messy. It struck me that most of my friends' flats were not that tidy. Maybe obsessing about tidiness came with middle age – I didn't know anyone in their twenties who put plastic covers on the arms of their sofa, or over lampshades. Maybe your home reflected your mindset and most of us were all over the place.

There was a conspiratorial air in the room. Picture a scene from a film about the Resistance: smoky atmosphere, darting eyes, low voices. Sitting in a crescent, sharing an enormous spliff, were the girls, Miriam, Lou, Sadie and now Amanda, who all looked like they'd be more at home in an opium den than at the Stitch and Sew Convention. They were drinking wine and listening to Led Zeppelin. They had all been members when I'd joined and were working towards launching an interiors label called 'I Want You', for which they'd made cushions and throws and wall hangings with words like 'PIN-UP' and 'STOP STARING' and 'STARLET' and 'SIT DOWN' crocheted across them.

'Hi,' I said to the girls. They smiled and waved back. Amanda patted the free seat on the sofa next to her. I collapsed into the cushions and instantly relaxed.

'Juliet was just telling me that Simon has been a fuckwit and slept with Hanna,' Amanda said. 'Remember that blonde girl? The one with white hair? Can someone please give the girl a glass of wine.'

Sadie poured me a glass and handed it to me. I took a deep drink.

'Are you surviving?' Sadie said. 'It's a nightmare, isn't it? But I promise you'll start to feel better. You might need a few nights out first, though, or a couple of one-night stands for good measure.'

'I've done that already,' I said, blushing.

'Good going!' Amanda said. 'Anyone we know?'

I shook my head and waved a hand in the air, dismissing the image of Philip from my thoughts.

'Have you been making anything?' Miriam said. 'When I broke up with my ex I started to knit. Instead of sitting on the sofa staring at the TV with him by my side, I sat on the sofa and stared at the TV with a ball of wool by my side. I hardly noticed the difference and I managed to make scarves for everyone's Christmas presents.'

I sat down and pulled my apron hesitantly out of my bag.

'I've made something that I wanted to show you,' I said quietly. 'It's just from a pattern in my grandma's old home-making book. They're nothing, really, I—'

Amanda looked up at me and cut me off.

'It's gorgeous,' she said, inspecting it. 'You know we've got that stall in Spitalfields now? Why don't you sell your aprons there? You could be part of "I Want You", or think up your own label. What do you think?'

'I've only made four,' I said. 'Are you sure they're not too gimmicky? I have to get more fabric too.'

Amanda listed the best places to find fabric and told me about a website called Cash's where I could get labels printed up – the sort you'd sew into school uniforms – once I'd thought of a name. Then Miriam showed me the iced fairy cakes she'd made that evening, all shaped and decorated like breasts.

'They're for a women's sex-shop launch party I'm doing tomorrow night,' she said. 'I've just started doing that, too – baking alternative cakes. Have you got time to help me make some more? I've got to make a hundred and fifty breast buns.'

A bottle of red wine later, I was standing in the kitchen, in a throng of drunken girls, under the glare of a main light that was just a swinging bulb, moulding breast shapes out of fairy cakes and pink icing. A whole fresh cherry made up the nipple, and inside the cake was a 'surprise' – a blob of jam. The cakes covered every kitchen surface and tabletop. There were fake breasts everywhere – every man's fantasy? When we were done, I scooped up a fingerful of icing, put it in my mouth and let the sweetness slide over my tongue. Maybe it was the dope, or the company, but now life didn't seem so bad. I felt incredibly rational, as if I could forgive anyone anything.

'Oh, we forgot to ask you – what's the worst or best act of revenge you've committed?' Amanda asked. 'We were discussing it before you turned up but couldn't think of anything original.'

I searched through catalogues of memories for a decent anecdote. Violet flashed into my mind.

'I was bullied for a while at school for not living with my parents,' I said, rolling my eyes. 'So my grandmother decided to take revenge on the bully. It was pretty drastic. We lived in Cornwall and she had this huge old fisherman's net. She set it up so that when he was walking home, she caught him up in it, securing it so he couldn't escape. She wanted him to understand what it was like to feel hunted.'

'Wow,' said Amanda. 'Did it work?'

'Everyone found out at school and took the piss, so he never even looked at me again,' I said. 'But it was strange. I ended up feeling kind of sorry for him.'

Amanda drank from her glass and poured herself more.

'My ex has a new live-in girlfriend,' she said, pulling a pissed-off face. 'When I dropped by to collect something, I went to the bathroom, found her toothbrush and scrubbed the toilet seat with it.'

Everyone laughed. I clinked glasses with hers.

'You have to look for someone's Achilles' heel,' said Zoe, who was laid out on her back. 'My boyfriend is a photographer and has a studio full of equipment. If he cheated on me, the only way I could get him back would be to smash it all up with a sledgehammer or torch the lot. Then he'd be ruined.'

I burst out laughing mid-swallow. Wine shot through my nose.

'Zoe!' I said. 'You're impressively scary. I wouldn't want to cross you. With Simon, my revenge is trying not to beg him to come back. I'm pathetic, aren't I?'

Amanda clucked sympathetically.

'Nothing really works,' said Zoe. 'The best revenge is to get happy again. And not just a bit happy, but deliriously, ecstatically happy, like you've never been before.'

'And find someone else,' I said. 'Someone that doesn't wear trainers like boats or talk about Ofsted reports.'

'Absolutely,' Zoe said. 'Let's drink and smoke to that.'

I did as she said. And at around eleven, the cupcakes were spinning, or I was. I began to think about everything I was worried about, and wanted desperately to talk to someone who really knew me. A terrible idea came into my head, and, because I was drunk, I convinced myself I'd had the best idea in the world.

'Can I call a taxi?' I said. 'Do you know a number?'

I left, thanking the girls and promising to come to Spitalfields Market with my aprons as soon as I'd made enough.

'Where are you going?' Amanda asked when the taxi sounded its horn. 'You have icing sugar on your nose.'

'Home,' I lied.

In Simon's parents' back garden, my heels sank into the lawn, so I took them off and put them in my bag. It was too late to enter the building conventionally, so I threw stones up at Simon's window to get his attention. Eventually a light snapped on and Simon's face appeared.

'Is that you, Juliet?' he whispered, peering down at me. 'What on earth are you doing?'

He was smiling, and I liked that. I was glad my presence could make him smile, even though he cheated on me.

'I need to talk to you,' I said.

He said he'd come down, so I sat on the step by the back door, near an old bathtub filled with rosemary, chives, mint and parsley.

'Hello,' Simon said, coming out of the door and sitting on the step beside me. He had a bare chest but was wearing tracksuit trousers. I took a long look at him: he looked the same – softer round the edges, perhaps. Maybe there wasn't room for his rowing machine in this eight-bedroom house.

'This is the one place in London where it's dark enough to see the stars,' I said, looking up at the sky, a black sheet with glitter spilled over it. 'What privilege.'

'Why are you here, Juliet?' Simon asked, shuffling his slippers on the steps. 'It's the middle of the night.'

'I know it's the middle of the night,' I said, suddenly irritated. Simon could be so needlessly obvious. 'But I need to talk to you about my family.'

Simon hummed and sighed. In the course of our relationship, I'd only talked about my family a handful of times, but whenever I'd brought it up, he'd treated me as if I had 'issues'. (Maybe I had, but it was his job to pretend I was fine.)

'The year my dad died,' I said, 'Ava left and went to Sydney. I found this letter from her to Violet saying that she had had a baby and had her adopted.'

I waited for Simon to gasp. I waited for him to throw his arms around me and offer to help in whatever way he could. Maybe I thought he'd want to come back. I counted to fifteen before he answered.

'Yeah,' he said. 'I know.'

I hadn't expected that.

'*WHAT*?' I shouted, springing up from the step. '*YOU KNOW*?'

Simon grabbed my hand and put a finger to his lips.

'Ssshh,' he said. 'You'll wake my folks.'

I flopped down hard next to him. I faced him full on and asked him again.

'You know?' I said. 'How do you know? And didn't you think to tell me?'

A fox sidled across the lawn in front of us and drank from the pond, which had a sculpture of a naked woman in the middle of it. Simon picked a sprig of rosemary from the bush and pulled at the needles. He paused a while. I wanted to scream a blood-curdling scream.

'I only know because I found the letter the day we moved into the flat,' he said. 'I was going to say something – I tried to say something – but then I couldn't. Not after what happened with Hanna.'

I stared at him, incredulous. He held his hands upwards, like it was all beyond his control.

'I just assumed you'd find it,' he said. 'I know you love those old books. I knew you'd flick through and find it. I'm sorry.'

'Simon,' I said. 'I literally cannot believe you wouldn't tell me something as big, as major as that. What planet are you on?'

'We've been through this,' he said jokingly. 'Men are from Mars, women are from Venus.'

Deflated, I picked up little stones from the steps and threw them on to the lawn. I knew Simon wanted to tell me to stop.

'Look, I'm sorry. What will you do?' he said instead. 'Have you asked your mum about it?'

I shrugged. Suddenly I didn't want to talk about it. How could Simon have not told me about the letter? It showed that he totally lacked humanity. I wished I'd never come.

'Juliet,' he said quietly, resting his hand on my knee. 'Can you ever forgive me for Hanna?'

From behind us, the door suddenly flew open. Standing in a red dressing gown, her black hair loose over her shoulders like liquorice sticks, was Simon's mum, Anne. We'd been pretty close for the years Simon and I had been together, so I stood up to give her a hug.

'Simon?' she said, ignoring me. 'Are you OK?'

'Yes,' he muttered, looking extremely uncomfortable. 'Juliet's just going.'

'I . . . I . . . how are you, Anne?' I started, trying to catch her eye. 'I'm sorry we haven't seen each other. I—'

'Juliet,' she said, cutting me off. 'I have nothing to say to you. I'm so disappointed in you for cheating on Simon. You, of all people, should have realized what a great catch my son is. Do you realize he won a scholarship to Sandhurst? This is how you repay him? Leave him alone.'

She glared at me, then slammed the door shut. Simon looked sheepish.

'Eh?' I said, stunned. 'Simon, did you tell . . . does your mum think I was the one who— You absolute bastard!'

But Simon just placed his head in his hands. Hiding his face, hiding his guilt.

'If this is what you're like, I'm pleased we're not together any more,' I said. 'Really, I'm pleased. Delighted.'

I pulled on my heels and walked away from Simon, perforating the lawn, imagining that the grass was Simon's backstabbing flesh.

Chapter Sixteen

If you are leaving your house for a period of time, put
the house in good order before you leave – a house that
is clean and shipshape will be a pleasure to return to.

America's Homemaking Book,
Marguerite Dodd, 1957

Violet once told me that a real test of a relationship is whether
a couple could live happily in a caravan together. I wasn't sure
she had ever tested the theory out. Her husband Aaron had
been killed when they'd been married only three years, so she
barely got to live with him at all. After he died Violet cleaned
like crazy, bleaching everything within an inch of its life, making their house absolutely perfect, as if he might be coming
back. Sad, perhaps, but I guess that was all she had: a half-empty
home to fill with half-empty hope.

I looked around the flat. Even though Philip had had it
cleaned, it was already returning to its default setting: abom-
inable. I stared at the dirty plates, unwashed clothes and

takeaway containers on the floor and wondered where my good intentions had gone. It wasn't socially acceptable to live in the apocalyptic state I lived in. But I simply didn't have the inclination to freshen up my bathroom with lemon peel, crochet a doily or plant herbs in ramekins. I zipped up my overnight bag and looked out of the front window over Lovelace Avenue. The sun shone brightly. I stood there for a moment and watched a mother smearing sun cream on to her baby's face and a man wearing only boxer shorts push his dustbin into the road. I wondered if I had too many clothes on. I checked my watch: six forty a.m., so there was no time to change. Dylan was due any minute to pick me up for our trip down to Cornwall.

I walked into the bathroom and checked my make-up. I needed more mascara. And lipstick. God, I was nervous. Why was I so nervous? It was ridiculous, but the prospect of spending six hours in a car with Sylvie and Dylan made me anxious. I wanted Dylan to like me, but worried it would put Sylvie's back up, plus I hated being the singleton gooseberry. It was hard to be sweet when people assumed you'd be sour.

I heard a horn sound outside. A glance out of the window confirmed it was him. Closing the door on unwashed laundry and a tower of dirty plates, I ran down the communal stairs and flung open the front door.

'Morning,' I said, waving to Dylan. He smiled back and opened the passenger door for me.

Dylan's camper van was dark red with a white roof. Like his Converse, it looked one hundred years old. But climbing inside, I had to give it to him – Dylan's camper was cool. Behind the front seats was a self-contained living space with green and brown tartan-covered seats that pulled out into a bed, a small pull-down table and a kitchen area complete with sink and cooker. It was surprisingly homely. There was no sign of Sylvie, unless she was clinging to the undercarriage.

'Where's Sylvie?' I asked. 'Are we picking her up?'

Dylan shook his head. His crow-black hair was looking especially glossy and kicked out at the ends. His orange-hazel eyes shone out from his freckles and his eyelashes seemed excessively long. I suddenly felt extremely shy.

'She got an invite to a party at Soho House,' he said, looking unimpressed. 'Of course, that's far more appealing than a trip down to Cornwall with me.'

I felt quietly relieved and just a little bit excited.

'Whose party?' I asked, then immediately regretted it. By the look on Dylan's face, I was clearly missing the point.

'I have no idea,' he said. 'Some idiot she works with, probably. Who would rather drink champagne in a pretentious bar than be by the sea?'

Given the chance I would, I thought, but shrugged unconvincingly. I was filled with questions about Sylvie. Where did she work? Who were her friends? What would she wear to a party at Soho House? Did she really love Dylan? Did he really love her? Of course I didn't ask any of them. I put on my seatbelt and rested my bag on my knee.

'All set?' he said, turning the key in the ignition. He fiddled with the radio controls, but nothing happened. He banged it with the palm of his hand.

'Sorry, I need to fix this radio – it's temperamental,' he said, glancing at me apologetically. 'We'll have to make our own entertainment.'

I nodded and smiled, wondering what on earth we'd talk about for six hours solid.

I needn't have worried. Unlike Simon, who drove in funereal silence, leaving me with nothing to do but stare out of the window at electricity pylons and the occasional cow, Dylan was a great conversationalist. He talked to me about his rock 'n' roll collection, the music venues he liked in London (mostly intimate, dark places where you could actually get near the musicians). He told me how he liked to go to Columbia Road market in Hackney really early on Sunday mornings to buy Sylvie fresh flowers (not that she deserved them, in my eyes), and that he had a love–hate relationship with city living.

'I'd love to live by the sea,' he said. 'But London has got under my skin. I sometimes feel like London is living in me, rather than I'm living in London.'

He said that though there were some parts of his job he loved, he couldn't tolerate all the egos in TV.

'Everyone is writing a script in his or her spare time or making an unpaid award-winning documentary about heroin addicts,' he said. 'There's a real sense of creative one-upmanship, but as far as I can tell, it's the people who don't go on about it that are really worth their salt.'

'Are you one of those salty types, by any chance?' I asked jokingly.

He turned to smile at me.

'How did you guess?' he said sarcastically. 'Everything I do or say is right, you must know that by now?'

His face lit up when he talked about surfing, telling me that he had travelled to the ends of the earth in pursuit of the perfect wave. My existence seemed rather dull in contrast. I tried to muster up interesting snippets, but was still tired after my party and the ill-advised trip to Simon's house on Monday night (I still couldn't believe what he was like) that I failed miserably.

'Have you ever surfed?' he asked me. 'We could go while we're down in Cornwall. I listened to the forecast before I set off and the waves should be great.'

My heart plunged into my gut. I had known he'd suggest this, but I couldn't possibly agree. I looked out of the window, blinking at the passing cars, fields and trees.

'I don't like water much,' I said quietly. I stopped talking. I didn't want to go into details. I never did.

Dylan looked at me quizzically and, sensing my discomfort, I think, he changed the subject. He asked me lots of questions, far more than Simon ever did in our entire relationship. He seemed genuinely interested in what made me tick. When I told him I belonged to the Home Help Group and had started making aprons and headscarves from patterns I'd found in Violet's book, he was incredibly enthusiastic.

'You should start your own business,' he said. 'You can't really shine when you're just a tiny cog in a vast machine like Rosendale's, can you?'

When I shook my head, he grinned.

'Actually,' he said, 'I take that back. Juliet Rice could shine anywhere.'

I laughed self-consciously, muttered something incoherent and offered Dylan a humbug.

We arrived at April Flaxman's hotel – Honeysuckle House – at lunchtime, aching all over from sitting in the van for six hours. Honeysuckle House was incredible, a sprawling country-style manor, with landscaped grounds rolling down to the sea. It was so picturesque I half expected Hercule Poirot, dressed in an impeccable pale blue suit, to be taking high tea. And the smell of the air! The scent of honeysuckle was almost overwhelming. This was a million miles away from the merciless bustle and stink of London. I took a deep breath of fresh air and felt my shoulders drop an inch.

'Shall we?' Dylan asked, holding open the main door for me. I walked in, immediately bumping into an enormous porcelain vase of white lilies.

'Got it!' Dylan said, catching the vase, most likely a priceless antique, just in time. I smiled gratefully and blushed (again) as Dylan introduced himself to the girl on reception.

While she called April Flaxman, Dylan and I waited in the drawing room, a grand space filled with spectacular antique furniture you'd expect to be cordoned off in a National Trust stately home. Dark wooden tables shone like mirrors, the carpet was deep claret and the walls were covered with portraits in huge gold frames, lit from below by soft ceramic lamps. I sat down on the leather Chesterfield nestling in a window bay, warm from the sun, and Dylan chatted to a fellow hotel guest. I admired that about Dylan – how easily he spoke to strangers. I always felt nervous and unsure of what to say, unless I'd had two glasses of wine, and then it was as if someone had pressed play and I couldn't shut up. Closing my eyes for a moment, feeling the heat of the sun on my face, I thought about Simon's complete lack of backbone. He was a jellyfish. I'd seen him in a new light, and although the circumstances of our break-up still hurt like hell, I was genuinely relieved now that we weren't together. Who needs a spineless idiot as a boyfriend?

I snapped open my eyes when Dylan nudged me. He nodded towards the doorway, where April Flaxman was standing. Deeply tanned, dressed in an eggshell-blue dress, a simple string of pearls around her neck, her golden hair laquered solid, she was desperately glam. She extended her arms towards us, and, with the light shining through the window like a spotlight behind her, was momentarily lit up.

'It's the Virgin Mary,' Dylan whispered to me out of the corner of his mouth.

I suppressed a giggle, while April paused, then swept over the carpet to us. She kissed and hugged us both, then gestured at us to sit down. Up close I saw she had virtually no lines on her face, which she later put down to a daily dose of Starflower, whatever that was. I suspected the surgeon's scalpel had played a role.

'I've saved the best room for you two,' she said in a polished upper-class accent. 'It has a four-poster bed and a balcony overlooking the cliffs. You can have your breakfast out there tomorrow, scrambled eggs and smoked salmon, perhaps?'

Dylan grinned at me.

'Excellent,' he said. 'That sounds phenomenal, but I'm afraid we're not together. Well, we're together, but we're colleagues, not lovers. Juliet can have that room. I'm happy to sleep in my van.'

I mentally recorded the way Dylan said 'lovers'.

'Oh, you absolutely will not sleep in your van,' she said in mock horror. 'My mistake, but when I saw you both, I assumed you were together, probably because you look rather alike. Young and pretty.'

She pantomimed drawing dots over her face.

'All those freckles,' she said. 'They say you're attracted to someone who looks like you, don't they? Something like that. But anyway, I've said enough, my mouth runs away with me. I'm so excited about filming for Channel 4 – it's awfully glamorous.'

'And so are you, April,' Dylan said.

I tried not to cringe, and watched her enjoying Dylan's flirtation. He was good at this charming business.

'Would you like to know something exciting?' she said, leaning in close to us.

'Yes,' Dylan and I answered in unison.

'I have more of Marilyn's things,' she said. 'Upstairs I have some absolute gems, but I'm never going to sell them. They're too close to my heart to do that. I'll show them to you, but first you must settle in and let me know what you want to film.'

My bedroom was spectacular. April insisted I have the Tudor four-poster bed, despite being alone. For half a second I wished Simon could be there to see the splendour, then I remembered how foul he'd been and felt glad he wasn't.

I put down my overnight bag and pushed open the French windows that led out on to the balcony overlooking the sea. A breeze made the long ivory lace curtains billow around me. On the bedside table stood a decanter of brandy, with two crystal glasses and a bowl of fresh figs. A silk flower lay on each pillow and a silk quilt covered the bed. This was fabulous!

I sat on the quilt, feeling the springiness of the mattress. Whichever angle I lay at, there remained acres of bed all round me. I leaned back into the stack of square white pillows, twiddling a purple silk flower between my finger and thumb, listening to the sound of seagulls. I thought about Rosie. What was she like? Where was she now?

The whole thing felt completely unreal, as if it was all happening to someone else. I shook my head. Right now, I was in the most beautiful hotel with Dylan, who I liked quite a lot, so I forbade myself to ruin it with worries. I shut my eyes and listened to the sound of the sea. I wished I found it comforting, like everyone else in the entire world, but it just made me think of the day Dad died. For hours after he'd drowned, I had sat on the beach while divers searched for his body. I kept expecting one of them to shout out that they'd found him, alive and kicking, but there was nothing, only the hypnotic lapping of the waves, the divers' heads bobbing in and out of the water like black marbles, the tick-tock of time passing. I snapped open my eyes and sighed.

'Juliet?' came Dylan's voice from outside my door. 'Can I come in?'

I swung my legs off the bed, smoothed down my dress, pinched my cheeks and opened the door. He put his hand on my upper arm briefly, which, in such close proximity to the bed, felt incredibly intimate. I thought: warm hands, warm heart. Embarrassed, I lurched away from him, flapping round the room like a trapped sparrow, showing him the en-suite bathroom, marvelling at the chrome legs and feet on the bath. He laughed at me and told me I was like a kid in a sweet shop.

'Come on, then,' he said, raising an eyebrow, 'we'd better get down to business.'

I don't know whether it was a deliberate attempt to embarrass me – I was beginning to think he enjoyed basking in the glow of my red face – but this time I told myself not to blush and to fight back.

'I agree,' I said, with as penetrative a stare as I could muster. 'Let's get on with the job in hand.'

We filmed for four long hours for what would eventually be edited to just a few minutes of the documentary, if that. I asked April the questions, while Dylan filmed. Wow, could she talk. What we really wanted to know was how she'd got hold of Marilyn's vanity case, but she insisted on telling us her entire life history first, which was seventy-six years long.

The only way to survive was to drink the champagne that April had had delivered to the room. Finally, she came to the point, telling us that she used to work as a make-up artist in Hollywood and had worked with Marilyn on *The Seven Year Itch* and *Gentlemen Prefer Blondes*.

'That scene in *The Seven Year Itch* – you know, the one with the dress being blown up in the air from the breeze wafting up from the sidewalk?' April said. 'I was there when that was filmed on Lexington Avenue in New York. But the New Yorkers who came to watch got so worked up, the director couldn't use any of the footage because of the noise of the crowd! She had to do it again in a studio, but then it was cut for being too steamy. Imagine that! Oh, those days. Anyway, what was I saying?'

'About her possessions that you've donated to the Rosendale's auction?' Dylan prompted, giving me a little smile, because, finally, April was getting to the point of the interview.

Apparently they had become close, and before April returned to England Marilyn had given her a few of her things as a kind of thank you. In an attic room at Honeysuckle House, where little windows overlooked the coastline, she opened an enormous rosewood wardrobe and showed us what other treasures she owned: a fantastic emerald ring, two diamond necklaces, a selection of clutch bags and a long black evening dress. We weren't allowed to film these because she didn't want collectors bothering her, trying to buy them.

'I adore this stone,' April said, pushing the emerald ring on her finger and holding it up to the light. 'I love imagining what she might have worn this for – cocktails at the Copacabana perhaps? Glamour in the Fifties was so different from what it means these days. Now it's fake tans and cocaine habits; then it was pure style and grace.'

April stopped talking and sat down on a floral chaise longue, her slender ankles neatly crossed. Dylan sat next to her, drinking his champagne. From the flush in his cheeks, I thought he was probably a bit drunk. Suddenly April stood up and crossed the room to where the black dress was hanging. She draped it over her arm and looked at me.

'Why don't you try this on, Juliet?' she said. 'If I had the figure, I would.'

I shook my head and said, 'No.' I was wearing a pink sundress with red sandals and a red headband, and hardly any make-up. There was no way I—

'Go on,' said Dylan, smiling at me. 'Model it for your captivated audience. We'd love to see you all scrubbed up. I reckon you could give old Marilyn a run for her dollars.'

I gave him a look – he was teasing me again, but his eyes were kind. We'd all had a few drinks, so I thought, Oh, why the hell not? I slipped behind an old-fashioned dressing screen in the corner of the room, took off my pink sundress and pulled Marilyn's gown over my head. The intricate beading made it incredibly heavy. Somewhere in my befuddled mind I'd imagined it would fit me perfectly. I'd imagined being transformed into a Marilyn lookalike – but it swamped me at the top and was too tight around the waist. I came out from behind the screen, pulling a horrified face.

'I'm not quite the right shape, am I?' I said. 'I'm clearly not a Hollywood starlet.'

'Of course you are,' April tutted. 'It's almost right, but that dress never fitted her properly either. It's probably why she gave it to me!'

I smiled gratefully. Dylan pulled his mobile phone from his pocket and took a picture of me. I frowned.

'My God, you look great,' he said, inspecting the picture rather than looking at me in the flesh. 'You know, Sylvie would die for that dress. I'm going to send her this picture and maybe she'll realize Soho House isn't the only glamorous place in the world.'

'Oh no,' I said, returning to my safe place behind the screen. 'Please don't send her that picture, not of me. She'll wonder what I'm doing trying dresses on in front of you. I don't want her to hate me.'

Dylan shrugged and put his phone back in his pocket. I heard April asking Dylan about Sylvie and him sighing, telling her she was driving him crazy. Suddenly glum at the mention of Sylvie, I unzipped the dress, took it off and draped it over the screen. It must have been too heavy, or I knocked it with my elbow, because the screen toppled over and crashed to the floor. I stood in front of Dylan and April in my knickers and bra – not my best set, either. Dylan cracked up laughing.

'Oh, I'm sorry, April,' I said, yanking my sundress up from the floor and holding it round my body. 'I'm so clumsy, I—'

She waved an elegant hand in the air dismissively and lifted up the screen to shield me. Dylan was laughing so hard he was holding his sides and the vein on his temple was throbbing. My cheeks blazed. Suddenly I hated him.

'Don't laugh at me,' I said to him coldly. 'I'm not a joke.'

Eventually he displayed an iota of self-control and managed to stop.

'I'm sorry – it was just your expression,' he said, wiping his eyes. 'I'll go downstairs and put the camera away.'

April gave me an understanding woman-to-woman smile. She rolled her eyes at Dylan.

'We've had a long day,' she said gently. 'I think it's probably time for dinner.'

Dinner was an awkward, stilted seafood meal of locally caught bream and scallops, with Dylan making small talk and trying to make me laugh with comments like 'Life's a bream' and 'Cod, I'm hungry'. I sat there, burning with a mixture of irrational anger and shame. Eating in front of a guy when they've just seen you in your worst M&S underwear is not easy. I was relieved when it was over and April sent over two large brandies and a plate of home-made truffles dusted in cocoa. I drank my brandy down in one gulp and polished off the truffles. Dylan asked if I wanted to go for a walk along the beach, and wouldn't leave me alone until I agreed.

Outside, the air was warm and clean. The sun was melting butter over the water. Seagulls soared overhead. There was no one else on the beach besides us. I hated the sea, but I loved the feel of the sand on my soles. I took my shoes off and walked barefoot.

'I think we've had our first lovers' tiff,' Dylan said, grinning.

He had changed into a thin grey jumper and dark brown cords, all charmingly ragged at the edges. He threw his arm casually over my shoulders. Again I didn't know how to interpret this surprisingly intimate gesture and it annoyed me. Why did he assume he could throw his arm around me without asking?

'Why are you constantly winding me up?' I said, shrugging him off. 'You love taking the piss out of me, don't you?'

His face dropped and he stopped walking.

'No, I don't,' he said curtly. 'I don't mean to wind you up. It's just the way I am. It's only because I like you.'

I knew I was being uptight and oversensitive. I scolded myself for spoiling the evening.

'Oh, I'm just being stupid,' I said apologetically. 'I've got too much going on in my head at the moment.'

Dylan turned to face me and narrowed his eyes. He chewed the inside of his cheek for a moment, as if he was plotting something. Then, just as I opened my mouth to say I was going to go back into the hotel, he whipped off his jumper and trousers, revealing a wiry, taut body. I held my breath in anticipation.

'Now you can laugh at my underwear,' he said, before picking me up by the waist and throwing me over his shoulder. Suddenly the world had turned on its axis. Blood rushed to my head as my nose banged against his back. He started to run towards the sea. I dug my fingers into his waist, clinging on, my heart pounding in panic.

'Dylan!' I screamed. 'What are you doing? Stop! Stop!'

But Dylan wasn't listening. He was laughing and splashing into the water, his bare feet sinking into the seabed. He loosened his grip, threatening to drop me in. It was only the second time I'd stepped into the sea since Dad had drowned. My body stiffened and I fell silent as fear squeezed my heart. I wanted to cry, but I was too frightened to breathe. I curled my hands into fists and pushed one into my mouth. I bit down hard and the pain of it helped me forget for a moment. Then came a horrible low moan that I didn't recognize as my voice.

'Juliet?' Dylan said, suddenly calm, taking me out of the water and placing me down on the sand. 'Oh God, what's wrong?'

I sank down on to the sand and put my head in my hands. Embarrassingly I started to cry, to really sob. To Dylan, who had surfed and swum in the most dangerous waters, I must have seemed utterly pathetic. But something in me had been undone – I couldn't stop the tears flowing.

'I'm so sorry,' Dylan said, kneeling down beside me, brushing strands of wet hair away from my eyes. 'I've just remembered, you said you didn't like water. I didn't realize you really hated it. Do you have a proper phobia? That was so stupid of me. Do you want to tell me why you're so frightened? I might be able to help.'

'I'm not usually like this,' I stuttered, using the cuffs of my cardigan to wipe the tears from my cheeks. 'You must think I'm always crying, but it's this, the water, I . . . I . . .'

'What is it?' he said.

I looked up at Dylan's concerned face. He was genuinely worried and I could tell he would really listen. I had never told anyone the whole story, but something about Dylan and being far away from my life in London made me do something I'd never done.

'This is so strange,' I said. 'But I want to tell you this story. This awful story.'

'Go on,' he said softly, quickly pulling on his jumper and trousers, sitting right next to me in the sand, his little toe almost touching mine. 'Tell me.'

So I did. I told Dylan my awful story. I told him the truth.

Chapter Seventeen

Ultimately, a family makes a house a home, no matter
how well you housekeep. Otherwise it is just a tidy house.

Homemaking Hints for a Happier Home, 1959

The morning of the day I killed my father, he and I were at the
kitchen sink, washing up. The radio was on, so we worked
companionably listening to a programme about honey bees.
Our white cat Samuel sat on the draining board frowning at
the water in the sink. Outside, dark clouds bundled over the
garden, threatening rain.

'On we toil, eh, Juliet?' Dad said cheerfully, pushing his
sleeves further up his arms. 'Whatever vulgar crap life throws
at us.'

My dad had greyed young and wore his pale hair long,
sometimes held back by a headband. He was not a conventional man, nor was he a clichéd 'artist'. I used to think that,
with his white hair and weathered skin, he looked more like a
seadog than a painter.

That morning at the sink, I smiled up at him hoping his cheer was genuine. I tried hard to keep his spirits up, but my silly attempts – dances, songs and poems – weren't enough. I knew he was unhappy. It was the way he stared wistfully out of the windows, the long periods of silence, and the fact he never seemed to sleep. If I woke during the night and crept downstairs to get a drink, he would be sitting alone in the dark, staring at his hands, or smoking roll-up cigarettes. More than once, when I surprised him at night and he quickly switched on a smile, I saw his cheeks and eyes were wet.

'What are we going to do, eh, Juliet?' he said, hanging his dishcloth over the tap halfway through the pile of dirty plates. 'We're going to have to do something, aren't we?'

He often asked these vague questions to which Samuel and I had no answer. I opened my mouth to say something, but was silenced by the clip-clop of Ava's heels on the path outside. Ava had been out all night, apparently at a friend's party. She was the teenager in the household, Dad and I the concerned parents, even though I was just nine years old.

Ava opened the door to the kitchen and stood there in the door frame, lit up by a sudden burst of sunshine behind her, as radiant as an angel. Even though Dad was upset with her, I knew she took his breath away. She took mine away too – sometimes I couldn't believe I really belonged to her at all.

'Good morning, wife,' Dad said sardonically. 'And where have you been?'

Ava's eyes were wild, her hair now cropped short. She put down her bag, walked to the sink, poured herself a glass of water and smiled. She patted my head and pulled me by the shoulders to her legs. I hugged her waist, searching for warmth.

'You know where I've been,' she said, popping out painkillers from a packet and swallowing them. 'At my friend's party, remember? It's what young people do. You should have come too, instead of being such a big bore.'

I hoped Ava was teasing Dad, but there was no humour in her voice. I checked Ava's face to see if she was smiling. She wasn't. Dad put his head in his hands.

'Ava,' he said. 'I couldn't have come. I was looking after Juliet here. One of us has to be a responsible parent. Anyway, I'm sure you wouldn't really want me there.'

Ava shot him a dark look. 'What are you saying?' she snapped. 'That I'm a bad mother? At least I have a life. At least I haven't sold out.'

'So I've sold out now because I don't party every night?' he said. 'I don't need to party because I want to be with you and Juliet, not a bunch of strangers. But we don't seem to be enough for you, do we?'

'I feel like you're trying to suffocate me. Why do you have to be so possessive?' she said. 'It's so unattractive.'

'I'm not possessive!' Dad shouted, pushing back his chair. 'That is not what I said! You always twist things. I'm trying to say that I love my family but you seem to want something else. What else do you want, Ava? Tell me, because it's driving me insane!'

Ava was standing at the sink. Her back was as stiff as a board. I saw her hand trembling. Without a word, she picked up a saucer and threw it at Dad's head. 'Ava!' he screamed. 'What are you doing?'

'Don't you know anything about me, you stupid bastard?' she shouted at him. 'I want my freedom! I don't want to be trapped by all this domesticity bullshit you've lured me into! Why can't you just let me go!'

Trembling, standing in the doorway, my heart beat loudly in my chest. I gnashed my teeth together, not knowing what to do.

'You're pathetic, Charles,' she said, her voice as hard as stone.

I looked at my father, his lips quivering. I shook with anger and hated her more than ever before. I knew what she was like. I knew the truth. Running towards her, slapping and hitting, I yelled, 'Don't say that! I hate you!'

Ava pushed me away and ran up the stairs. I listened as she slammed the bedroom door. I moved over to Dad and put my hand on his arm. He picked me up and sat me on his knee. I watched tears stream down his face.

'I've let your mum down somehow,' he said. 'I love her so much, but I'm just not enough for her. I think she's beginning to despise me, and that's an awful thing, a terrible thing. I must have done something wrong.'

I felt rage boiling and burning inside my belly. I couldn't let him believe that was true. I decided that I was the only person who could put a stop to his misery. I could tell him the secrets I'd discovered about Ava, I could tell him that she was having an affair, that she'd bought my silence and that she was not good enough for him, not the other way round. I took a deep breath.

'Dad, she has another boyfriend,' I said quickly. 'She stays there at night. I've seen them together. That's probably where she was last night. You should tell her you know. That will make her sorry. That will make her sorry and realize that she's a horrible person.'

Dad leaned back in his seat and let out a long, slow sigh. He covered his eyes with his hands and sobbed like a baby. I tried to put my arms round him, but I wasn't big enough to hold him properly. I felt hot with panic – maybe I shouldn't have said anything.

'Charles?' said Ava, suddenly there in the room with us.

'What's wrong?' she said. 'Why are you crying like that? I was out of line. I shouldn't have said . . . I know I haven't made things easy—'

Dad lifted his hand to silence her.

'Go to your room, Juliet,' my dad said, lifting me off his knee. 'Go now, please.'

I went upstairs and locked my bedroom door and sat on my bed. Even with my hands over my ears I could hear them arguing, then screaming at each other. I started to hum the hymns we sang at school. I heard the sound of struggling. I knew they were fighting – I'd seen them do it once before, grabbing each other's hair and arms. My stomach turned in on itself. I stood on the bed and stared out of the window at people walking past the house. A couple looked up, noticed me, smiled and waved. I didn't wave back. I stood still, listening for The End. Eventually it came, and there was silence.

Creeping down the stairs, I saw Ava lying face down on the sofa, crying into the cushion. She looked like a doll. Dad was outside, marching towards the garden gate. He looked as wild as the slate sky above him. In his hand there was a whisky bottle. He hardly ever drank alcohol.

'This is all your fault,' I said to Ava before running through the door after Dad.

'Daddy!' I called, as it started to rain. 'Daddy!'

But Dad was in a world of his own. In driving rain, he marched down our street, straight down to the beach, swigging from the whisky bottle as he went. I chased after him, my sandals slapping on the wet path. At the beach I watched him throw the empty bottle down and start running towards the sea, shouting at the top of his lungs. I ran after him as fast as I could, but he was so far ahead. He couldn't hear my voice above his own. He ran into the sea, where waves were crashing all around him.

Pulling off my sandals, I ran to the water, calling him at the top of my voice. He wasn't a strong swimmer. I looked frantically around for help. Along the beach was a man walking his dog. Dad just swam out, over and under the waves. I ran in after him, shivering in the freezing water, but the waves were too strong for me. They crashed over my head, filling my mouth with water. I coughed and spluttered, trying to dig my feet into the sand to get balance. When I surfaced, I couldn't see my dad any more. My lungs ached from shouting and swallowing water. I stood waist-high in the sea, rain slicing the black clouds above. Crying hysterically, I clambered out of the sea and collapsed on to the sand. The man with the dog ran towards me.

'My dad's in there!' I screamed. 'And I can't see him!'

The man ran out into the sea looking for Dad, but he soon turned back. I could tell by his face it was no good.

'My God, I'm sorry,' he said. 'I just can't see him out there. It's too rough. Let me call the coastguard.'

We both knew it was too late. The waves were enormous, the current fierce, the sky black with storm. We both knew that my father had drowned.

I thought: This is my fault. I killed him.

'I was to blame,' I said to Dylan now, tears soaking my cheeks and neck. 'I killed him.'

I rested my chin on my knees and waited. Now that I'd said the words out loud and couldn't retract them, I had never felt so exposed.

'Juliet, please listen,' Dylan said softly, taking my hand and holding it. 'You didn't kill him.'

I faced Dylan and he smiled warmly.

'Please,' he said. 'You've got to believe it. You did not kill him.'

'But if I hadn't told him about Ava's affair, he never would have run into the sea and drowned in those waves,' I said, shivering. 'My parents would have carried on as they were, happily unhappy.'

Dylan shook his head.

'I don't think anyone is happily unhappy,' he said. 'He may have already known about Ava's affair, or he may have already been contemplating suicide.'

I swallowed hard.

'But that's worse,' I said, my voice thin and high. 'If I didn't kill him and it's true that he committed suicide, that means he deliberately abandoned me. He never loved me enough because . . .'

Dylan put both his arms around me and hugged me. I relaxed into his chest. I needed the warmth. I loved his warmth.

'Hey, hey, I'm sure he didn't want to abandon you,' he said. 'I expect he was suffering beyond anything we can understand. You were just a little girl and it wasn't your fault. Seriously, you're not responsible for your parents' actions. And of course he loved you.'

I tried to let Dylan's assurances sink into my brain. I was hungry for them.

'Yes, I know that,' I sighed. 'What makes it all worse, what makes me even more angry, is that I found out a few days ago that when he died, my mum was pregnant by another man.'

I paused to take a deep breath.

'I found this letter and a photo which said she had given birth to a little girl called Rosie, but she'd put her up for adoption,' I told him. 'I don't know if Dad knew about it, but perhaps he did, perhaps that's why he did what he did. Perhaps it wasn't all my fault after all.'

'It wasn't your fault,' Dylan said. 'Do you know who the father was? Whether *he* knew she was pregnant?'

'A guy called Stephen,' I said, lifting my eyebrows. 'That's all I know. I doubt he knows, but again, that's not clear from the letter I found. I've got to ask my mum. She's the only person who can tell me what I need to know, or maybe my aunt Joy. Half of me doesn't even want to ask.'

Dylan puffed out his cheeks, then expelled the air.

'I understand that,' he said. 'You know, when I was a little kid I was such a geek. I had a bowl haircut, spots all over my chin and this weird walk, where I kind of bounced along the road. I was always wondering why I looked like that and whether I was like my dad, who left when I was three. My mum had his sister's address and I spent years thinking about contacting him, and once, when I actually did contact him and we agreed to meet, at the last minute I decided I didn't want to meet him. I thought, I don't want to know. I just don't want to know what he's like and if I'm like him. The fact is that he disappeared and he's chosen not to be a part of my life.'

'Wasn't that just fear?' I asked.

'Maybe,' he said. 'Or maybe it was a form of taking control. For me, it was like saying I don't need this person in my life to have a good life. I was making a choice to be without him, to be just me – a little geek.'

'You're no geek now, though,' I said, smiling.

'Oh, I don't know,' he said. 'I've been collecting vintage toy cars since I was eleven – that's pretty geeky, don't you think? Actually I've sold most of them now, but I loved them!'

'That's a shame,' I said. 'Shouldn't you have held on to them rather than flog them?'

'Maybe,' he said, suddenly dismissive. He turned away from me and looked back at the hotel. The air between us had cooled and I didn't understand why.

I smiled a weary smile at him and stood up. It was getting dark now, so I gestured towards the hotel. Dylan nodded.

'I'm sorry for loading you with all this,' I said as we walked back. 'I hope you don't think I'm mad.'

He grabbed my hand, squeezed it, then let it go again.

'On the contrary,' he said seriously. 'I think you're pretty fucking scarily amazing.'

It was the most romantic thing I'd ever heard.

Back at the hotel, I said goodnight to Dylan, then went up to my room and flopped down on to the mattress to wait for sleep. I stared at the ceiling, feeling alternate waves of relief and anxiety. It was a massive relief to have told Dylan something that had burdened me my whole life. But I felt anxious that I'd finally put the truth out there, to circulate and breathe new life. I had just closed my eyes to shut it all out when there was a knock on the door. I opened the door to April, in elegant night attire, holding a tray of raisin cookies and a mug of hot chocolate. She looked at me sympathetically.

'Someone called Philip has phoned for you three times this evening,' she said. 'I thought he sounded rather drunk, or crazy – one of the two.'

'Oh God,' I said.

'He's no help whatsoever,' she said sardonically, looking up to the ceiling. 'Take it from me – I've asked him for help before. But nothing.'

I laughed and took the tray from her hands.

'Thanks for these,' I said. 'I'm ravenous.'

'Carbohydrate,' she said, turning to go and waving a small wave. 'One needs carbohydrate at times like this.'

I closed the door, turned the gold key and climbed back

into bed. What times like these? And what the hell did Philip want? I ate all four of the cookies (they were warm and soft) and gulped down my hot chocolate before pushing my head into the pillows to block out the world.

Chapter Eighteen

If you're out of mice, you can still use the mousetrap.
Paint it and nail it to the wall, spring up, to hold your
unpaid bills or old love letters.

The I Hate to Housekeep Book,
Peg Bracken, 1962

I have this silly, slightly sick superstition where I believe that
if I think of the worst possible scenario, it means it won't
happen. So if I imagine all my friends perishing in a car crash,
they won't. The problem with this theory is that I have to
spend a lot of time thinking negative thoughts to cover my
back. And sometimes life can throw things at you that are so
ridiculous, you'd never even contemplate them, like that
morning in Honeysuckle Hotel when a phone call from Philip
woke me up. I looked at the clock and groaned. It was seven
forty-six a.m.

'Philip?' I said. 'It's the crack of dawn.'

'Oh shit, hi,' he whispered. 'Listen, I'm going to speak in code for a couple of minutes.'

I sat up in bed, mystified. The edges of the curtains were lit up with sunshine. A flashback of spilling my guts to Dylan sent a nervous tremor through me. I blinked.

'So,' he said in a loud voice. 'Have you booked the meeting rooms for nine a.m.?'

I heard the sounds of small children and a woman in the background – Angela?

'Sorry, Philip, I don't understand,' I said. 'Is there a problem? As you know, I'm not at work today.'

'And I'd prefer bagels to sandwiches,' he said. 'Smoked salmon and cream cheese would be excellent. With a selection of fruit.'

I sighed. There was the noise of a slamming door in the background.

'Philip,' I said. 'Why don't you ring me later? This is really irritating.'

'Fantastic,' he said. 'Just give me one minute.'

I sighed.

'It's OK now,' he said. 'She's gone. Listen, babe, I've got something to tell you.'

Did he just call me 'babe'? I pulled a face at the receiver.

'I've made a decision,' Philip said quickly. 'I'm finally leaving Angela and so I'll be able to be with you.'

My mouth hung open. I stayed silent and still. I squashed the phone against my ear to make sure I could hear him properly.

'What?' I said. 'What did you say?'

Philip breathed heavily.

'Isn't that what you wanted?' he said. 'For me to leave her so you wouldn't have to be the so-called mistress? I know you didn't feel comfortable with the way things were, and I wanted to show you I've got feelings for you, so I'm changing my situation.'

I was flabbergasted. Not in my wildest negative thoughts had I imagined this one. I kicked off the duvet and swung my legs over the side of the bed.

'No,' I said, feeling desperately sick. 'I didn't want that, I definitely didn't want anything like this. You're just using me as a scapegoat, and—'

Philip chose to ignore me.

'I'm moving out of our family house,' he said, his voice catching slightly. 'And I need somewhere to stay. I'm going to New York for a week, but could I crash at yours for a few nights when I get back, perhaps? Aren't you pleased that we can get to know one another properly now? Give ourselves a chance.'

'Hang on a minute,' I said, my heart pounding in my chest. 'We spend one drunken night together and you're leaving your wife for me and now you want to move in with me? Are you completely crazy?'

'For you and your marvellous breasts, yes,' he said. 'Aren't you just a tiny bit pleased?'

I pulled a disgusted face and shook my head. I would have laughed if it weren't so shocking. I thought of his children's faces when they heard their daddy was shacking up with a girl from work. What was he on?

'No,' I said firmly. 'No, no, no, no, no and no.'

Surely he would get the message now?

'I'll work on you,' he said smugly. 'I love a challenge.'

I couldn't believe his conceit. Was his ego really so enormous that he couldn't believe I didn't want him?

'If you want a challenge, climb Everest,' I said before slamming down the phone and screaming into my hands.

After showering, muttering furiously in disbelief at Philip's phone call, I straightened up my room, shaking out the towels and sheets with a viciousness reminiscent of Ava. Maybe we had something in common after all. I gathered up my bags, wondering what the hell I could do about Philip. How could someone who seemed so sane be so completely mad? After one last check around the room, I went downstairs to the lobby to meet Dylan. I tried to put Philip out of my mind, but couldn't help thinking I'd have to get another job now. How could I continue to work under a man who wanted to be on top of me? The thought repulsed me.

At reception, Dylan stood talking to April, glamorous in a simple white sundress and shawl. She handed him a basket of food and kissed his cheek.

'Lunch,' she said when she noticed me. 'I thought you two would get hungry on the way home and I don't want you to have to go to Mc-whatever-it-is.'

I smiled and thanked her. I doubted she'd ever stepped into a fast-food outlet in her whole life.

'I can't stand those ghastly fast-food outlets at those hideous motorway service stations,' she said, reading my mind. 'The one awful time I visited, I didn't even speak to a person. I spoke to a machine to order my meal. It's like everything these days, isn't it? Where have the bloody people gone? I sometimes wonder if I'll have an automated priest at my funeral.'

Dylan and I laughed. Then he turned to face me and smiled while April spoke to another guest.

'Hi,' he said. 'How are you this morning?'

'Fine,' I said, lying. 'And you?'

'Not fine,' he sighed. 'I was on the phone to Sylvie most of the night. She was doing most of the talking and crying.'

'Oh . . .' I said. 'Is everything OK?'

'Does it sound like it?' he said. 'Our conversation last night seemed to signal "The End". You know how it goes. She's sorry and all that, really sorry, but she thinks she needs some space. She needs space? But hey, such is life. I hate relationships. I'm done with them.'

I looked at Dylan but didn't know him well enough to work out whether he was seriously upset. He was doing a good job at being flippant.

'I know what you mean,' I said. 'I'm done with them too.'

We glanced up at each other and April, who was now listening in, chuckled her throaty laugh. She hugged us both, thanking Dylan for agreeing to name the hotel in the documentary. She scribbled something on her business card and handed it to me. On our way out to the van, I looked at it. In a scrawl, she'd written, 'You're not done', underlined and followed by four exclamation marks. I tucked the card into the pocket of my jeans. It would be safe in there.

Dylan agreed to drive along the coast road to Violet's house before we started back to London. Though most of her furniture was in storage, I hadn't yet cleared out her attic. With buyers interested in the cottage, I needed to find out what was left up there. Though it was unlikely, I secretly hoped I might discover letters or photographs to help me find out more about Rosie. I knew Joy must know, and I had left various rambling messages on her answerphone, but she hadn't yet called back. And as for Ava – well, I couldn't face talking to her about it at all. We'd never been able to talk about anything remotely emotional. We spoke quietly and calmly about safe, anodyne subjects while my blood boiled underneath. Just thinking about what she might say when I opened this can of worms filled me with waves of panic and nausea. I tried to push it out of my mind. As Dylan drove along the winding road, I watched the trees and sky whizz by in a blur.

'Oh, fuck!' he shouted, suddenly slamming on the brakes, as a rabbit leapt out of the hedgerow in front of the van. I gripped the dashboard, clenching my teeth together as the van screeched to a halt.

'Christ, that was close,' I said, sitting back in my seat. The rabbit stood still in front of us for a moment, fixed us with a stare, then bounded off into the bushes.

'My heart!' Dylan said, resting his hand on his chest.

He lifted my hand and put it against his heart.

'Feel that,' he said, grinning. 'Nearly had a bloody heart attack!'

Dylan's chest was solid and warm. His hand, wrapped around mine, was hot. My hand started to tingle. I held my breath and smiled.

'There's probably the entire cast of *Watership Down* under those bushes,' I said.

Dylan burst into an operatic rendition of 'Bright Eyes' from the film.

'Oh, don't. I'm welling up!'

Dylan stopped singing and cracked up.

He let go of my hand, grinned enormously and drove off. We sat together in silence for a few minutes. Then Dylan looked sideways at me and asked about Simon.

'What was he like, then?' he said. 'Simon.'

I thought for a few moments.

'Childish,' I said. 'Which is good and bad. He was charmingly childish at times, but painfully immature at others. Then he slept with my flatmate, Hanna, and that was it, I hated him. Since then he's called me a few times wanting to be "friends", but that will never work.'

'You couldn't forgive him?' Dylan said. 'I'm not saying you should, I'm just asking the question. Some couples get through an infidelity, don't they?'

'I couldn't,' I said, shaking my head. 'The fact that she was my friend and we all lived together felt like the ultimate betrayal. I'd never be able to forget it. And his timing – Jesus! We had just moved in to our new flat together, and when I was getting all excited about having a home together, he was confessing to sleeping with Hanna. I hate talking about Simon. How about you? How did you meet Sylvie?'

'Oh,' he said. 'On a beach in France. There was a group of surfers I knew and she was with them. She seemed to find everything I said absolutely hilarious and appeared quite captivated by me. Then she suggested skinny-dipping and that was it. Being the fool I am, I fell for her, hook, line and sinker.'

He laughed a bitter laugh.

'Could you live in a caravan with her, or is it really over?'

I said. 'That's what my grandma said is the ultimate test of love.'

'No way,' he said. 'I think I thought I could – live with her, I mean. Not in a caravan, though – which is why I've stuck with it. But I sometimes wish I'd never met her. After our conversations last night I definitely wish I'd never met her. It's over. It's been over for a while, if I'm honest with myself.'

He sighed heavily. I wanted to say something knowing and reassuring, but could only think of useless platitudes. Plus we were almost at Violet's house and I had a horrible nervous feeling in my stomach. Coming to the cottage, now it was empty, was heart-wrenching. Whenever I'd come to see Violet in the past, it had felt like coming home. Now her cottage was a shell.

'Violet's cottage is just round this corner,' I said, craning my neck forward and pointing left. 'About five hundred yards down.'

He indicated left into her narrow lane, where leafy trees on either side leaned over the road, forming an arch that didn't quite meet in the middle.

'Great,' he said as the tyres crunched to a halt on the gravel. 'I badly need a smoke.'

'Oh my God,' I said, unlocking Violet's front door and pushing it open. 'What is that hideous smell?'

An overpowering stench of rotting flesh hit us. My eyes watered. I covered my nose with my hand and looked at Dylan.

'I think there's a dead animal in here,' he said, standing behind me. 'A very dead animal.'

I took a gulp of fresh air from outside, then held my breath while I located a can of air freshener under the sink and sprayed until the air was thick with Woodland Pine. We coughed and I buried my nose in my elbow as Dylan found the source of the stink in the pantry – a dead rat writhing with maggots.

'That is disgusting,' I said. 'Violet would be horrified. I feel awful. I should have put down mouse traps or something.'

The cottage was in a state of neglect. Water had dripped out of the taps and stained the sink, post had gathered in a heap by the letterbox, grit or soot or brick dust had slipped down the chimney and spilled on to the carpet and it smelt bad. I felt guilty, for Violet.

'It looks like the only one in here – I'll get it out,' Dylan said. 'You go and do whatever you need to do. This is a job for a man. Deer, rats – I can cope.'

He jokingly flexed his arm muscles. I laughed.

'Are you sure?' I said. 'You don't need to do that, I could call someone in or something. There's a shovel in the shed if you want one ...'

'I was thinking of using my bare hands,' he said sarcastically. 'Thanks all the same.'

Dylan flapped his hands at me, instructing me to go away. Light-headed with air freshener, I climbed the stairs and stood in the upstairs hallway. With no furniture in any of the bedrooms, it looked like a different house. I closed my eyes and remembered Violet's wardrobe, stuffed with beautiful hand-made clothes. When I was small, I'd often hide in there, burying my face in her skirts and dresses, which smelt faintly of her Chanel N° 19 perfume. I wrapped my arms around myself. This had once been my home, my sanctuary. Now it was just a collection of bricks.

Pulling down the ladder from the attic, I climbed up into the loft and flicked on the light. I scanned the space to see what was left up there. Digging through the boxes, I found oddments, a selection of sewing titles – *The Singer Sewing Book*, *The Modern Encyclopedia of Sewing*, *Glamour Fashion Sewing* – and a stack of *Homemaker* magazines from the 1950s, school notebooks, a globe, a canvas and a collection of china teacups and saucers. Near the boxes was a huge package wrapped up in brown paper. I stuck my finger through the paper and pulled it back. Fabric. Lots of gorgeous fabric. Violet was still looking out for me, even from the heavens. Grinning, I shoved it through the attic door on to the floor below. I could use that to make my aprons.

'Dylan?' I called. 'Can you give me a hand, please?'

Dylan's hand popped up through the attic entrance, followed by his head. I handed him the boxes to throw out.

After an hour we were done and decided to move into the garden to eat our lunch. I noticed Dylan look at the scar on my arm. I tried to catch his eye, but he was fishing through the basket of food April had given us.

'Shall we eat now?' I said. 'Are you hungry?'

We shared out the baguette, Brie and tomatoes. Dylan told me cheese and biscuits were his staple diet back in London. Sitting side by side on the grass, I surveyed the garden – the flowerbeds were overgrown, but with flowering red poppies all around, it looked wild and beautiful. I missed this, living in London. If you had outside space with your property in London, it was rarely bigger than a postage stamp.

'How did you get that?' Dylan asked, pointing at my arm. 'Your scar?'

I put my bread down and ran my hand up and down my arm self-consciously.

'I fell through a glass door,' I said. 'When I was nine.'

I didn't tell Dylan the truth. That after Dad's funeral, I'd been so angry, so furious, so lost that I'd slammed my arm through the glass to punish myself for what I'd done. I couldn't tell Dylan because he'd write me off as a lunatic.

'Did you mean to do it?' he said, gently running his finger along it. 'It feels like ribbon.'

My heart throbbed in my teeth. This close, Dylan was even more alluring. I tried to be calm. I put my head to one side, but didn't give him an answer. He gave a slight nod of his head – acknowledgement, I think – and took away his hand. I wanted to say something but couldn't find the words.

'This is what life should be like,' he said suddenly, changing the subject. 'The sea's a stone's throw away – sorry, I know you hate it. I'd move here like a shot if London wasn't so annoyingly addictive. Hey, look, there are some wild strawberries over there. Shall I pick some?'

'Who are you?' I said. 'Hugh Fearnley-Whittingstall?'

'I'd love to be,' he said. 'Have you seen that house he lives in, River Cottage? That's actually my dream house. One day I'll live in a place like that, with my vegetable patches and the sea on my doorstep, so I can surf to my heart's content.'

'When you retire?' I said.

'And then some,' he said, opening his palm in front of me to reveal strawberries. I took one and bit into it, juice filling my mouth.

'I get the impression you don't much like your flat in Tower Hamlets,' I said. 'Couldn't you move somewhere else?'

Dylan stood up and brushed the crumbs off his jeans.

'No,' he said, curtly. 'But I try not to think about it.'

Dylan looked irritated. I finished my strawberry and opened my mouth to say something apologetic, but my mobile rang. Dylan picked it up from the top of my bag and glanced at the screen.

'It's Philip,' he said, handing it to me. 'Jesus, he's phoned about six times since we got to Cornwall!'

I held the phone and frowned. My cheeks were blazing.

'Oh, I see,' Dylan said with a slight smile. 'Is there something going on with you two?'

I pressed REJECT and threw the phone down into my bag.

'Absolutely not,' I said quickly as the phone beeped with a voicemail. 'I couldn't think of anything worse.'

On the long drive back to London, I fell asleep and woke up in a traffic jam on the outskirts of the city with my mouth open. I glanced at Dylan, hoping my tongue hadn't been lolling out or something equally hideous.

'Wow,' he said. 'You slept like a baby for hours.'

I pulled my compact mirror from my bag and checked my face. Red marks crisscrossed my cheeks from where I'd been lying on a rolled-up jumper.

'I'm mortified,' I said, covering my skin with my curls. 'Did I dribble?'

Dylan laughed.

'Not that I noticed,' he said. 'Look at this traffic. I should have taken a different road. Profound, eh?'

He gave me a quick smile and then we were quiet for a while.

'I'm sorry if I snapped at you earlier when you asked about my flat,' he said out of the blue.

'That's OK,' I said. 'I didn't even think anything.'

'It's no big deal but just a slightly sore subject,' Dylan said. 'One of those things, you know?'

I didn't know, but there was something ever so slightly vulnerable about him, so I told him I did.

'I know what you mean,' I said. 'There are some things you just don't want to talk about.'

'Absolutely right,' he said.

I smiled. It was as though there was an understanding between us, but I wasn't sure what that understanding actually was. Perhaps we recognized something in one another, some underlying chink in our armour that we were unwilling to divulge.

Eventually the traffic started to move, and as we edged our way into London, Dylan talked about the documentary. Apart from filming the actual auction in ten days' time when the auction documentary would air, Dylan had all the material he needed for the film. He would spend the next week editing in the studios at Channel 4, so we wouldn't see each other until auction night. Outside my flat, I gathered up my jacket, handbag and overnight case. I grinned and hugged Dylan goodbye.

His hug was so firm and warm and so safe, it made me want to hang on to him and not let go.

'You know I'm arranging a hen night for my best friend next Saturday,' I said, climbing out of the van and holding the door open. 'Would you like to come?'

'Aren't you missing something?' he said, rubbing his hand across his jaw. 'My five o'clock shadow is a clue.'

I looked at the bluish shadow of stubble covering his jaw. I wondered what it would be like to kiss him.

'It's mixed gender,' I said. 'Five o'clock shadows are welcome.'

'Thanks,' he said, holding my gaze for a second longer than necessary. 'Send me an email and I'll try to make it.'

I slammed the door shut and gave him a wave. He started to move off, then stopped and rolled down the window and stuck his head out.

'What about a camper van?' he called.

'What do you mean?' I shouted.

'Could you live in a camper van?' he said. 'Or does it have to be a caravan?'

I held my breath. I smiled uncertainly. He didn't wait for an answer. He gave a laugh, put his foot down on the accelerator and roared off down Lovelace Avenue, his exhaust banging into the night sky like a firecracker. I beamed.

Chapter Nineteen

If you've barely had a moment's notice that someone
is arriving unexpectedly for cocktails, keep your cool at
all costs.

Ladies' Home Journal Art of Homemaking,
Virginia T. Habeeb, 1973

What is your idea of hell? Mine is arranging a hen party for a hen
who doesn't want to marry the cock. A week after the filming trip
in Cornwall, I stood in Ann Summers on Oxford Street staring
desolately at pink furry handcuffs and gold vibrators.

'Should I really buy these?' I asked Imogen's younger sister
Zoe, who was trying the handcuffs on for size. 'Imogen will
absolutely hate them.'

I had spent the morning curled up in bed with buttered
toast and Violet's *Homemaking Hints for a Happier Home*
book, sniggering at the chapter on marriage entitled 'How
to be a Happy Little Wife'. Holding the gold vibrator, I
remembered the points of advice:

* put a flower in your hair to brighten up your
  husband's day
* never leave red lipstick marks on cups
* offer to take off your husband's shoes
* never create a drama out of baking a sponge cake
* wear a simple pearl necklace to demonstrate style

The book was a world apart from the crotchless knickers and nipple tassels on display in Ann Summers. Or was it? Ultimately both were about satisfying your partner – though the meaning of 'pearl necklace' had altered somewhat...

'Yes!' Zoe said, snapping the handcuffs shut and blowing her thick red fringe out of her eyes. 'We have to buy as much tack as we can.'

I looked in the shopping basket. We already had diamanté-studded thongs, a flashing vibrator, L-plates and badges with obscene slogans on them. I would never have considered buying any of it, but Zoe seemed hell-bent on arranging the most hideous hen night we could muster. I felt incredibly anxious about going ahead with the party, but what could I do? Imogen was insistent that she would marry Jonathan, even though she was still having an affair with Cath. It was a ludicrous situation, but Imogen was refusing to confront it. Meanwhile her family was busy choosing flowers, wedding cakes and musicians for the ceremony. My only hope was that by inviting Cath to the party, Imogen would realize it was her she wanted and make a decision to cancel the wedding.

'Are you sure about all this?' I said. 'I don't think it's such a good idea, you know.'

Zoe rolled her eyes at me and folded her arms over her chest.

'Surely you know why I'm choosing these things?' she said, holding up a tin of chocolate paint. 'The more tack we buy, the more freaked out Imogen will get, and the less likely she'll be to actually go ahead with this ludicrous wedding. Hopefully she'll take one look at the handcuffs and realize that she can't walk down that aisle.'

I raised my eyebrows.

'I see,' I said. 'The handcuffs are a metaphor for marriage to Jonathan?'

'Absolutely,' she said. 'And the rest of it will make her feel ridiculous. I think it will work.'

'Why not just be honest, sit her down and tell her she has to cancel the wedding, at least in the short term, until she's sorted out her head?' I said. 'Wouldn't that be better? Coming from you, she'd have to listen.'

'I've tried that,' she said. 'It didn't work. She just got majorly defensive and told me I didn't understand. I'm sure you know what I'm talking about – Imogen's not one to be told. I know my sister, and I have to be cruel to be kind.'

Zoe and Imogen had always been really close and she did probably know her better than anyone. I had to trust her.

'You're right,' I said. 'Anything's worth a go.'

I joined the queue, a snake of slightly crazed-looking women. I stole glances at their baskets of underwear and sex toys. There were all sorts – busy young professionals, middle-aged ladies, giggling teenagers and a mother pushing a sleeping toddler in his pram. I thought of Violet's book and felt suddenly exhausted. So many roles to fulfil! Tammy Wynette was right. Sometimes it was hard to be a woman.

Pinning up the last pink balloon under the disapproving gaze of the landlord, I checked my watch. We'd paid £150 to book the upstairs room in the Village pub in Greek Street from seven-thirty to midnight. Zoe's boyfriend Chris was playing records, currently to an empty room. Our hen night paraphernalia was hidden in carrier bags underneath the tables. It was already eight o'clock and no one else had arrived.

'They'll all come at once,' said Zoe, noticing my anxious face. 'Don't worry.'

We had invited forty people between us, and I was beginning to regret it. Maybe we should have kept it to a small, private party. Then, if it did all blow up there and then, it wouldn't be so embarrassing for Imogen and Cath.

'I'm really not sure about this,' I told Zoe. 'This could be a disaster.'

Zoe, dressed in a short black dress and footless tights, put her hand on my back.

'Everyone will be pissed and enjoying the party,' she said. 'If we'd invited fewer people they'd all be watching Imogen, wouldn't they? This way, people will leave her alone and she'll have the opportunity to talk to Cath and hopefully decide that marrying Jonathan is the worst idea she's ever had. I think seeing everyone will make it real. She needs context.'

I gulped my wine. I wasn't only nervous for Imogen. I wondered if Dylan was going to turn up. I'd emailed him an invite earlier in the week and hadn't heard back. I'd put on my favourite green pencil dress and heels, just in case.

'Will you take those balloons down before you go?' the landlord asked, suddenly appearing beside me.

'God,' I said, clutching my chest. 'You made me jump. Yes, of course I will. Every single last one of them will be removed, deflated and destroyed.'

'OK, OK,' he said, lifting his hands up as if for mercy. 'Only asking.'

'Sorry,' I said. 'I'm really nervous.'

The landlord huffed, but before I could apologize again, the door burst open and a flock of Imogen's friends arrived adorned in feather boas, on Zoe's instruction. Twenty minutes later the room was full. The only person not there was Imogen. Speaking to Cath, who resembled Dita Von Teese, I tried to pretend I didn't feel sick with nerves. When Imogen finally arrived, pale and uncertain, everyone screamed '*Surprise!*' She did a good job of feigning joy, but I could see she was bewildered. I rushed over to her and threw my arms around her.

'Sorry, Imogen,' I said into her hair. 'This may have been a bad idea.'

Imogen hugged me back and, noticing Cath behind me, blushed. Her face fell and she exhaled loudly.

'We can call it all off—' I started, but Imogen interrupted me.

'I need a drink,' she said. 'And I think you will too.' She pulled a concerned expression and gestured to the door.

I looked over to where she was pointing, and there stood Hanna and Simon, smiling and smooth, like Barbie and Ken in their heyday. I tried to be brave, but I felt gutted.

'What the fuck?' I gasped. 'What are they doing here?'

Imogen explained that Zoe had bumped into Hanna and mentioned it without realizing what had happened between us all. But why had they arrived together? Were the two of them back together? My stomach flipped. This was the very last thing I needed. I turned away from them, aimed for the bar and ordered a Mojito. I drank it down and ordered another.

'Hello,' said Simon, suddenly standing by my side. 'You look wonderful.'

Simon had caught the sun – he always did if ever there was a glimmer of sunshine. He had on a light blue shirt and had pushed the sleeves up to his elbows as if preparing to milk cows, exposing tanned arms.

'Hi,' I said. 'You're brown.'

'I've got bikini marks, though,' he said with a quick smile. 'Look, Juliet, the reason I've come tonight is because I wanted to apologize about the other night at my mum's house. I'm sorry I've been so awful to you. I've behaved like an idiot.'

The music pounded in my ears and I wondered if I'd heard him right. I couldn't believe that Simon was actually apologizing to me.

'But didn't you arrive with Hanna?' I said, snorting. 'That's pretty high up on the thoughtless scale, isn't it?'

Simon opened his mouth to speak, but before he answered someone tapped me on the shoulder. It was Dylan, with a feather boa tied round his neck. My stomach somersaulted.

'I've come to be a hen,' he said, kissing me on both cheeks.

I kissed him back. I felt genuinely delighted to see him.

Simon's face darkened when I introduced them. They shook hands briefly, then Dylan looked Simon right in the eye.

'So you're Simon,' he said, before draping his arm over my shoulder. 'How could you let this one go? I just don't get it.'

Five rum cocktails later, I was dancing like a crazy person. The combination of Simon, Hanna and Dylan being at the same party was too much for me. Plus Imogen had barely said a word to me, so I was worried that she was annoyed about the party. And I had the awful prospect of seeing Ava the next day. I'd lost track of time, but guessed it was late from the Eighties pop tunes Chris was playing – guaranteed to get people up on the dance floor. Or me, anyway.

Cath and Imogen were squirrelled away in a dark corner, talking intently. God knows what everyone else made of Imogen – she'd barely looked up all night. Our bags of vibrators and handcuffs were untouched. I couldn't see Hanna anywhere and Simon was sitting alone, occasionally throwing black looks over in my direction. I was vaguely aware that I was far drunker than anyone else. I knew it was bad, because though I could see blood oozing from the blister on my heel, I couldn't feel anything. Eventually Simon took it upon himself to tell me the obvious.

'You're way too drunk, Juliet,' he said, steering me off the dance floor. 'I'm going now, so would you like me to take you home? You're in a state – you're embarrassing yourself.'

I shrugged him off. The tone of his voice and the look of disapproval in his eye made me suddenly furious. How dare he pass judgement on me when he'd abandoned me for a quick fuck with Hanna? What business was it of his if I wanted to get drunk and dance on my best friend's hen night?

'No thanks, Simon,' I hissed. 'I'd like it, actually, if you would piss off.'

My forehead was sweaty from dancing, my legs suddenly heavy from the booze. Simon threw his hands up in the air.

'Well, that's nice,' he said. 'Fine, I'll leave you to it.'

'Good!' I said, watching him stride out of the door.

Sighing, I sat heavily on a stool near the bar. I looked around. Dylan was nowhere to be seen. Since he'd arrived I'd felt stupidly nervous, but now I desperately wanted to talk to him. Could I tell him how much I liked him? Then, as if by magic, he was by my side, asking if I wanted to get some fresh air.

'I've found this ladder,' he said. 'It takes you up to the roof terrace. Want to climb up with me? Reach new heights?'

Linking my arm through his, clutching my cocktail, I let Dylan lead me to a back door, where a precarious-looking ladder hung from the roof. We ignored the sign saying 'Private – No Entry'.

'Let's go up,' he said, pulling a bundle of balloons from the wall by the back door, 'and liberate these balloons.'

The roof terrace was on two levels: the first housed disused chairs and a table in a large box, the second, higher level was empty except for a slightly broken bench. I sat down on the bench and looked out over the street.

'We're pretty high up here,' I said, nervously watching Dylan walk off and sit down in the middle of the roof. 'Maybe I shouldn't be this pissed.'

'Come and lie down over here,' he said. 'Look up at the stars with me.'

I moved over to where Dylan lay, near the chimney breast. Lying down next to him, I stared up at the sky. Even though the streetlights made the stars difficult to see, I could make out the brightest ones.

'The moon looks close enough to touch. Did you know there are dark stars up there? Ones that don't actually shine?' Dylan said, craning his neck to finish off his pint.

'I know how they feel,' I said, half joking, half serious.

'What?' he said. 'You're a one-off! Don't be down on yourself.'

'I'm not normally,' I said. 'It's Simon and Hanna – they make my skin crawl.'

'Ignore them,' he said. 'Shall we let these balloons go?'

He handed me two of the balloons, and from where we lay, with our thighs and arms almost touching, we let the balloons go. I swear I could feel electrical currents passing through our skin.

'Be free, balloons!' he said as we released them. Carried by the breeze, they bobbed off across the roofs and out over London.

'I wonder where they'll end up?' I said. 'Probably in the Thames.'

'I wonder where we'll end up?' he said. 'Hopefully not in the Thames.'

We laughed, and then were quiet for a while, listening to the music below.

'So, here comes a Big Question I only ask when I'm drunk,' Dylan said. 'What makes you happy? What do you want from life?'

I ran through a list of things that I supposed would make me sound cool. Then I told him the truth.

'A home,' I said. 'A home with some people in it I love. Not very cool, I guess.'

Dylan nodded and rolled himself a cigarette.

'I can understand that,' he said. 'We all need a place to be ourselves. My studio flat has never really felt like a home because I can't fit any possessions in there. When I wash my face in my tiny bathroom, with the avocado sink beneath me, I sometimes wonder who Dylan really is.'

'Maybe you're still finding out,' I said. 'Isn't that what your twenties are for? Self-discovery? The decade of finding yourself, or some such bollocks.'

He turned and gave me a lovely smile. We shared a look. I knew we understood each other. And sitting next to him, staring out over the streets, listening to the muffled sounds from the pub below, I felt an immense sense of freedom. I thought: Dylan gets me – he can really see who I am, the real me. I closed my eyes and felt the air on my skin. For the first time in weeks, I felt happy.

Back inside, we split up. By midnight, I was beyond drunk and my blisters felt like razor blades in my shoes. I needed to go home. I hadn't seen Dylan for a while and I guessed he was smoking, so I went outside to the garden to find him. There were no lights on out there, only tiny tea-lights burning in glass jars. I strained to see.

'Dylan?' I said quietly. 'Hello? Dylan?'

There was no answer, so I found an empty table, sat down and rested my chin in my hands. My head was banging. At least Simon had gone – and hopefully Hanna, the bitch. I thought about sitting up on the roof with Dylan. Did he just want to be friends? He had never made a move on me – but maybe it was too soon after Simon. Or perhaps he was still with Sylvie, in his heart. I couldn't work it out – I just felt we had an unspoken connection. From his behaviour, I thought he felt the same.

There was a noise nearby, so I looked up, and, with sickening realization, I noticed them. Leaning with his back against the wooden fence, a burning cigarette dangling between two fingers in his right hand, was Dylan. Pressed up against him, her arm curled around his neck, her white-blonde mane cascading down her back, her heels escaping from her sling-backs, her lips fastened to his, was Hanna the Unicorn.

'Oh my—' I gasped, slapping my hand over my mouth.

Jerking up from the table, I stumbled back into the bar and to the Ladies' toilet. I banged open the door of a cubicle and left it swinging. I knelt down on the floor and put my hands on each side of the toilet seat. With a dreadful lurch, I vomited.

Seconds later, Imogen's cool hands were holding back my hair.

'Poor you,' she said. 'You'll feel better in a minute.'

I burst into sobs and vomited once again, immediately sobering up. Imogen handed me some tissues, a glass of water and a mint. She looked worried.

'Thank you,' I said in a tiny voice. 'I'm sorry. I've had way too much. I just saw...'

I thought about what I'd seen and nearly vomited again. I realized I should ask Imogen how she was, but I felt too stunned, too dislocated from normality.

'I just saw . . .' I said again, then stopped.

'Simon and Hanna?' Imogen said, shaking her head sympathetically. I didn't correct her.

'They've got some nerve,' she said. 'Let's get you home.'

In the cab, Cath sat in the front seat, making small talk with the driver, while Imogen held my hand in the back. I opened the window wide, closed my eyes and let the cool air hit my face. I concentrated hard on not being sick. Why was this happening to me? I'd told Dylan about Hanna and Simon, so how could he kiss her? He was just like every other bloke – a sucker for blonde hair, long legs and a Swedish accent.

'How are you doing?' Imogen asked, squeezing my hand. 'We're nearly home now.'

I squeezed her hand back and tried to be brave, but I was desperate to cry. The hangover was hitting me already and I felt wretched. It was only when we were back in the flat and I flicked the lamps on that I realized how sober Imogen was. I poured myself a glass of water, while Imogen and Cath sat down on the sofa together.

'What a nightmare that was,' I said, calling through to the living room. 'I'm so sorry we went ahead with the party. It was supposed to help you come to the conclusion that getting married was a ridiculous idea.'

I found some crackers in the cupboard, smeared horseradish sauce on them (fantastic hangover cure, promise), walked back into the living room and flopped down on the armchair. Cath smiled at me and put her hand on Imogen's thigh. Imogen reached for her hand and held it, glancing at me.

'It's a bit more complicated now,' Imogen said, letting go of Cath's hand and lifting her handbag on to her lap. She unzipped it and looked inside.

'I know it's complicated,' I said, crunching into a cracker. 'But what are you going to do? It's not that bad to cancel a wedding. You're going to ruin your life if you make the wrong decision.'

'You think I don't know that?' she said crossly. 'Look.'

Imogen delved into her bag and pulled out a Clearblue box. She held it up in the air and waved it, a look of terror on her face.

'A pregnancy test?' I said, incredulous. 'Oh my God. So you're still sleeping with Jonathan?'

Imogen leaned her shoulder into Cath and exhaled.

'I slept with him once, six weeks ago, after I met Cath,' Imogen said dully. 'It was out of guilt, or maybe I was testing out my feelings one last time or something. I'm so stupid, I know I am.'

'You're not stupid,' Cath said. 'Relationships aren't simple, are they? There's no black and white with love. You were trying to sort your head out without hurting Jonathan. Sometimes sex helps.'

I covered my mouth with my hand.

'So you could be pregnant,' I said quietly. 'Do you know if you are?'

Imogen shrugged. Clutching the box, she stood up. Pushing open the door of the bathroom, she turned and gave us both a brave smile.

'I'll tell you in three minutes,' she said.

Three minutes passed as slowly as thirty. I found a dribble of milk in the fridge that was still in date and made Cath a mug of tea, slowly stirring in a teaspoon of sugar. I gulped down another pint of water and two paracetamol. I shivered as I remembered Hanna's arm hooked round Dylan's neck. My cheeks burned with embarrassment that I thought I'd stood a chance with him. I was shocked he'd gone for her, though – I hadn't thought she was his type. Then again, Hanna seemed to be everyone's type. But none of that mattered now. I glanced at the bathroom door.

'Thanks,' Cath said when I handed her the tea. She held the mug against her cheek.

'By the way,' she said. 'I really like your aprons. Where did you find the fabric?'

'Oh,' I said. 'My grandmother was a dressmaker and she had lots of lovely vintage fabric. She died last year and I found a few bundles of some great prints.'

'What a find,' Cath smiled. 'You'd pay a fortune for that now from a fabric dealer. Have you got a label yet? You know, I could try selling them for you in the shop. It's so "now", all this home-made stuff. If you can't sew or make things yourself these days in this city, you're nobody.'

I saw Violet's book on the table and had a flash of inspiration.

'I want to homemake,' I said.

'Excuse me?' she said.

'"I want to homemake",' I said. 'That's my label. It just came to me, when you asked. Any good, or is it terrible?'

Cath smiled. We heard the toilet flush and shared a look.

'It's spot on,' she said. 'If you can make me fifteen aprons, we'll see how they sell, OK?'

There was a noise from the bathroom. Cath and I stared at the door. Slowly, Imogen emerged. She was deathly pale, but her cheeks blazed like cherries. I knew from her expression what she was going to say. Her lips quivered. I held my breath.

'Pregnant,' she said, wrapping her arms around her waist.

Later, I offered Cath and Imogen my bed while I slept on the sofa. From what Imogen had been saying to us, I had a horrible feeling she would keep the baby and go back to Jonathan, even though she was clearly in love with Cath. But that was only her kneejerk reaction, wasn't it? I desperately wanted to talk to her more, but I'd have to wait. The two of them had wanted to be alone.

My brain was buzzing so frantically, I could almost hear it working. I kept thinking of Dylan and Hanna. I'd had a text from Dylan saying 'Where are you?', but I'd ignored it. He was probably enveloped in Hanna's limbs by now, lucky cow. What did they matter, though? It was Imogen, with her life turned upside down, who I was most worried about now. What would she do? I wished I could spend the following day with her, but, irritatingly, in a few hours I'd have to face Ava for lunch at Joy's flat. What would she say about Rosie? What would I say? I wasn't sure I had the strength to hear her excuses.

I rolled on to my stomach and pushed my nose into the sofa cushions. I listened to the sounds of people arriving home after their Saturday night out: laughter, banging doors, coins being dropped on the pavement, an argument, the hushed tones of Imogen and Cath. I longed for sleep, for dreams.

Chapter Twenty

There are excuses for everything one does not like to do,
but procrastination can become a disaster. Mending is
as inevitable as dusting and almost as easy.

Ladies' Home Journal Art of Homemaking,
Virginia T. Habeeb, 1973

I knocked on Joy's front door and waited. I was clutching a
bunch of yellow tulips and blue irises wrapped in crinkly cel-
lophane. My hands were clammy and my breath shallow.

From inside the flat I heard the rise and fall of women's
voices. My heart banged in my chest – Ava was there already.
Joy had probably primed her about the photograph of baby
Rosie I'd seen, and Ava had most likely invented a thousand
lies to tell me. My stomach churned with resentment. I
dreaded seeing her, even after six months. This time it was so
much worse. There was no point pretending otherwise.

'Darling!' Joy exclaimed, opening the door and pulling me
close. 'Such beautiful flowers!'

I stood there in her hallway, looking past Joy to the slight figure standing behind her. Every time I saw Ava she looked different in hair and dress, yet she was consistently strikingly beautiful. Today her hair was chin-length, gold and wavy. She wore a simple black dress, gold sandals and gold bangles up her arm that tinkled as she came closer, her arms outstretched and her palms upturned, as if she was saying, 'And who's this?' Her eyes were underlined with her trademark kohl. She smiled an uncertain smile and kissed both my cheeks. I gave her a tight grin and put my hand on my chest, as if to say, 'It's your daughter, remember me?'

'Hi,' I said, leaning into her briefly. She smelled of peppermint. 'You smell nice.'

'Juliet,' she said, pulling me in for another hug. 'It's been months since I saw you – is that the best we can do?'

I chewed my bottom lip. Ava always managed to make me feel responsible for our terrible relationship, even though she was the one who travelled all over the world relentlessly and had abandoned me aged nine. Silence fell. I fumed internally. Joy clasped her hands together and looked anxiously from Ava to me.

'We have so much to talk about,' she said, gesturing to the living room. 'Let's go and sit down and have a drink. I've made home-made lemonade to mix with vodka. It's the one thing I'm good at. Fresh mint leaves are the secret.'

Joy's living room was uncharacteristically immaculate. Her dining table was laid out with cheeses, meats and deli-style salads. My stomach groaned with hangover. I didn't think I could eat a thing.

'Here,' Ava said, giving me a small wooden statue of a

giraffe. 'It was handmade in Kenya by a group of villagers I got to know. Isn't it wonderful?'

I stared at the giraffe and ran my fingers up and down its long, thin neck. I put it on the arm of the sofa.

'Marvellous,' I said. 'Absolutely marvellous.'

Joy shot me a warning look. She sprang up from her seat and clapped her hands together.

'Lemonade!' she exclaimed. 'Coming up!'

While Joy clattered glasses in the kitchen, Ava and I made pointless conversation about her journey from Kenya to London. I watched her mouth move, but didn't listen to her words. I thought, How could she not tell me about Rosie? I realized I was trembling.

'Here you go,' Joy said, handing me a glass. I drank deeply, my heart banging loudly. Could they hear it? I felt as if it was going to burst out of my chest. I had to speak. I had to ask Ava about the letter, I had to know the truth. I took a deep breath, but Ava spoke first.

'Juliet,' she said. 'I know that you've seen a letter from me to Violet about baby Rosie. Joy told me you'd mentioned it to her.'

Joy gave me an apologetic look. She fiddled with her green beads and sipped her vodka lemonade. Ava sighed and leaned her head back into the sofa cushions. She stared up at the ceiling and crossed her ankles. I steeled myself for what she would say.

'It's all true,' she said slowly. 'You won't like this, but when your father died, I was pregnant by another man. I decided to leave for Sydney, have the baby there and give it up for adoption over there too. I have never told you all

223

this, because I wondered what the point was. Rosie is adopted and on the other side of the world. She's only your half-sister.'

'But how could you not tell me?' I said. 'Did Dad know you were pregnant and that the baby wasn't his? I've always longed for a brother or sister.'

Joy put her hand to her mouth and shifted in her seat. Ava jangled her bangles up her arm and cleared her throat.

'When I was young,' she said, her voice faltering, 'I was extremely naïve. I didn't realize how being beautiful can be a curse.'

'What?' I scoffed. 'How can you turn this into a discussion about your looks! You're so unbelievably vain! This isn't about you!'

Ava lifted her hands and flapped them up and down, a gesture to calm me down, I suppose.

'I know you're going to be upset,' she said. 'But please, hear me out. Please, Juliet. I want to tell you how it was. I should have told you years ago, but I've never wanted to make it all worse.'

'Come on then,' I snapped. 'Tell me how it is.'

Ava stood up and moved to the window. With the sunlight behind her, she was beautiful. I was reminded of the day my dad died. A sudden sadness hit me.

'When I was young,' she said again. 'I thought that because I was attractive I had power over men, but in fact the opposite was true. Men told me they had feelings for me when they just wanted to sleep with me. I fell for it every time, and when they'd got what they wanted, off they'd go. I soon got a name for myself, much to my mother's embarrassment.'

'God bless Violet,' Joy said. 'My lovely sister. Sorry. Go on, Ava.'

'So there I was, sleeping my way through half of Cornwall,' continued Ava, 'until Charles came along, offering to love me for me, not for my body. He was different. He was older, wiser, talented and I loved him. But – and this doesn't make me sound like a nice person – I'd got used to sleeping with men. I'd got used to the attention, the thrill; I was addicted to it, perhaps. Even when I'd married Charles, I still occasionally slept with other people, and that one time, I fell pregnant. Charles had had a vasectomy after we had you because I didn't want more children, so we both knew the baby wasn't his.'

'So he did know about Rosie?' I interjected. My eyes welled up with tears.

'Yes,' she said, quietly and sadly. 'And he couldn't accept that I had betrayed him. That's why he killed himself. I suppose the other option was for me to have an abortion, but even though I didn't want another child, I couldn't go through with it.'

I looked up. My chin wobbled. Ava's eyes were glassy.

'Killed himself because of Rosie?' I said. 'But I thought it was my fault. I thought I'd driven him to his death by telling him you were seeing someone else. I told him you were seeing another man, just before he ran into the sea. Wasn't it me? Didn't I kill him?'

Ava shook her head. She was crying now. Tears dripped down from her eyes.

'No,' she choked. 'I didn't know you'd told him that. He knew already, he knew it all from the start. That day was just the final straw because I'd been to a party and I was rude and horrible. I'm sorry, Juliet, I'm so sorry. If I hadn't been so stupid, your dad would still be alive. He loved you so much. It has taken me a long time to accept full responsibility for his death, but it's true. It was all me.'

My shoulders slumped. Ava looked at me sympathetically.

'He once told me he could never understand people taking their own lives, because, if it were him, at the last minute he would hear a bird or see a person smile or feel the breeze in his hair and that would make him stop,' I said, stuttering with emotion. 'So I have always thought it must have been me that killed him – indirectly, but I still did it. I must have, because I don't believe he wanted to commit suicide.'

'No!' Ava said. 'Of course you weren't responsible! I was. It was all my fault, and it's hard to believe, very hard, but it was suicide. I'm so sorry you thought that. Dear God, I didn't know you thought that.'

'Perhaps if you hadn't left so soon, you would have known. Why did you go to Sydney?' I said. 'Why did you leave me and not stay with us to have Rosie?'

'I was desperately unhappy about what I'd done to Charles,' she said. 'Violet was ashamed of me. There were other reasons. I didn't think I could ever be a good mother to you. I was young, stupid and scared. I longed to run away – it was my only option.'

'Violet was not ashamed of you,' I said, voice breaking. 'She loved you. She always told me she loved you.'

Ava sighed and wiped her eyes. Joy handed us both tissues.

'I was so young and ill-equipped to deal with any of it,' Ava said. 'Violet was an upstanding member of the village. She'd lost her husband, and I didn't want to make it worse by giving birth to another child by another man. She loved you and was a better mother to you than I could ever be.'

'And what about Rosie?' I said. 'Did you tell the father – Stephen, was it? – about her?'

Joy and Ava shared a worried look.

'What?' I said. 'What's wrong?'

Ava shook her head.

'Oh, I'm sorry you read that letter,' Joy said. 'I wish Violet had never left it in her book. She knew very well you'd find it.'

'Why?' I said. 'What is it?'

'Stephen was having a relationship with Joy at the time,' Ava said. 'I seduced him from under her nose. Now do you understand why I live on the other side of the world? I'm the black sheep of the family.'

'You stole Joy's boyfriend?' I said. 'Your own uncle?'

'Don't be ridiculous,' said Ava. 'He wasn't my uncle. Joy didn't ever marry – she had a succession of boyfriends and one of them we shared. He didn't know about the pregnancy and doesn't know to this day.'

I shook my head in disbelief.

'You're unbelievable,' I said. 'Why couldn't you say no? Have more self-control?'

Ava shook her head. Joy shook her head.

'It's one of those terrible things,' Joy said. 'It's a big old fat mess.'

Outside, clouds had covered the sun. The room had gone dim. Joy stood up and flicked on a lamp, then walked over to me and cupped my face in her hands.

'But don't be too furious with your mum,' she said gently. 'It all happened a long time ago.'

I didn't speak. I was still trying to digest the information.

'I know you must detest me,' said Ava meekly. 'It's all my fault that your dad died. And I've let you down terribly. I don't think I was ever meant to be a mother. As soon as I held you after you were born, I realized you were too precious and that I was bound to let you down. And when you were a little girl, you were far more like your dad than me. I wanted to be free and adventurous, not accountable or responsible.'

Ava shook her head.

'It's different now,' she said. 'I've grown up. I've realized a lot of difficult truths about myself. But I've thought about you and Rosie every single day. I've wished I'd done it differently every single day. I do love you, Juliet. I've always wanted you to be happy, but I didn't know how to do that.'

I nodded. I felt deflated. Until now I'd convinced myself that Ava was a wicked, hateful person, but now I could see that it wasn't entirely true. I had to remember she was only twenty-seven when my dad died and she gave birth to Rosie – not far off my age now.

'Oh, Juliet,' Joy said. 'Tell us what you're thinking. It's a lot to take in, all this.'

'I feel lonely,' I said in a small voice, picking fluff from the arm of Joy's sofa. 'I miss my dad and Violet. I wonder what Rosie is like. Everything feels screwed up. I'm not sure who I'm supposed to be any more. It's so strange, because you're my mother, but we seem to be complete opposites. All I want is a home, with people in it I love. I want a family, a real family.'

'You'll have one, darling,' Ava said. 'You can make that happen, of course you can.'

I started to cry, and Ava walked over to me and crouched down by my side. She held my hand. Joy walked over to the table and picked up the jug of vodka and lemonade, poured three large glasses and handed them out. I tucked my feet up under my legs, drank deeply and rested my head on the back of the sofa.

'So how come you didn't tell Stephen?' I said, recovering. 'Did he not want to be a dad?'

Joy cleared her throat.

'He did, actually,' she said. 'We were trying to get pregnant before your mother came along and put a spanner in the works.'

Ava looked at the floor, then at Joy.

'I'm sorry,' she said.

'How can you forgive her?' I said to Joy. 'I would never be able to forgive her. She wrecked your life!'

Joy shook her head.

'She hasn't wrecked my life,' Joy said. 'My life has been wonderful, and I don't regret a moment of it. Yes, your mother and I fell out for a while, but ultimately she's my niece, and she had her reasons for behaving as she did. Her father died when she was tiny, and Violet was a broken woman for years. She wasn't always the woman you knew her as, Juliet.'

'Yes,' Ava said. 'But that doesn't excuse what I've done. There's no explanation, no justification. It's the way I've done things. I'm not normal, am I? I don't have a home like this, or a normal job. I've never stopped travelling, I've never settled. I've never wanted to settle. It's just—'

'Life,' said Joy, finishing Ava's sentence. 'That's what this is. Life.'

Joy lifted her glass and stood up.

'Cheers!' she said. 'Here's to life. What's that saying? Life is like an onion: you peel it off one layer at a time, and sometimes you weep.'

'Life is just one damned thing after another,' Ava said sullenly. 'Wouldn't you agree?'

'I'll drink to that,' Joy said. 'Come on, let's drink – it's the only way to cope. We're not your average family, are we? But who wants to be normal?'

'Me,' I said. Ava and Joy smiled kindly, but I could tell by their eyes they were thinking I had a lot to learn.

'You're right at the beginning of your life, Juliet,' Ava said. 'There's so much to come. Let's raise a toast to your future.'

We raised our glasses and clashed them together. I drank thirstily, feeling the vodka burn my throat. I was taken aback by what had just happened. The air in the room felt different, fresher, light. I looked at my mother and my aunt and was struck with wonder. When I reached their age, would I look back on a tangled history similar to theirs? What had they wanted when they were young women? As if reading my thoughts, Ava looked straight at me.

'All I ever wanted,' said Ava, 'was to feel free, whatever freedom is.'

'I can understand that,' I said, and she smiled – gratefully, I think.

Chapter Twenty-One

Many interesting textures can be provided by 'natural'
items such as brick [which] can blend with both
modern and traditional schemes, but should not be
overdone.

Sure & Simple Homemaking,
Jill Blake, 1975

When Philip returned from New York and phoned me from
Gatwick airport to invite himself to my flat, I panicked.

'I've got shingles,' I lied. 'And it's contagious. I won't be
able to come in to work for a few days. I can do preparation
for the auction from here. Make calls to the press, that kind of
thing. Sorry.'

Philip wasn't stupid. I knew he didn't buy a word of it,
but I didn't waver. I couldn't think of anything much worse
than Philip turning up on my doorstep clutching his suitcase,
regaling me with glamorous stories of the Big Apple. I imagined him on the flight home, reclined in his business class

chair, champagne bubbles bursting on his tongue, plotting his entry into my bed. I shuddered.

'You'll need a doctor's note,' he said frostily. 'HR insist on it these days.'

I told him I'd sort it out and cut off the conversation before he could say anything else annoying. I'd blame it on bad reception – that was the beauty of mobile phones.

I sighed noisily and looked over at Imogen. She had decided to stay with me for a few days. I'd given her my bedroom and moved into the box-room, which was just what it said on the label – full of boxes – but she looked completely exhausted.

'Shit,' I said to her. 'Where will I get a doctor's note from?'

'What?' Imogen said, blinking up at me. 'Sorry, I wasn't listening.'

Imogen was curled up on the sofa, her head resting on her hands. Dressed in pale yellow pyjamas and my dressing gown, she was quiet and listless. I'd never seen her like this. Normally she was an explosion of colour and couldn't keep still. I walked over to the sofa and sat down next to her feet.

'Why don't you get dressed?' I said. 'We could go out for a coffee or just have a walk in the fresh air? I've heard it's good for you, fresh air.'

Imogen didn't move. She shook her head and sighed.

'I don't want to,' she said sadly. 'Sorry.'

'Do you want to talk yet?' I said tentatively. 'About the pregnancy? You know, you've got choices. You don't have to have . . .'

I tailed off. She shook her head again.

'Not yet,' she said. 'Sorry.'

I wondered how long we had before Jonathan discovered Imogen was here. When he did find out, I knew I'd be bombarded with phone calls. Their wedding was supposedly only five weeks away. I'd been encouraging Imogen to cancel or postpone, but she was paralysed with fear.

'Don't worry,' I said, squeezing her foot. 'There's no rush.'

Imogen hadn't yet said anything about the pregnancy. After Cath had left on Sunday morning, she'd completely withdrawn and had hardly eaten a thing. I'd tried tempting her out of herself with (pointless) challenges: could she help me sort out my apron fabric, or help cook dinner. But she simply stared into the middle-distance and shook her head. I didn't think the environment was really helping. My tip of a flat and row of untouched packing cases was hardly mood enhancing.

'What about eye-pillows stuffed with flax seed?' I said.

'What?' she said, brow furrowed in annoyance. 'What's that?'

I had been scouring the pages of Violet's surprisingly resourceful book for ideas for things to occupy us. I turned Violet's book round to show her the diagram.

'Or a headboard for the bed?' I said, turning the page for more diagrams of DIY homemaking. 'All we need to do is thread cushions on to a curtain pole and suspend it above the bed. How does that sound?'

Imogen pulled a face. 'Ludicrous,' she said. 'It sounds ridiculous. You can just buy one.'

'I know,' I said. 'But so can ten million other people. That's what I hate about all this IKEA stuff Simon made me buy. Yes, it's cheap, but it's devoid of personality, just like Simon. How many people have a home-made headboard? Do you want to make one with me?'

I was struggling – we both knew that. Imogen pursed her lips.

'I know you're trying to distract me or get me to talk,' she said. 'But no, sorry, I'm not interested in headboards unless it involves banging my head against one.'

'I know!' I said, flicking past a recipe in Violet's book. 'I'll make chocolate truffles. Then we can eat them all and watch *Chocolat* on DVD and forget about everything else. How's that sound?'

Imogen's lips moved into a tiny smile shape.

'Better,' she said. 'That sounds better.'

I found the well-thumbed recipe and ran my finger down the list of ingredients. I had everything except for whipping cream. I popped out to the local shop for a tub, then raced back to the flat and cleared the kitchen surfaces with unnecessary drama, trying to get Imogen's attention. The more I moved, the less fearful I felt of everything going on around me – not only with Imogen, but the thoughts of Dylan and Rosie that popped into my head every few seconds.

Chocolate Truffles

Ingredients
7 oz dark chocolate
7 fl oz whipping or double cream
2 tbsp butter (unsalted)
nuts or raisins (optional)
cocoa powder and/or chopped nuts

Method
Break up the chocolate and set aside.
In a pan, gently heat the whipping cream until just beginning
    to boil, then add to the chopped chocolate and stir.

When the chocolate has melted and the mixture is smooth,
add the butter. Mix until smooth.

Add nuts or raisins now.

Leave mixture to cool (you can hurry it up by putting it in
the fridge) then, when firm, spoon out small portions to
roll into truffles.

Roll in cocoa powder and/or chopped nuts.

Delicious served with a dollop of whipped cream laced with
brandy.

Imogen moved off the sofa and came to stand by me in the
kitchen. She put on one of my aprons and helped make the
chocolate truffles, though she still didn't say anything. When
they were finished, we took a plate of them to the sofa and sat
there, side by side, in our aprons, eating.

'Look at this,' I said. 'Domestic bliss!'

'I'm not sure you should go that far,' she said. 'I'm gay,
pregnant by my ex-boyfriend, and I've got a wedding ap-
proaching. You're hiding from your stalker boss, your mum
used to be a sex addict who stole your aunt's boyfriend, and
now we're going to get fat. Is that bliss?'

'As near as I'll ever get,' I said drily.

Imogen rested her head on my shoulder. 'Oh God,' she
said. 'Do you think Jonathan would take me to court or
something if I had the baby?'

I turned to face her. 'So you're going to keep the baby?' I
said. 'But not marry Jonathan?'

'I think so,' she said with a sigh. 'I keep changing my mind.'

She started to cry. I put my arm round her shoulders and
hugged her close. I hated seeing her this upset, but there was

no easy answer. Then the doorbell rang. My stomach twisted. I stood up and said a silent prayer: please don't let it be Philip. I went over to the window and lifted the blind.

'Oh fuck,' I said, turning to Imogen. 'It's Jonathan.'

'Shit!' she said, wiping her eyes. 'Tell him I'm not here. Stick your head out of the window and tell him you're in the bath or something and you haven't seen me for ages. Please don't let him in – I'm not ready to face him yet. I can't tell him . . .'

There was terror in her eyes. I grabbed the nearest thing – a tea-towel – wrapped it round my head and pushed open the window.

'Jonathan, sorry,' I said. 'I was in the shower. Are you OK?'

'No, I'm not OK,' he shouted. 'I'm fucking terrible! I know Imogen's in there with you. Why won't you let me see her? I'm supposed to be marrying that bitch in five weeks.'

He was really loud. The neighbours living opposite looked out of their window. I heard Imogen muttering behind me and walk across the room.

'Don't call me a bitch,' Imogen said, appearing over my shoulder.

Jonathan's face turned to stone and his shoulders dropped. He looked like the weight of the world was bearing down on him.

'I need to talk to you,' he said. 'I need to know what's going on. You're being such a fucking bitch!'

Imogen leaned right out of the window and spoke in an icy voice.

'I'll talk to you when I'm ready,' she said. 'Now leave me alone.'

She slammed down the window and we stood there, looking at the blind, expecting . . . I don't know what. After a couple of moments we sat down on the sofa again with the plate of chocolate truffles. Neither of us said a word. I think we sensed something bad was about to happen. We just sat there in silence, when suddenly there was a tremendous crack as a brick came flying through the window, shattering shards of glass all over the place. It made an unbelievable noise – like nothing I'd ever heard.

'Christ!' I screamed, jumping up. 'What's he doing?'

After the first brick came another brick – he must have picked them from the pile in next door's front garden. Imogen and I hid in the bedroom while glass flew over the living room. We were both shaking.

'Shall I call the police?' I said.

'Wait a few minutes,' Imogen said. 'I'm so sorry, Juliet – he's got such a temper on him.'

We listened to him kicking the downstairs communal door so hard I wondered if he'd actually be able to kick it down. For a wafer-thin person, he made a lot of noise. Then silence. We stood stock-still, not knowing what to do. Eventually, my heart pounding behind my ribs, I walked into the front room, my feet crunching over broken glass, and looked out of the window. I scanned the street for him, but there was no sign, just a couple of neighbours looking worried. I waved to them and called down that we were fine, you know how it is, ha ha, men, eh? and all that. They quickly dispersed – no one wants to get involved in other people's dirty laundry in London. You never know what you might come up against.

'Look at this,' Imogen said from behind me, picking up one of the bricks he'd thrown. 'What kind of maniac does that?

There was glass all over the place – on my sewing machine, which sat on the table underneath the window, over my apron fabric, in my shoes and bag, over the chocolate truffles. I leaned down and carefully began picking up the larger pieces of glass.

'Will you cancel the wedding now?' I asked Imogen.

When she didn't answer, I spoke again.

'If you don't, I will.'

Chapter Twenty-Two

Homemaking isn't so bad, compared to the drudgery of a woman's other career options. Women should buckle down, stop dreaming of a career or even an office job, and get those toilets scrubbed and cakes baked.

The I Hate to Housekeep Book,
Peg Bracken, 1962

I managed to stretch out my shingles lie for an entire week, but I had no choice but to go back to work on the day of the charity auction. I'd checked my emails several times a day, quietly hoping I'd hear from Dylan, but somehow knowing that I wouldn't. Instead, there were numerous messages from Philip, some work-related, others irritatingly personal – I ignored all of those. But the more I ignored him, the more emails I received. I kept them all in a folder on my desktop – I had a nagging suspicion that one day I might need to use them against him. I had never regretted sleeping with anyone more than with Philip.

'Cath's coming over again tonight,' said Imogen over her Weetabix and strawberries as I got ready to leave for work. 'Is that going to be OK?'

I wondered if Imogen needed more space to make her decision about the pregnancy, but she and Cath were as thick as thieves. Cath's toothbrush was in the bathroom, and her clothes were hanging in the wardrobe. Her touch was everywhere – sweet williams in wine bottles, honeycomb candles by the bath, a seemingly endless supply of monkey nuts to crack open and nibble. She was like the grown-up in the house, and had even boarded up the window with plywood before I paid for a man to come and fix it properly.

'Send Jonathan the bill,' Imogen had said crossly. 'He should pay.'

But I didn't. Because of Simon and Hanna's affair, I kind of understood where Jonathan was coming from. If I had been more of a rebel, perhaps I would have taken a brick to Simon's rowing machine – or head – the day I found out he cheated on me. And anyway, I was hardly out of pocket right now. The sale of Violet's cottage had just gone through and the money – all £100,000 of it, after debt repayments and some for Joy – was sitting in my bank, sparking a flurry of calls from the bank manager asking what I was going to do with my assets. It was an incredible amount of money, and I felt bound to give a chunk of it to Ava, even though, or perhaps because, Violet hadn't left anything to her, but the rest I would save. This was not like me at all. Previously I'd have gone on a massive shopping spree with Imogen in Liberty – our spiritual home – but now I knew I should hold on to it.

'Juliet?' Imogen asked again. 'Is it OK for Cath to come over again? We're going to make a plan about what to do next, finally, so we'll be out from under your feet.'

'Of course it's OK,' I said. 'You don't have to ask. Come and go as you please – and you're not under my feet, honestly. You're my best friend.'

I was going to ask about the pregnancy, but I shut my mouth again. Every time I broached the subject, she closed down.

'I know,' she said, then with a sly grin, continued: 'Those monkey nut shells drive you up the wall though, don't they? You and me both.'

I glanced up at her.

'So is everything not all rosy in the Cath-garden?' I asked.

'Oh, monkey nuts are nothing,' she said with a small laugh. 'At least she's not actually nuts, like Jonathan.'

'And Philip,' I said.

'Loon-bags, the lot of them,' Imogen said. 'I think what we should do is run away and start all over again somewhere new where no one knows who we are.'

I picked up my bag and shuddered. The thought of running away and starting all over again made me feel exhausted. At least this way, with the truth out, I knew what I was working with. I was tired of feeling lost in a maze of lies. I wanted to be found.

Back at Rosendale's, I felt totally out of the loop. The first thing I did was Google 'shingles'. Armed with anecdotes of itching welts, I doubted my immediate colleagues would question the absence of a doctor's note. Besides, they'd be rushing around today like headless chickens in preparation for tonight's Sale of the Century.

Philip was a different matter. I'd spent the tube journey worrying about seeing him again. If he continued to harass me with his sexual advances, I'd have to tell him where to go.

'So,' said Philip, suddenly behind me, his hands on my chair. He swung me round to face him and flashed a smug smile. 'Did you miss me?'

No, I thought. Not at all, not in the slightest, not for a single second. I didn't smile.

'Oh,' I said, deliberately ignoring his question. 'I'm glad I've seen you this morning. I wanted to check the journalist from the *Telegraph* magazine had called you back. I had an email from him and he wanted to do an interview with a Rosendale's rep after the auction tonight. I suggested you.'

Philip's face fell. My hair was pinned up and he brushed the back of my neck with his hand. Even though I'd worn the least provocative dress I owned, he gawped at my chest. I felt physically sick.

'Yes, I've spoken to him,' he said quietly, leaning his head to one side. 'Juliet, can we have a word, in my office?'

Reluctantly, I followed him into his room. Everything about him now seemed fake – the enormous family portraits on the wall, his gold wedding ring, the tan. I'd gone from finding him attractive to being repulsed by him. I tried to shake the image of the pig snout from my head.

'I know we're having a little power struggle here and things between us have become a little strained,' he said gently. 'But I think we should give us another chance.'

I opened my mouth to speak, but he lifted his hand and made a 'sshhh' sound. My blood boiled. I felt like a schoolgirl in the headteacher's office. I clamped my lips shut. Shame I hadn't done the same with my legs.

'Hear me out,' he said. 'I went one step too far with cleaning up your flat, didn't I? I understand that. But I have a fantastic surprise for you, a much better surprise than a neat living room. At the auction tonight.'

I stared at Philip. How could a person get it so wrong? I didn't see him as authoritative and impressive. I saw him as desperate. What was he talking about a 'power struggle' for? Watching his mouth move, I thought of it pressed against mine. I hated him.

'I really don't want any more surprises,' I protested, but Philip pointed to the door and gave a slight shake of his head. I looked and saw my colleagues arriving.

'Come here quickly,' he said, waving me over to behind his desk. For one awful moment, I feared he might have opened up his suit trousers. I eyed up the guillotine. Instead, he pulled open his top drawer.

'This is surprise number one,' he said, nodding down towards a small bag of white powder. So the rumours were true.

'Cocaine?' I said, stunned.

'Top marks,' he said, winking at me then slamming the drawer shut and locking it with a tiny key. 'I saw enough of it at your party to know you like it.'

'Did you?' I asked, incredulous. I struggled to think of anyone who might have had cocaine on them – Jonathan maybe?

Philip beamed at me, then called his assistant.

'Lisa! In here, please,' he said. 'Juliet, you'd better get on, we've got a big day ahead of us and a fantastic night.' He winked.

I said nothing and walked calmly out of the office and sat down at my desk. Philip had me so wrong. I had a new understanding of people who, without apparent warning, suddenly lose the plot. Last year I had heard of a girl who was so sick of her job working as a newspaper reporter with a bully for a boss that she picked up her computer and threw it out of a third floor window on to the pavement below. It smashed into a million pieces, as did her career. But it must have felt good.

Previously in my time at Rosendale's I'd felt hugely excited about celebrity auctions – I liked it that charities benefited, and it was so easy to get press coverage. The Little Black Dress celebrity auction for children's charities earlier in the year had raised the most I'd known, and this one was expected to raise a lot more. But today I couldn't muster an ounce of enthusiasm. I felt flat. The phone rang off the hook with journalists wanting to check details about what was being sold. I answered them in a monotone. When I wasn't speaking to journalists, I was stuffing press packs in slow motion. It was the combination of Philip's unwanted attention and the knowledge that Dylan would be showing up later to film the auction for the conclusion of the documentary that was making me miserable. I didn't want to face Dylan again. What would I say? What could I say? I had no right to be upset with him – we were only friends, colleagues. But I had surprised myself by feeling desperately upset about it. I had secretly let myself think that something might happen between us. I'd let myself think he genuinely liked me.

'I need a breather,' I told Lisa, the press office assistant. 'Anyone want coffee?'

I took orders for coffee, got the lift down to the ground floor and walked to Caffè Nero. I pushed open the door and instantly noticed Dylan standing in the queue, looking stylish in a blue and black checked shirt hanging open over a T-shirt. He saw me before I could run out. I flushed with embarrassment, but swallowed my pride, waved and walked over to him.

'Hi,' I said with a smile. 'How are you doing?'

Dylan stared at me as if I was from another planet.

'I just don't understand you, Juliet,' he said quietly. 'You abandon me at a hen party you invited me to, where I know nobody. Then you ignore my texts and calls, and now you're all nice as pie. I just don't get it. What's your problem? I thought we were pals.'

I stood there looking at him, stunned. Dylan spoke softly, but I knew the other people in the queue could hear and were listening. I frowned.

'What do you mean, abandoned you?' I said. 'You seemed pretty busy when I left that party. One minute we were staring at the stars on the roof, the next you had my nemesis's mouth attached to yours. I didn't think I should interrupt.'

Dylan shook his head.

'What? You don't know what you're talking about,' he said before turning to order a latte. 'You have got that so wrong. Is that why you didn't answer my calls? Christ, Juliet, you're tough.'

Scolded, I shook my head, chewed my lip and sulked. I joined the back of the queue and stared at my shoes, tears stinging my eyes. Dylan paid for his coffee, then, without even looking back at me, walked out of the shop.

'Lovers' tiff?' the man standing next to me asked, a wry smile on his lips. 'Don't worry, you'll have fun making it up.'

'I doubt that,' I said. 'He hates me.'

Back at Rosendale's, Dylan and I avoided each other. I imagined myself going to find him to talk to him as he was setting up his equipment, but when I walked in his direction, my legs turned to liquid. I decided it was a better idea to give it up. The sooner this day was over and I could go home, the better. I kept myself busy organizing press information. Dylan could go to hell – all men could.

At six o'clock, Philip called me into his office again, rolled down the blinds and offered me a line of coke. How did he manage to hold down his job if he had this nosebag? Thinking about it, it explained a lot. My heart raced.

'It'll help with your nerves,' he said as he snorted a line in front of me.

'No thanks,' I said, my mouth as dry as chalk. 'Really, I'm not interested. I've got to get changed to do the meet and greet.'

Trembling, I walked straight back out of his office. I felt Philip's eyes boring into my back. I wondered if he was slightly crazy.

Hiding in the Ladies' to change, I stood perfectly still for a moment and sighed. Maybe if I had a drink, I'd feel better. There was a tray of champagne in the Press Room. I'd get dressed quickly and find a glass.

Locking myself into a cubicle, I changed into a simple black dress and heels. I heard someone coming into the bathroom and assumed it was one of the girls from the press office. But when I opened the door, Philip was standing there, leaning up against the sinks, his arms folded. I gasped.

'Look,' he said, smiling broadly. 'I just want to apologize for being an idiot. Do you forgive me? Will you come here and give me a hug? Don't be too hard on me.'

My eyes darted towards the door. I felt incredibly nervous – there was no one else in here. Shaking now, I told myself to be calm. But Philip was scaring me. I edged away from him, forcing a smile.

'I've got to meet the journalists now,' I said, my hand on the door handle. 'Don't worry about anything. It's all been a mistake. Let's forget about it.'

Relief washed over me when I'd got out of the Ladies' and was standing in a public space. Philip didn't follow me, but I didn't wait to find out why. I would have to make sure I was never alone with him, ever again. Maybe if I kept a very low profile for a few weeks, he would lose interest. Surely he didn't really believe we had a chance together? Perhaps because he was having marriage problems, he was going through a weird nervous breakdown. Whatever it was, I didn't want anything more to do with it. As far as Philip was concerned, I planned to disappear off the radar.

Two hours later the first part of the auction was under way. I stood at the back of the auction room, watching the auctioneer, Maurice Knight, a celebrity in his own right, working the crowd. Postcards of Bettie Page in various lingerie was the starting lot, and while the bidding got going, I sat at the back of the auction room watching Dylan filming. I decided I'd have to talk to him during the break – it had been immature of me to be angry about Hanna. Dylan could do whatever he pleased, couldn't he? So when Bettie Page's items were sold and Maurice called a break, I moved through the crowds over to Dylan and tapped him on the shoulder.

'Can we talk?' I said. 'Just for a moment?'

He followed me into the hall, outside the auction room, and pushed his hair away from his face.

'What is it?' he said curtly.

'I'm sorry that I didn't wait for you at the hen party,' I said. 'I guess I was a bit mad that you and Hanna were together. I don't know why, I had no right. I just hoped that if you weren't with Sylvie, we might—'

I couldn't finish my sentence. I suddenly thought I was being ludicrous. Perhaps, like Philip, I was way off the mark and Dylan had never liked me, not even a little. I waved my hand in the air dismissively.

'I'm so stupid,' I said. 'I get things so wrong sometimes ...'

Dylan broke out into a grin. He laughed gently.

'You thought we could what?' he said, grinning.

I blushed boiling red. Now he was laughing at the idea. He was laughing at me. I frowned. Suddenly Philip was next to me.

'Juliet,' he snapped. 'I need to speak to you. Now.'

I told Dylan I'd catch up with him later and followed Philip back into his office. I looked up at the family portraits, whose smiles now seemed demonic. I sighed noisily.

'What is it now?' I said. 'The auction's about to start up again and I'd better be there in case any journo wants quotes or—'

Philip's face was as black as night. His eyes were thunderous. He thumped the desk with his fist. I glanced out of his door and into the office to see if anyone else was there.

'You're a little prick-tease,' he said, nastily. 'Aren't you?'

I don't know if it was the pure injustice of this statement or the champagne, but my fear disappeared and I felt furiously angry.

'No, I'm not a prick-tease,' I hissed. 'You're a bloody fool, Philip. You won't leave me alone and I've had enough of it. You've no right to keep on hassling me like this. I just need you to back off and leave me alone. I've never given you any signals to suggest I'm interested in you.'

'You slept with me,' he smirked. 'That's a signal, isn't it? And now you just want to pretend it didn't happen? Is that right?'

I looked at him coldly.

'That's right,' I said. 'I want to pretend it didn't happen.'

I felt exhausted. I wanted Philip to go away, but he wouldn't. He wouldn't lie down and die. Suddenly he grabbed my wrist and held on to it tight.

'How dare you lead me on like that?' he hissed. 'I've given up so much for you, and now you're treating me like I don't exist.'

'Get off,' I said. 'Get off – you're hurting me.'

Philip was strong. He stared right at me.

'No, I'm not,' he said. 'Don't be a silly girl. Now come here.'

He yanked me towards him. What the fuck? Philip made me sick. I pushed and wriggled free from him, but he still had my wrist.

'Juliet,' he said. 'Relax before this gets out of hand.'

Before it gets out of hand? I couldn't stand it any longer. I just wanted to go home.

'I'm leaving,' I said coolly. 'I quit.'

Without letting go of my wrist, Philip squeezed my breast with his free hand. My heart pounded. I took a deep breath and screamed at the top of my voice.

'GET OFF ME! GET THE HELL OFF ME NOW!'

I was aware that someone else was in the room with us, and, turning, I saw Dylan standing by the door, holding up his camera.

'Smile, Philip,' he said. 'You're on camera.'

'Fucking fantastic,' he said. 'That's illegal.'

'No more illegal than what you're doing,' Dylan said.

Philip let go of my wrist and pushed past Dylan. At the door he turned back to face me. I was shaking.

'Do you really?' he said. 'Do you really quit?'

I rubbed my wrist. Dylan put his arm protectively around my shoulder.

'Yes,' I said, taking off my Rosendale's name badge and throwing it on the floor. 'I quit ten million times over.'

'You don't have to do that, Juliet,' Dylan said. 'He's the one who should lose his job, not you.'

'Why don't you shut your mouth?' said Philip, turning to Dylan.

'Why don't you shut yours?' he said to Philip.

Philip shoved Dylan and left the room. We stood there together, alone. I was shaking violently.

'You'd better get back,' I said as I heard the bell ringing for the second part of the auction. 'Thank you for that.'

'Any time,' he said, concerned. 'Are you sure you'll be OK? I think you've got a strong case against Philip if you want to keep your job, or at least get Philip to lose his. I'll keep this recording.'

I shook my head.

'I want out,' I said. 'I don't want to have anything more to do with him or this place. Yes, maybe I'll report him to HR, but I need a fresh start, a new life. It wasn't meant to be like this.'

Dylan pulled a sad expression. He put his hand on my shoulder.

'Can I call you later?' he said. 'I'd like to explain, about the hen party. That's what I was coming to say when I found you and Philip. Will you promise to answer this time?'

'Yes,' I smiled. 'You'd better get back in. Can you tell Lisa to help out with any journalists' enquiries? I've got to get out of here.'

Holding back tears, I cleared out my desk, stuffed my things into a carrier bag, left a Post-it note on Lisa's desk and walked out of Rosendale's and into the street. Rain was falling, but it was warm. I stood still for a moment and looked back at the building. From the auction room there was uproarious applause – probably someone had paid a fortune for Marilyn's possessions. I couldn't make myself care. I just wanted to get away from there – a long way away.

Walking towards the tube, I reeled from the shock of Philip's behaviour. I knew I should report him – he would probably get the sack. I would. But for now, I needed to calm down. I'd quit my job. I sat on the tube, vowing to get my life together. I really needed to talk to someone. But who?

When I reached my flat it was almost dark. I looked up at the window. The living room was lit up. I saw Imogen and Cath, their heads close together. I felt estranged, as if I didn't belong. Where did it come from, that feeling? I knew Imogen loved me, but she had other, bigger, issues on her mind and I didn't want to get in the way of her blossoming relationship.

After a few moments standing there, I turned away and carried on walking. The rain was heavier now, pattering on the leaves of the trees, streaking across car windows and sloshing down the gutter. I lifted my face up and let the drops fall on my skin. I thought, I could collapse into a hedge and sleep there and nobody would know. Instead, I decided to go to Joy's place. Picking up a bottle of wine from the off-licence, I got a cab to her flat, praying she was in and alone. I knocked on her front door.

'Hello, darling – you're soaking wet,' she said, concerned. 'What's happened?'

She reached out her hand to me and pulled me inside. By now, I was feeling extremely sorry for myself.

'I've lost everything,' I said in a small voice. 'I've lost my career, my boyfriend, my flat, my friends.'

'You haven't lost your mind,' she said, handing me a fluffy dressing gown from a pile of clean washing. 'Be grateful for small mercies.'

Chapter Twenty-Three

[A homemaker] has an easy job. She spends hours looking at television or listening to radio soap operas but doesn't deduct this time from her workday. She includes as labour even the naps she takes during the day and still says her job is killing her.

'Your Wife Has an Easy Racket!', Robert J. Knowlton,
American Magazine, November 1951

Wrapped in the dressing gown, I watched the Rosendale's documentary from behind one of Joy's velvet cushions. Seeing myself on TV demonstrating the lots up for auction, even though I appeared only for a few minutes, was painful. I switched it off before the coverage from the auction came on, or anything from our stay in Cornwall. Thinking of Dylan made me unfathomably sad. Though he'd 'rescued' me from Philip, he was clearly annoyed with me. I should never have snubbed him after Imogen's party. He hadn't done anything wrong. I covered my face with my hands. Joy patted my knee.

'I think we should open a bottle of bubbly and celebrate, don't you?' she said, jumping up from the sofa and walking through to the kitchen. 'New beginnings?'

I sat still, hugging my knees, which were tucked under my chin. My wet clothes steamed on the radiators. I murmured my agreement.

'There,' she said, handing me a glass. 'You know, all this that you're going through – you'll look back one day and think how awfully exciting it all was. At least you're really feeling something, experiencing real life.'

I smiled thinly. Joy moved across the room and picked up a snowstorm dome from her mantelpiece. She shook it.

'How come you've got so many things?' I said, gesturing to her living room. 'I always wonder where you find it all.'

The room was a cross between a museum and a junk shop. It reminded me of the antiques market I used to love in Greenwich. There was an eclectic mix of furniture: a blue leather three-piece suite, too many lamps throwing out a yellow glow into the room, framed photographs everywhere, ornaments on every surface, stones thrown on to a plate, framed butterflies, hat boxes, a collection of walking sticks, each with a different handle, and silk and lace cushions thrown about. Piles of *Stage* magazine were stacked up in the corner of the room next to a collection of hardback children's books.

'Oh,' Joy said. 'Over the years I've bought bits and pieces I like. I couldn't bear to live in a blank room with no per-sonality. All of these things say something about the person I am, don't they? I can be myself in here – it cheers me up. I read something about a designer that said your home should be like a good dose of Prozac. Do you know what I mean?'

My chin wobbled. I couldn't help myself. My flat was depressing. I'd had a horrible day. Joy was looking at me so kindly. I burst into tears.

'No,' I sobbed. 'My flat is a disaster area and now I've quit my job I can't afford it anyway. I hate my life. It's all Simon's fault. It's all Hanna's fault, and then there's Dylan . . .'

I sobbed so hard my back arched, like an angry cat. Joy held my hand and made soothing sounds. Eventually I stopped sniffing and apologized.

'Oh, Juliet, why don't you come and let me look after you for a while?' she said. 'Until you get your feet back on the ground? I'd love to have you here, to keep me company.'

'What about Jack?' I said, wiping my eyes with a tissue.

Joy creased up her nose.

'Who's Jack?' she said with a clap of laughter. 'I've moved on, darling. Jack's history. Ancient history.'

Later that night, my phone rang. Dylan? I fished it out of my pocket and looked at the caller ID. It was Imogen. I walked into Joy's spare bedroom and flopped on to the single bed. It was covered with a patchwork quilt Violet had made when I was young, each square a beautiful piece of fabric I strongly associated with a feeling of home. I lay back on the pillow and held the phone to my ear.

'Hi,' I said. 'Are you OK? I came over to Joy's so you and Cath could have some peace and quiet.'

'You didn't need to do that,' Imogen said. 'I've made a decision, a big one. I can't talk about it now, so I'll tell you all about it when I see you, but I'm phoning to say that a parcel just arrived for you by courier. Do you want me to open it for you?'

I looked at my watch. It was eleven o'clock. No one sends parcels at this time of night.

'Yes please,' I said. 'Be careful that it's not a horse's head or something. I've just quit my job. I wouldn't put anything past Philip right now.'

'You've just quit?' she gasped. 'What happened? Are you OK?'

Joy stood in the doorway, holding my glass of champagne. She pantomimed pouring me more. I nodded and smiled.

'Long story,' I said. 'I'll tell you when I see you. I'm more intrigued about what's in the parcel. Will you open it up?'

I heard the sound of paper ripping. Joy passed me my refilled glass.

'It's not a horse's head,' she said. 'It's cupcakes. Big ones, covered in icing.'

My mind raced. Philip. It had to be from him. He had probably got scared that I'd report his outrageous behaviour. He was trying to buy me off.

'Oh God,' I said. 'I think they're from Philip – he's unbelievable. Don't open it up any more. I'll have to return them. There's no way I can accept them.'

'They're gorgeous, all decorated differently with stars, flowers and hearts,' she said. 'I'll wrap them up and leave them on the table in the living room. Juliet, I'm sorry, I'm – we're – still in your flat. I should give you some money towards the rent or move out.'

'I was going to talk to you about that,' I said, sitting up and dangling my feet over the edge of the bed. 'Joy has offered me a bed here and I wondered if you and Cath would like to sublet the flat? If not I'll put my notice in, but I thought I'd check with you first.'

'Good idea,' Imogen said without another thought. 'I'd love to do that. Even if Cath doesn't want to, I'll rent it. Give me your bank details and I'll pay the money in. You can still stay here though, you know.'

'No,' I said. 'It's never going to feel right. I've never made it feel like a home. It wasn't meant to be for me on my own. I need to sort my life out. I'm not sure what I'll do now.'

'Cath loves the aprons, by the way,' she said. 'She sold two in the shop today. She sold them for forty pounds each. You should make more. That's what you can do. Aprons are the future.'

She laughed. I heard Cath agreeing in the background.

'Yeah,' I said despondently. 'I'll think about it.'

Yawning, I hung up and lay back on the single bed, staring at the ceiling, with my glass balanced on my stomach. I checked the time. Nearly midnight. My head was buzzing. How could Philip believe I would be so easily bought? So much for Dylan calling me back. I thought, after our trip to Cornwall, that he'd understood me, but I clearly meant nothing to him. Perhaps he was with Hanna. I envied her. She could, apparently, get any man she wanted. Or any man I wanted.

I put the glass on the bedside table, turned on to my side and closed my eyes. I didn't stir when Joy came in, turned out the light and pulled Violet's quilt up over me. Forget about them, I told myself, drifting off into sleep. Forget about love. Think about aprons. Aprons are the future.

Turns out I was right. Without a job to go to, I was at a loose end the next day. I wrote to HR, tendering my resignation at Rosendale's. I hadn't decided whether to make a complaint about Philip – because I'd slept with him, I didn't rate my chances. Joy told me I should, without doubt. I knew she was right, but I wasn't quite ready for the fight.

In the meantime, I had nothing to do but make aprons. I picked up some clothes, the parcel from Philip, my sewing machine and the rolls of fabric from Lovelace Avenue and piled them into a taxi to take back to Joy's. The driver sat in his seat chewing gum while I hauled everything down the stairs and into the boot, nearly breaking my back. After ten minutes, I collapsed into the back seat and asked him to drive.

If it's not too much trouble, you git, I wanted to add, but I stared blankly out of the window instead.

Back at Joy's flat, I felt terribly aware of my solitude. Except for the occasional whoosh of a passing car or bus, everything seemed to be eerily silent and still. I decided to sew. At least, when I sewed, I was producing something and had something to show for my waking hours. If I made enough, I could sell them in Cath's shop or at the market stall. And while I was sewing, I didn't have to face the horrible truth: that I felt desperately alone, without a job and without anywhere to call home.

I thought about Dylan a lot. I imagined what it would be

like if it had all turned out differently and Hanna hadn't got in the way. I'd only known him a few weeks, but I knew there was something special about him. When, after making three aprons in four hours, I felt absolutely exhausted, I had a nap on Joy's sofa and dreamed of him, stripped down to the waist, running along the beach in dappled sunshine.

I woke with a jolt. My phone was ringing. I grabbed it from the table and saw Simon's name. I didn't pick up, just waited for him to leave me a message. Then I listened to it.

'Imogen told me you're moving out of the flat,' he said. 'It's made me worry about you. I've been doing a lot of thinking. Will you give me a call?'

Simon's call was followed by one from Imogen.

'Are you eating?' she said. 'You're not depressed, are you?'

I told her that I was eating, that Joy had a well-stocked fridge, and that I didn't think I was depressed, only maybe suppressed.

'I feel like I've entered another world,' I said. 'There's no one to talk to and all I do is eat cake. How are you? Have you made any decisions?'

'I've decided to keep the baby,' she said. 'When it comes out I'll have nothing to do but breastfeed, so we can sit together eating cakes and talking all day long.'

'That's a brave decision, but I'd do the same,' I said warmly. 'Remember when we looked after your cousin's baby that afternoon? He weed all over the place, didn't he, because we couldn't work out how to put the nappy on. We'll have to do some training. It'll be great. I'll help you, Imogen. I promise.'

After we'd said goodbye, I walked into the kitchen and poured myself a glass of Joy's lemonade. A tiny part of me missed Simon and I wondered whether to call him back. Then I noticed the parcel on the table. I hadn't even opened it up properly yet. I put down my glass and stripped off the paper – I'd have to rewrap it before I sent it back to Philip. Pulling off the tissue paper and opening the lid, I looked at the cakes. They were from the Hummingbird Bakery in Notting Hill, each cake a tower of sponge and buttercream icing, sprinkled with colourful sugar stars and flowers. I smoothed out the packaging and noticed a small card with a handwritten message. My stomach turned. What had Philip written to me? I picked it up and read.

It said: 'To enjoy in your caravan . . . Dylan.'

I dropped it in surprise. Dylan had sent me these cakes? I blushed all over. Moving from room to room, I wondered what I should do. I picked up my phone and called his mobile, but it went straight to an automated message which said the number was not currently available. I phoned the production office he worked in at Channel 4. A girl answered and told me that the day of the auction had been his last day there.

'He's flown out to California,' she said. 'While we're all trapped in this dark studio, he's gone in search of the perfect wave. He's making a documentary about rookie surfers. What a job.'

I thanked the girl, but when I put down the phone my hand was shaking. I'd missed him. He'd gone. She hadn't said for how long. What if he'd gone for good? What if he'd gone with Sylvie? I didn't even know where he lived in London –

somewhere in Tower Hamlets, that's all I knew. What if he'd changed his mobile number? I only had his work email.

I picked up his card and pressed it against my chest. So he did like me. But what about Hanna – where did she fit into all this? I decided I had to see her. Ironically, she was probably the only person who could help. I sat down at Joy's computer and sent an email to Hanna. An out-of-office email pinged straight back.

I'm in the States, but will get back to you on my return.

My skin blazed. In the States?
I typed a furious reply:

Hanna, if you're in California, I will gouge my own
eyes out and yours. I have never hated anyone so much
right now as I hate you.

What was wrong with me? I'd lost the plot. My finger hovered over the Delete button. But before I could do anything the computer crashed. I bashed the keyboard with my palm, swore at it and went to bed.

Chapter Twenty-Four

Remember to take off your apron and turn off the
kitchen appliances before your husband returns home.
He will not want to be reminded of domestic drudgery
the minute he returns from the office.

Homemaking Hints for a Happier Home, 1959

Weeks went by and I didn't hear from Hanna or Dylan, so
I almost convinced myself they had disappeared into the
Californian sunset hand in hand. And here was I, Cinderella,
living with my ageing aunt in a small London flat – Joy's moc-
casin slippers the nearest I came to a glass shoe.

I thought about Dylan a lot. There was something about
him I couldn't let go of, an unspoken complicity between us.
I remembered the way he'd told me he thought I was 'pretty
fucking scarily amazing' on the beach in Cornwall, possibly
the most romantic thing anyone had ever said. Even if it was
paranoia, suspecting that he and Hanna might be together
made me feel furiously upset with myself. Why hadn't I

intervened when I saw them kissing at the party? Why hadn't I trusted my instincts and told Dylan that I really liked him when we were on the roof? I'd been shy and inert, saying not very much when I should have been bold and talked my head off.

Joy was a good sport. When I told her how I felt about Dylan and Hanna, she would go red in the face hurling acrid abuse at them, then hug me and say: 'We just have to carry on carrying on, darling girl.' We fell into a cohabiting rhythm. She was out most days, rehearsing scripts for her new play. While I had her flat to myself, I sewed my aprons in the living room, listening to the radio. When my fingers and eyes got bored with sewing, I stared into space or searched Violet's homemaking book for the more bizarre homemaking tips, then typed them on to brown cardboard tags with Joy's old-fashioned typewriter. And in the evenings, with Joy home, I cooked for her while she tried on the aprons, which she said were nicer than her Monsoon dresses, and tied on the tags with narrow velvet ribbon.

'I love this one!' she exclaimed, tying it on to an antique rose-print apron. '"Lemon juice will shine leather shoes if you don't have polish." Who would've thought? Shall we try it out? Or this one: "For creaky floorboards rub talcum powder into the cracks."'

Joy was easily distracted and, while I worked like a dog ensuring my aprons were ready for my first stall at Spitalfields Market in East London the following Sunday, she squirted lemon juice on her shoes and rubbed talcum powder into the floor.

'Do you think I'll actually sell any of these?' I said, resting my hand on a pile of twenty-six aprons I'd made, each in a different fabric.

'Yes!' she said. 'You'll have to wear one to model it. Put some heels on, red lipstick, do your hair all nice and retro. Youngsters love anything vintage, don't they? London's bursting at the seams with shops selling old clothes. It's very odd, this obsession with "vintage", especially considering how badly most young people treat vintage people like myself.'

I handed her a plate of spaghetti, a very big glass of red wine and the *Evening Standard* property pages. Since the sale of Violet's cottage had gone through, I was considering trying to buy a place. I had a big deposit, so if I found somewhere cheap, I could get a tiny mortgage.

'I actually really like living here, though, now,' I said as she read out the details for a flat in Angel, Islington – an area we both liked for its antique shops and good pubs.

'I like you being here too,' she said, peering out over the newspaper. 'But you're twenty-five and I'm sixty-three. And besides, you rather cramp my style. When I bring back a young chap, I don't want him to prefer my great-niece. We're rather in danger of history repeating itself here!'

'I'd never do that to you,' I said. 'I'm not like my mum.'

'I know you're not, darling,' she said with a kind smile. 'But you're every bit as beautiful and irresistible to men as she was.'

There was a vulnerability to Joy's normally strong voice when she said this. I wondered if she was really able to forgive and forget what Ava had done to her. I found it embarrassing, almost as if I was somehow responsible.

'Hardly!' I snorted. 'Anyway, I'm not interested in men any more – they're bad news.'

She raised an eyebrow and peered at me over the top of her spectacles.

'Don't close your mind to the opposite sex just yet,' she said, returning to her newspaper. '"All men are bastards" and all those miserable clichés make for an awfully boring life.'

The following Sunday morning, I woke to my alarm at six a.m. I lifted up a corner of the bedroom curtain and saw a bright blue sky. I smiled. I loved days like this. I'd arranged to meet Sadie from the Home Help Group at Spitalfields Market at seven. As I set off with a suitcase packed full of my aprons, plus business cards I'd got printed up by a friend of Joy's, I didn't know what to expect. I'd spent lazy Sundays sauntering through the market with Imogen before, but I had no idea what it would be like to be there all day, actually selling.

'I have got the worst hangover,' Sadie said, pulling a sick face. 'It's a miracle I'm here at all. I might have to have a nap under the stall later.'

Sadie didn't have a permanent stall, so we had to wait with a huddle of other traders to be allocated a spot by the market manager. It would cost £60 for the day. A man with a big blue-veined nose and slapped cheeks, dressed in jeans and a leather jacket, ran his finger down a clipboard.

'Home Help Company?' he said. Sadie raised her hand and he nodded at her.

'Stall number ten,' he said. 'I'll come round for the money later.'

'Thanks,' she called, and dragging her bags behind her gestured for me to follow.

Watching other traders setting up their stalls of everything from screen-printed trousers to organic beauty products to hand-made jewellery and vintage clothes, I felt a flutter of excitement in my gut. Nobody else was selling aprons. Was there a bad reason for that, or was my idea unique to this market? I'd found various sites online, mostly in the States, of individuals who made retro-style aprons, but on the whole aprons were sold as personality-free utilitarian garments. Mine, I hoped, were fun fashion accessories with an old-fashioned twist. Even if I sold just one today, I'd be happy.

'Do you want a coffee?' Sadie said, dumping her bags on the tabletop. 'Before we dress the stall? We've got a good hour before anyone turns up.'

'Yes please,' I said. 'A mocha would be delicious.'

I watched Sadie walk towards a coffee shop, stopping to talk to other traders on her way. I stood by our stall and started to unpack my aprons and hang them on wire coat hangers I'd threaded with multicoloured beads.

'What are you selling?' asked a Spanish-looking guy setting up a stall opposite. 'What are they?'

He was staring at my aprons, unsmiling. He wore red braces over a striped shirt, in an ironic way, I supposed. He was very tall and quite fat, with lots of dark hair, and made me think of a bear in fancy dress.

'Not your thing, then?' I asked.

'Is it clothes?' he asked, swinging his dark hair out of his face.

'Aprons,' I said, thinking, *obviously*. 'How about you, what are you selling?'

'Jack-in-the-boxes,' he said. 'And other hand-made toys. I make them all myself. It's my passion in life. Toys are my passion. I couldn't do anything else. I never want to grow up and get a proper job, answering to a suit in a Mercedes. That would be my worst nightmare.'

I thought about my career to date: working in an office, answering to a suit in a BMW. Nightmare.

'Great,' I said. 'What's your name?'

'Andre,' he said. 'Pleased to meet you.'

'Juliet,' I said, holding out my hand.

'Oh no,' he said, lunging in to kiss each cheek with his big wet lips. 'Like this.'

At midday I sold my first apron. I was so delighted I half expected a fanfare. The lady, a young, smiley mother, chose one in a strawberry print with a green lace tie and big pockets. Putting it in a paper bag and taking the money made me feel absurdly happy. I'd made that apron! This lady wanted it! My label, I Want to Homemake, was sewn into the apron and repeated on the business card I nervously handed her. By the sixth sale, I was almost hyperventilating with excitement. Then an older woman chose to buy two.

'Do you sell wholesale?' she asked, picking up my card. 'Can I be in touch?'

I didn't know what to say, but Sadie stepped in to rescue me and told the lady that I would be happy to sell wholesale, but which shop would it be for?

'I own a chain of kitchen shops nationwide,' she said.

'We're called Home and we sell products from lots of different contributing craftspeople. I'm just taking a look at the markets to see what's out here and hope to make some orders. This is exactly what I'm looking for – something with a retro edge.'

I stood frozen to the spot.

'The only issue is the price,' she said. 'We'd want to buy them for much, much less than thirty-five pounds.'

'We'd be happy to talk about that,' Sadie said. 'Just give us a call on that number and we'll get our figures straight.'

The lady thanked us and left to talk to another stallholder.

'Did that really just happen?' I said. 'Did she really just say she wants to put my aprons in her shops?'

'No,' Sadie said with a laugh. 'She didn't say that. She said she'd think about it. And listen, that's happened to me before a few times, so don't get your hopes too high. This lady from a line of boutiques based in Dorchester wanted me to crochet a load of animals for her, but it never happened. But let's cross our fingers. And toes.'

At six o'clock, when the market started to close, the Spanish guy, Andre, invited us to join him and some other traders at the Golden Heart pub I knew to be a favourite haunt of Dylan's. Sadie couldn't cope with another drink, and I wasn't sure about Andre, but I decided to give it a go. Sitting in between Andre and his girlfriend Felicity, who didn't seem to speak or have any facial expressions at all, I shocked myself by, completely out of context, telling them about Dylan.

'I wasn't looking for a relationship at all – in fact I've just come out of one – but I somehow feel like I've missed out on Dylan,' I said. 'That he was the one who got away, you know? I hate that feeling – that it was me who messed it all up.'

Felicity said nothing, and Andre was boyishly awkward at first. He squirmed in his seat like a fidgety boy, but then answered.

'Personally I would try to contact him,' he said. 'Otherwise you'll be wondering for the rest of your life, won't you? Where's the harm in finding out?'

I thought for a moment. Since meeting Dylan, I'd thought about him an inordinate amount. I wondered what he thought about when he was falling asleep, whether he liked dark or milk chocolate, what his favourite films and books were. I felt convinced he'd love my *The Wonder Years* DVDs.

'The problem is, I think he's in the States with my ex-friend,' I told Andre. 'Well, actually, I have no evidence of that, I've just put two and two together and got five.'

'Are they *together* together?' he said. 'Or just friends?'

'I don't know,' I said, shaking my head. 'Maybe they're not even out there at the same place, but I'm too scared to ask.'

'Isn't it better to confront these things and deal with them now?' Andre said. 'There's no point procrastinating too much, is there? Oh, I don't know – I'm no good at these grown-up conversations. They make me feel old. I don't ever want to grow up. It's too difficult.'

Felicity looked at Andre and spoke for the first time.

'You have to grow up – you can't be a kid for ever,' she said.

I raised an eyebrow and gave her a look: you think so too? Then she stared hard at me and spoke in a low, serious voice.

'We're a long time dead,' she said, and I nodded sagely. 'That's what you have to remember,' she said more emotionally. 'We're a long time dead.'

Later, I decided to walk home to Joy's house. I loved London on summer evenings, when the setting sun drenched the streets in neon pink and its inhabitants sat outside to drink and smoke and talk. Dragging my suitcase of remaining aprons behind me, I peered into the windows of the houses I passed. I wondered what was going on beyond those front doors. Were people having similar dilemmas to me, pondering their uncertain future? Were they deciding what to do with their lives? How did people really know what to do anyway?

Before I reached Joy's flat, I passed a flat that looked so homely, I wanted to walk in and take up residence there. It had the antique vibe of Violet's home, but on a much smaller scale. I felt a flutter of excitement. Now that I was planning to buy a flat with my inheritance, I could make it equally homely, couldn't I? I just needed to find the right place, a home that I could make my own and that Violet would have approved of too. Climbing up the steps to Joy's flat, I bumped the suitcase up behind me and found myself wishing I could have told Violet about the aprons. I knew she would have been proud that I was following in her footsteps.

When I unlocked the front door, Joy was waiting at the door with a glass of champagne in her hand ('Always time for a glass of fizz!'). She seemed uncharacteristically nervous, moving round the flat within an inch's radius of me.

'How did it go?' she said. 'Did you sell your aprons?'

'I sold six,' I told her. 'And a woman who works for a kitchen shop asked about wholesale. Are you OK? You seem edgy. Why have you got the food processor on?'

'Oh, I'm making some crushed ice for cocktails,' she said. 'Kitchen shop, eh? You're going to need a flock of assistants.'

'I don't think it'll come to that,' I said, walking into the kitchen to confront the food processor. 'Shall I turn it off now? It sounds like it's going to explode.'

'Yes, dear,' she called through. 'If it's ready.'

I opened the food processor and stuck in a spatula.

'It is,' I said, and walked back through to the living room to find Joy. 'It was a good feeling you know, to imagine that I could make money another way, apart from being in an office. So what have you been doing?'

My computer was on. She was wearing her glasses on a string round her neck and one of my aprons over her dress, and there were papers spread over the floor.

'Oh, not much,' she said meekly. 'I think there are airmails for you on here. A little envelope keeps bursting on to the screen and it's terribly irritating. I don't know what was wrong with carrier pigeon.'

'Emails,' I said.

I set down my suitcase and opened up my email. I swallowed when I saw that Hanna had written to me. My heart in my mouth, I opened it, dreading that I would hear she had set up home with Dylan in California.

> So you want to gouge my eyes out? I've been in New
> York for an audition, but I'm back on Wednesday.

> If you need to talk, let me know. There are some things
> I'd like to tell you. I'd prefer it if we could talk face to
> face.

I slapped a hand over my mouth. Bollocks. She'd got my email! I'd never meant to actually send it. Joy was at my shoulder, wringing her hands.

'Are you OK?' she said. 'You look shocked.'

'I accidentally sent an email to Hanna,' I said. 'I accidentally told her I wanted to gouge her eyes out.'

'Oh, don't worry about that,' said Joy lightly. 'That's nothing compared with the one I sent her.'

'What?' I said. 'You've emailed her?'

Joy projected an apology by pulling her lips into an upside-down smile. She spoke quietly, as if to herself.

'I just didn't like that she stole Simon, then Dylan, from under your nose. When your mum stole Stephen from me, I was so pathetic I hardly made a squeak. I got the address from your airmail account and told Hanna exactly what I thought, and she was awfully regretful. I messaged Dylan too.'

She said 'Dylan too' almost inaudibly. My eyes widened. I was appalled.

'You emailed Dylan?' I said. 'How could you do that? You don't know him or anything. That's so embarrassing! What did you say? Has he answered?'

'I told him you'd been bitten by a poisonous asp at London Zoo,' she said quickly. 'I wanted to get a reaction.'

'YOU DID WHAT?' I said. 'Did you hear back?'

She smiled uncertainly.

'No,' she said sadly. 'Not a word.'

I was trembling. It was all I could do not to scream at Joy. How dare she meddle with my life like this, and what the hell would she have said to Dylan? My blood ran cold at the thought. She made an exit into the kitchen and opened the fridge. I heard the sound of ice being poured into glasses. An asp?

'This isn't Anthony and Cleopatra!' I shouted. 'This is my life!'

'Yes,' she said, appearing with two cocktails. 'I know it is. But if it was left up to you, nothing would happen. You like this Dylan, you've talked of little else, yet you've let him drop off the face of the Earth. I wanted to see if he really liked you, so I found his email address and told him about the incident you had. You know, I've not taken this apron off all day.'

I was mortified. I felt sick. I was so angry with Joy I couldn't speak. I didn't even want to see what she'd written. Dylan was history now. If I hadn't nailed the coffin shut, Joy now had. It was all over, finished. Dylan had no interest in me, alive or half bitten to death. I had to forget him and move on.

I sighed heavily, stood up from the computer chair, my mood thunderous. Yet from somewhere deep inside came the desire to laugh my head off. Joy sat in my place at the computer, clicking the mouse, muttering under her breath.

'I spent an hour on the phone to India getting this Internet thing sorted out, and now I wish I hadn't bothered for all the trouble it's caused,' she said. 'To think that when I was young, we had no phone, no television, no car! We had to make do with walking, knitting, sewing and the wireless. Of course wireless has a different connotation these days, as does gay.'

She turned to face me.

'Oh, Juliet, do you absolutely detest me now?' she said. 'I only had your best interests at heart, unlike the men in your life right now. Sod Bob Dylan.'

She stuck out her bottom lip and raised her eyebrows into her hairline, then held out her arms for a hug. I walked into her embrace and rested my cheek on her shoulder.

'It's just Dylan,' I said with a little laugh.

'Precisely,' she said, kissing my hair.

'No, I mean – ' I said. 'Oh, it doesn't matter.'

Chapter Twenty-Five

When arranging coffee mornings, if you're behind with
your chores, push for your friend's house as the venue.
Then you can avoid the dreadful early morning panic,
when you stuff all the mess into a random cupboard and
hope that the door holds up.

Homemaking Hints for a Happier Home, 1959

Hanna had said she'd be in Caffè Nero on Old Compton
Street at twelve-thirty. When I arrived a fashionable ten minutes late, she was halfway through a latte and talking into her
mobile phone. Tanned and slim, wearing a pink skirt with
stars all over it and a white vest, she looked like she'd been
airbrushed. If she weren't human (which I had questioned
before now), she would have made a perfect fairy on top of
the Christmas tree, or one of those enamel brides perched
atop a three-tiered wedding cake. Noticing me, she put down
her phone and raised her hand into a half wave. She smiled,
but it was a watery smile and quickly trickled away.

'Hi. Right, I'll get a coffee,' I said, my voice shaky, putting my bag down on the chair opposite her. 'Do you want another?'

'No thanks,' she said. 'I'll be awake all night if I do. Those jeans look good on you. What make are they? Have you lost weight?'

I never liked this question. There was an implied criticism that you used to be a lardy lump, even if you weren't now.

'No,' I said. 'The opposite, I think. I'll just get the coffee...'

From inside the café, I watched the back of her head. The wind blew her hair up into the air and into her eyes. She pulled it away and turned to look for me. I stared down at my nails until I thought she'd looked away. What did I hope this meeting would achieve? I guess I just wanted to know her side of it all. Did Dylan make a pass at her at the hen party? Had she seen him since? Had they (gulp) slept together? Why was she intent on ruining my life?

I carried my coffee outside and set it down on the table.

'Before you ask,' Hanna said. 'I'll tell you everything. I owe you that much.'

I sat down and perched on the edge of the chair, feeling too nervous to drink my coffee. Shoppers bustled past our table and into the café.

'I only really want to know what happened between you and Dylan,' I said. 'Are you ... ?'

I struggled to make myself say 'together', but the word stuck in my mouth like a lump of bread. Hanna shook her head.

'No!' she said. 'If you let me speak, I'll explain.'

She took a sip of her coffee and pushed her sunglasses up on to the top of her head, narrowing her eyes in the sunlight.

'Simon made me do it,' she said, rolling her eyes. 'Since you two broke up and I refused to get with him, Simon's been full of regret about losing you. He knew that there was something between you and Dylan—'

'There wasn't,' I interrupted. 'Not really. I just really liked him, and when I saw you I—'

'When you saw us you were meant to run back into Simon's arms,' she said. 'You were supposed to realize that I was out of the picture and Dylan wasn't interested so you'd rethink your relationship with Simon. I told him it wouldn't work.'

'That's so manipulative,' I said, screwing my nose up, anger rising in my voice. 'Wasn't it enough that we broke up the way we did? God, I just don't get Simon, or you. Why did you agree to do it?'

Hanna shrugged and adjusted her bra strap.

'I guess I felt guilty for splitting you two up,' she said. 'Simon and I, we should never have slept together – it was a drunken, foolish few minutes. I thought maybe you two still had a future.'

I considered this for a moment. Was Simon an evil manipulative bastard, or was he trying to win me back – and wasn't that rather romantic? A memory of his mum, Anne, scolding me for dumping him, flashed into my mind. I shook my head.

'Simon's a spineless idiot,' I said. 'I'm not interested in him any more. But I am interested in Dylan. What did he do when you did whatever you did—'

'Seduced him?' she said.

I scoffed. 'Seduce' was a bit OTT for a quick snog in a pitch-black pub garden, wasn't it?

She gave a brief smile.

'He said he wasn't interested,' she said in mock surprise. 'He was pretty pissed off, actually, but then I did lunge at him. Before I saw you coming, we were talking about travelling in America. I only lasted in Sweden for a weekend – then I went to the States to see some friends, so I was talking about that. He must have thought I was very weird. He told me he'd only just split up with a girl – Sylvie or something.'

The mention of Sylvie made my heart stand still. There I'd been imagining, albeit irrationally, that Dylan was in California with Hanna, when most probably he was with Sylvie.

'You are weird,' I said. 'Do you say "row" properly yet?'

'Not yet,' she said with a small laugh. 'It's a mental block.'

We sat in silence for a few minutes, me digesting what she'd said, Hanna scanning the streets, probably for her next conquest.

'I'd better be going,' I said, swilling the last of my coffee around the cup and drinking it. I stood up, looped my bag handle over my shoulder and half smiled.

'Thanks,' I said. 'For telling me the truth.'

She lifted both hands up in the air, her palms facing me.

'No hard feelings?' she said.

This was a tricky question. I did harbour lots of cold feelings towards Hanna – ice cold. But though half of me hated her, one quarter felt grateful that she'd given me good news about Dylan, and the other quarter wanted to forgive her so that I wouldn't have a person in my life that I hated. But I couldn't be that big-hearted.

'Maybe it'll all work out for the best?' she said, trying again.

'Hope so,' I said. 'Right then – goodbye, Hanna.'

I was tempted to follow with 'you treacherous bitch', but she waved and smiled a small sad smile before pushing her sunglasses down over her eyes and sipping more of her coffee.

'Sorry, Juliet,' she said as I turned my back and left. 'I am sorry...'

Walking away, mingling into the crowds, I knew I'd never see Hanna again. I thought, that snapshot of her sitting in the café will be my lasting memory of her. Once she was my friend, now she'll be a person I talk about as having changed the course of my life. Funny, that – how other people can change your life so dramatically; how their actions can kick-start a chain of events that help determine your future. I didn't like that feeling – that I wasn't in control of my own life. But maybe I was. Maybe I subconsciously chose Hanna to be my friend because I knew Simon wouldn't be able to resist her, because somewhere in my psyche I wanted to sabotage my relationship with him. Freud, eat your heart out!

Snaking through the maze of Soho's grubby, narrow streets, I jumped as a rat shot across the path in front of me. What was it that Dylan had said? There's a rat or mouse within ten feet of you everywhere you go in London. Grim. I turned right on to Tottenham Court Road and was toying with the idea of shopping, when my phone rang. Nipping into a book-shop doorway, I answered, hoping it would be Rosendale's HR – they'd promised to call me back about the protocol for making a complaint against Philip – but it was the lady from the market. I listened, awestruck, when she asked if I could make a hundred and fifty aprons within six weeks. She made me an offer and I agreed without once thinking to negotiate or ask about contracts, or whether I'd have enough time, fabric or energy to make that many aprons in forty-two days, or asking any of many other questions I should probably have thought of.

'Yes, I'd love to,' I heard myself saying, ever the hard-nosed businesswoman. 'I can do that, no problem.'

I was trembling slightly as I finished the call. I walked to the tube grinning madly, thinking: Oh fuck, what have I agreed to? I wondered if this was how Richard Branson felt when he sold his first student magazine, or Sir Alan Sugar when he boiled and sold his first beetroot at a market stall. Whatever, it was a good feeling. I remembered Imogen's words: aprons are the future.

Chapter Twenty-Six

When buying a new home consider this: Are there suf-
ficient bathrooms and fixtures to handle the morning
rush?

Ladies' Home Journal Art of Homemaking,
Virginia T. Habeeb, 1973

A few days later I viewed a flat in Columbia Road in Hackney
that overlooked the Sunday flower market. The flat, situated
between a bike shop and a grocery store, stood out from
all the others I'd seen for being so incredibly shabby. The
majority of places I'd been shown by the estate agent were
converted, newly renovated flats, painted magnolia, filled
with chrome bathrooms and pine kitchen units. They all
blurred into one characterless showroom, which made me feel
depressed.

But this place, number 32a Columbia Road, was a different
kettle of fish. Lived in for forty years by the previous owner,
recently deceased, it hadn't been touched in about as long.

Spread over the first floor and ground floor, it had some original Victorian features that I loved: sliding sash windows, timber shutters, French windows, and a fanlight in the Brunswick-green front door which was glazed with decorative coloured panes. Original features apart, the estate agent clearly didn't rate it much. In his grey shiny suit, stinking like a perfumery, he hurried me through the rooms, talking about a new development around the corner he thought I'd prefer.

'It's really a project for a developer, isn't it?' he said, poking at the crumbling plaster around the fireplace. 'Can I show you something else more suitable for a single girl about town like yourself?'

Single girl about town? What was I, a street worker?

'How do you know I'm single?' I said. 'Do I emanate singleton vibes or something?'

'Absolutely not,' he said. 'It's that you're buying this place on your own and you just seem it – independent, I mean. But what do I know? Perhaps you have six husbands and ten children.'

I ignored him and knelt down and pulled up the edge of the carpet. Underneath were original mosaic floor tiles in black and white. I walked to the other end of the room and found more of the same. In the bedroom, there were French windows leading out into a very small garden, thoroughly overgrown but magically full of wild flowers: daisies, poppies and cornflowers. I threw open the doors and breathed in their scent.

'Perhaps this was a waste of time,' he said. 'You're not saying much.'

I shook my head and smiled. An enormous butterfly

flapped its wings in my gut. I looked up at the ceiling and, beyond the yellow staining from a lifetime's smoking with the windows closed, saw original light fittings and picture rails in each room. I could imagine myself living in that flat – I felt connected to it, despite the tired carpets and the peeling wallpaper and the tiny mould-speckled bathroom with no shower and the kitchen that dated from the 1960s and smelled greasy. Yes, it needed a lot of work, but the longer I stood there the more I realized I had fallen in love with it, hook, line and sinker. But could I do this? Could I really buy my own place – a run-down old place like this – on my own?

The estate agent sighed and looked at his wristwatch.

'I love it,' I said, as boldly as I dared. 'I'd like to put in an offer.'

There was no chain, no complications to hold me up, and luckily I had an enormous deposit, so four weeks later, after pulling up the carpets and painting the walls with a fantastic range of Farrow & Ball colours, I moved in.

I got a tiny mortgage based on the earnings I expected to make with my apron business and freelance press office work. Adrian – a man with a van that Joy knew – helped me move. He had arms as thick as tree trunks, wore a singlet to show them off, and made sexual innuendoes in his thick Welsh accent from start to finish. He annoyed the hell out of me, but I couldn't move a wardrobe on my own, so I had to be sweetly appreciative. When we were done with heaving (or humping – his word) boxes around, he asked if I wanted to share a bottle of wine and a pot of hummus. He flicked off the plastic lid and dipped his finger into the hummus pot and sucked provocatively. He was disgusting.

'We could fool around a bit,' he said, running his hand down the strap of my dress. He picked up one of my aprons. 'You could wear this?'

I laughed in his face.

'I don't think so,' I said, showing him to the door and slamming it behind him with such force that I feared for the property's foundations.

'*I'd rather die,*' I was tempted to shout through the letter-box, but I had to give the guy a break. He had just spent four hours helping me move. What was it with men and aprons anyway? Maybe if I didn't sell many in the conventional market, I could leave holes where a woman's breasts would be and target fetish stores. Or maybe not.

Left alone in my new, old flat, I felt a sense of wellbeing I'd never felt from a building before. Not in Joy's flat, or Violet's house, or in the flat I'd hoped to share with Simon. In here I could breathe. This was a place for me to make my own that already felt safe and familiar, despite the dodgy wiring and ancient bathroom suite. I was desperate to breathe new life into the property, to wake it up and start afresh. I wanted it to tell stories about my life, for us to get to know each other.

Sorting through the few boxes of possessions I had – it didn't take long to unpack them all – I found Violet's ashes and put them up on the mantelpiece. I found her book, *Homemaking Hints for a Happier Home*, and placed it on the shelf alongside photographs of her, Joy and my dad. I put up a small one of Ava and the faded Polaroid I had of Rosie. I stood back and admired them – the motley crew that were my family.

'What do you think, then?' I asked the pictures. 'Do you like it here?'

I imagined their responses. Dad would wonder where he could set up his easel and paints, Ava would search for a decent mirror in which to gaze, Rosie . . . well, I had no idea what she would say and Violet would scold me for not having matching cushions and curtains. She would thrust her homemaking book into my hands and tell me to study every last word.

'Yes we do!' squeaked a voice from behind me, followed by raucous laughter. I turned on my heels to see Joy and Ava standing in the doorway, clutching carrier bags stuffed full of food and booze.

'We wanted to give you a proper welcome,' Joy said, putting her bags down and kissing my cheek. 'The door wasn't locked, did you know? Any old loon could come in, and I'm not talking about myself.'

Ava put her arms around me tentatively, her eyes sweeping over the pictures of herself and Rosie. I suddenly felt ashamed – even if she'd had her adopted, it must still hurt to see that picture.

'And I wanted to see you before I went back to Kenya,' she said firmly. 'I hope you don't mind me coming here unannounced.'

Since our meeting in Joy's flat, Ava and I had spoken on the telephone, but she'd been travelling around Britain visiting various old friends. I hadn't thought I'd see her again.

'No,' I said, a smile creeping over my lips. 'Not at all. I can show you both round.'

As we walked through the flat, Joy and Ava made all the appropriate exclamations and I felt thoroughly proud of my new home, even if it was in a bit of a state.

'Right then,' said Joy when we came back into the living room. 'I know I always say this, but shall we have a drink? Then we can talk about what else you're planning to do with this place. I would recommend investing in some furniture at some point. Is that terribly old-fashioned of me?'

Ava and I followed Joy into the kitchen, where at least I had a small kitchen table and four chairs. We sat down while Joy poured wine into plastic cups she'd brought. Ava unpacked crisps, nuts and olives and put them on the table, her eyes continually flicking up at me. I could see she was nervous.

'Juliet,' she said, passing me a drink. 'Since I've been back, I've been meaning to tell you something.'

'Oh God, what now?' I said. 'Another love child?'

Ava pushed air through her nostrils and tipped her head back.

'No,' she said. 'I've been meaning to tell you that I admire you. Compared with me when I was your age, you are so much more clued-up about the world. You have a strong head on your shoulders, and, if you'd let me into your life a little more, I'd like us to get to know each other again.'

'Again?' I said, a little too harshly. I softened my voice. 'I don't feel I know you at all. My memories of you are vague and not very nice. I think that if we were to get to know each other, it would have to be as equals, not mother and daughter. I think that relationship is too skewed.'

I'd never been that open or honest with her before. It was a revelation.

'Maybe you're right,' she said. 'Equals sounds good to me. I'd like to make up—'

'For all that lost time?' I said. 'Bit late now.'

Joy looked at me and frowned. Her expression told me to go easy.

'Well, yes,' Ava said. 'I can see you're still angry with me. Perhaps I shouldn't have said anything. I can't expect anything.'

I sighed heavily.

'I'm sorry,' I said quietly. 'I don't want to snap at you. I don't want to be a bitch about all this. Yes, of course I'd like to get to know you. I've spent my whole life wondering what you're really like and whether we're remotely like one another.'

We shared an uneasy smile, while Joy, who was popping olives into her mouth ten to the dozen and spitting out the stones into her palm, suddenly stood up and moved over to the sink. Looking out of the window, she kept her back to us as she spoke.

'There's something I've been meaning to say too,' she said. 'And I need to say it before you go back to Kenya. I know you both think I'm some mad geriatric with skin as thick as an old boot, and to some degree that's true.'

'No one thinks that,' I protested. 'You're the opposite of geriatric, Joy—'

She lifted a hand to silence me.

'And I admit,' she said, 'that I do like my alcohol. But that's just the way I am and I don't ever intend to change. Anyway, my point. I've always liked to look on the Monty Python "bright side of life", but occasionally it's difficult. God, I've had to get over a mountain of shit in my life, but if we're all exorcizing our demons here, there's one thing I want to tell you, and that's how much I regret not having had a child. Juliet, you, of course, are a wonderful great-niece, and I love you dearly, but I did so want to have a child with Stephen. So, anyway, here's what I've done . . .'

She took a deep breath and turned to face us.

'I've contacted Rosie,' she said. 'She had her name on the register which lets adopted people search for their blood relations and vice versa. I've written to her, spoken to her, and she intends to come over to London in a few months' time.'

Joy screwed her eyes up and lifted her shoulders as if waiting to have something thrown at her. I looked at Ava, who sat there motionless, tears in her eyes, her mouth slightly open.

'This must be very shocking,' Joy said. 'And yes, I should have checked with you first, Ava, but, quite frankly, I couldn't face you. I did this for me. Rosie is the daughter of Stephen, who was the love of my life. She's also my great-niece. I wanted her to know she is loved. Isn't that what life is all about? Loving, in whatever ways you can.'

'Wow,' I said, eyeing Ava, who was staying silent. 'What's she like?'

'You,' Joy said without missing a beat. 'She's a lot like you in looks and manner. I think you'll get on famously.'

'You've seen a photograph?' Ava said, her voice croaky.

Joy moved over to Ava's chair and put her hand on her shoulder. Ava's body tensed.

'She's beautiful,' Joy said. 'Just as you were and are. Ava, are you outraged? Are you about to explode? I never can tell with you.'

Ava pulled a tissue out of her pocket and wiped her eyes.

'No,' she said. 'I'm ... I just don't know what to say. This is your thing, so I need to see it like that. I don't have to be involved and get in the way, do I?'

'The thing is,' Joy said. 'I've, well, I've ...'

'Don't tell me she's about to walk in,' I said, checking the door with my eyes.

'No!' Joy exclaimed. 'I'm not that much of a drama queen. But Ava, she did ask me to give you her email address. She so desperately wants to know who you are.'

Ava sipped her drink and nodded. I noticed her hand was shaking.

'And Juliet,' Joy said. 'You can think about whether you'd like to meet her or not.'

The kitchen fell silent as Joy's news sank in. Ava's face was pale and I could see she just didn't know how to react. I reached my hand across the table and squeezed her hand.

'We could all get to know each other,' I said quietly. 'That wouldn't be too terrifying, would it? No pressure or commitment or anything. We could just find out what we're all like and see what happens. There's no need to be scared.'

Ava opened her mouth and started to say she wasn't scared. Then she stopped mid-sentence.

'That's what it is, Juliet,' she said, squeezing my hand in return. 'I'm scared of what I've done – to you, to Joy, to Rosie, to your dad. I'm so scared that I've never stopped running. Maybe I should slow down a little, let the past catch up with me.'

Then, turning to Joy, she said, 'You will never cease to amaze me, Joy. Violet would be turning in her grave.'

Joy let out a burst of laughter.

'Violet would be dusting these skirting boards, ready for a fresh coat of paint,' she said, grabbing a packet of dusters from her carrier bag and handing them out to Ava and me. 'I've heard housework is cathartic. So – shall we?'

And we did. We dusted and then painted together, three women up to our elbows together. As we worked, sometimes talking, sometimes in silence, I felt warmth envelop me. I realized I felt closer to having a family than at any other time in my entire life.

Chapter Twenty-Seven

To impress guests, there's nothing more fashionable,
yet tasteful, than the Margarita. Just remember to go
easy on the measures; there's nothing fashionable about
a drunken hostess.

Homemaking Hints for a
Happier Home, 1959

Two days later, after Joy and I had seen Ava off at Heathrow
airport, Imogen and the girls from the Home Help Group
came over. I had made sixty of the hundred and fifty aprons
for my August deadline. They offered to help with apron
pattern-cutting, and I offered to prepare snacks and Margaritas from a recipe I found in Violet's book, torn out from
Woman magazine, December 1954. It was their 'Drink of
the Month', and I made myself smile imagining exhausted
housewives frantically mixing them for their hardworking
husbands before secretly knocking back several themselves.
This was the recipe:

1 shot of tequila (I doubled it, considering the modern girl's
   constitution)
a dash of Triple Sec
juice of half a lime or lemon
salt for the rim

Pour over crushed ice and stir. Rub the rim of a stem glass
   with the lemon or lime rind, spin in salt – pour and sip.

For Imogen, I made alcohol-free Margaritas with lemonade.
I bought cheeses, olives and bread from the deli at the end of
the road. I chopped fruit and broke up a load of dark and
white chocolate to serve in large bowls for dessert. By the time
the girls were due to arrive, I'd drunk a cocktail and I wished
I hadn't. I should have stuck to water. The alcohol made me
feel melancholy and I'd started to think about Dylan. Whatever I did, wherever I went, I ended up thinking about him.
It was as if he was in my blood.

Later, we all sat round the living room stitching name labels
on to the aprons I'd already made up. Imogen was typing
advice on to the cardboard tags, occasionally swearing at the
typewriter or stamping her feet when she typed inaccurately.

'I've got baby brain,' she said in her defence, with a smile.
Any mention of the baby was met with 'oohing' and 'aahing'
from the girls. We couldn't get enough of wondering whether
it would be a boy or a girl, how it would come out, whether
Imogen had cravings, what she was going to do for the rest of
her life.

'Are you looking forward to being a mother?' I said.

It was the first time I'd asked her that question. Previously we'd talked about the pregnancy in terms of Jonathan and Cath, or where she would live and what she would do for money. My question made me think of my own mum and whether she'd hated being pregnant as much as she hated being a mother. I imagined her glugging down a bottle of gin and floating in boiling water like a lobster.

'What I'm looking forward to most is letting myself go,' Imogen joked, looking immaculate as always. 'When the baby's born, I can forget about thinking about myself and concentrate a hundred per cent on this child. I won't have to worry about careers, or my hair, or my clothes. All I'll want to do is talk about baby poo and organic nappies. What a relief that will be.'

I looked at the clock. It was ten o'clock. The food was gone and we were working our way through the jug of Margaritas. Everyone, except for Imogen, was pretty pissed. I felt happy, but the talk of motherhood had made me strangely restless. Always – there was always this feeling I had, a kind of restless energy I couldn't put my finger on.

'What about you, Juliet?' Miriam asked. 'Do you want babies one day?'

I made a 'hmmm' noise as I thought about my answer for a minute.

'Yes,' I said. 'Definitely. But – and this is old-fashioned of me – I don't want to have them unless I'm really in love with the guy. I come from a broken home, and though I didn't have a bad time, I'd like to at least try to get it right.'

'So have you met him yet?' Miriam said. 'This perfect man?'

Dylan popped into my head and I blushed at the thought of him.

'You've gone red!' Sadie said. 'Come on, who is it? Have we met him?'

'Juliet?' Imogen said. 'Are you thinking about Dylan? The one that got away?'

They were all staring at me. I suddenly felt stupid for even mentioning Dylan. He wasn't remotely interested in me – his total lack of communication proved that.

'Tell us the story,' Sadie said. 'Come on, we're dying to know.'

I set my glass down on the rug and tucked my legs under my bottom. The alcohol and the heat had made my face hot. I peeled off my jumper and cleared my throat.

'OK,' I said. 'When I used to work at Rosendale's, I met this TV bloke. His name is Dylan and he has freckles, like me. There was something I liked about him straightaway. He's charming, cheeky, but funny. He seems like he's free, buoyant – you know? We went to Cornwall together to do some filming. I had to check that everything he filmed was in line with Rosendale's protocol, that kind of thing.'

'Yes,' Sadie said. 'Get to the good bits, then.'

'It was strange,' I said. 'Nothing physical happened between us, but I felt this inexplicable connection to him. We'd had similar life experiences, so maybe that bonded us, but it was more than that. When I was with him – and I'm in danger of sounding super-corny here – I felt complete. I wasn't looking for anything, or feeling empty or restless like I normally do – I just felt OK, like I could be me. I found myself blurting things out to him that I've literally told nobody.'

I saw Imogen glance up at me, looking slightly hurt.

'So what happened then?' Miriam said.

I stood up and dusted down the back of my skirt. I picked a thread off my black top.

'Oh,' I said. 'He disappeared off to California, probably with his ex-girlfriend, weeks ago now, and I've not heard from him again.'

'Unrequited love, then?' Sadie said. 'That's so sad. Where does he live in London?'

'Tower Hamlets,' I said, suddenly feeling like I wanted to burst into tears.

'It was more complicated than that though, wasn't it?' Imogen said. 'Dylan was supposed to ring Juliet, but he didn't. However, he did send her a tray of cupcakes before he went away, but when Juliet's aunt emailed him, he didn't respond. If you ask me, he's messing with her head. You don't know where you stand, do you, when someone blows hot and cold like that?'

Sadie poured us all another drink and handed the biggest glass to me.

'I believe that if you want something to happen enough, you can make it happen,' she said. 'Presumably he's going to come back soon. So when he does, as long as he's not back with his ex, just go for it. Invite him over here to this lovely flat, cook him dinner, court him. Everyone loves a bit of romance, don't they? Win him, but do it the old-fashioned way.'

After everyone had left, Imogen devised an email for me to send to Dylan, inviting him over for dinner when he returned from California. It went to his work address, so I had no idea if he would pick it up. My finger hovered over the Send button before Imogen sighed and hit it for me.

'You've nothing to lose,' she said, beaming at me. 'And a lover to gain.'

Chapter Twenty-Eight

If you have plenty of money and buy all your furniture
new from a shop, your home will lack personality and
you will miss out on fun! Collecting pieces of bric-a-
brac, restoring, painting, converting them to suit your
own needs and tastes; these are what homemaking is all
about.

Sure & Simple Homemaking,
Jill Blake, 1975

I was in a long queue at the checkout in Heal's in Tottenham
Court Road, holding a toast rack and a bread board, when
I realized that there are some voids in life you just can't fill.

No matter how many shiny new possessions you buy or
men you sleep with or tequilas you down, sometimes you just
feel empty and hollow inside. It didn't take a genius to realize
that my empty feeling stemmed from when Dad died and my
mum moved away. There was too much abandonment for
me to cope with, too much implicit rejection too early on in

life. And the deep, painful grief I'd felt from the moment I'd watched my dad walk into the sea was as strong as ever.

I had been so young when he died and Ava left that I hadn't understood the complexities of his death. I'd always blamed myself, but I knew now that it was possible that Dad, the man I had loved most in the world, had committed suicide for reasons that had nothing to do with me. The implied rejection in his death was paramount, but I was able to empathize with his suffering. My mum was different. Though I understood that she hadn't been up to motherhood when I was born, I fervently believed that a parent–child bond would, or should, be stronger than any other desire, even if it felt like a duty. Wouldn't you instinctively, selflessly, want to protect, shelter and keep your child safe? And not only did she abandon me, but she gave Rosie away too.

And standing there, in the queue at Heal's, I saw my life as if waking up from sleep. I had been chasing that missing feeling of safety when I moved in with Simon, despite knowing deep down that our relationship was flawed. I had been chasing that missing feeling of protection when I had had a one-night stand with Philip, the older man. And look where that had got me.

Now was the time to break free. I'd fucked up enough. Yes, our history helps to construct us, but it doesn't have to absolutely define us. With tears prickling my eyes, I put down my toast rack and bread board. I left the shop empty-handed and walked all the way home, vowing never to make the same mistakes again.

When Joy came over to my flat later that day, she gave me a housewarming present – a reclaimed chest that had been painted black and decorated with tiny pink and red flowers.

'I love it!' I said. 'Where did you find it?'

Joy shrugged.

'One of those antique stalls I love in Camden Passage,' she said. 'I couldn't resist it. You can keep all your most treasured possessions in there. Everyone needs a treasure chest, don't they?'

We went outside and sat in the garden on deckchairs and I told her all about my episode in Heal's.

'You had an epiphany,' Joy stated. 'You realized that a toast rack isn't going to make you happy.'

'Maybe,' I said with a quick smile. 'But seriously, I don't think I've dealt with all that stuff about Mum and Dad. I've just closed my eyes and ears to it and concentrated on forging ahead, building up walls around myself, distancing myself from it all. But now that you've found Rosie, and Ava wants to make an effort with me, I'm having to think about it properly.'

'You're probably right, darling,' Joy said. 'But that's OK – denial's not so bad, as long as you're vaguely aware of what you're doing, which you are. Don't analyse so much. I just think you're determined to be happy, which is a marvellous thing. You're like Violet – determined not to be beaten down by all the shit.'

I smiled at Joy and pinched a sprig of lavender from an enormous bush that spread over half the garden. Rubbing the needles between my fingers, I breathed in the smell.

'I've thought about Rosie, too,' I said. 'I would like to be in contact with her. Will you help me? I'm not going to think about the past or the future where she's concerned – there's no point. I'm going to live in the now and see what she's like.'

Joy pushed her glasses up on to her head and let her hands drop down on to her skirt.

'That's very Buddhist of you,' she said. 'If I had to be any denomination at all, I'd be a Buddhist. I could probably be Buddha's body-double these days. Look at my stomach! Yes, darling, of course I'll put you in touch with her, and we can all meet if she comes over – anything you want.'

I looked at Joy and thought about her life. I suspected she thought Ava was a shambles, but she had never bad-mouthed her. Instead, she had tried to fill in and patch up those voids in our family's lives, made by other people's mistakes, by being the mother Violet had tried her best to be too. She had done it in a humorous, unsympathetic way which could be translated as coldness, but most definitely wasn't. Out there, in the stamp-sized, uncut, wild garden, I felt overwhelmed with love for her.

'Thank you, Joy,' I said, welling up. 'Thank you for everything you've ever done.'

'Good grief, what's all this about?' she said. 'I feel like I'm on *This Is Your Life*. Remember that show? How I dreamed of being on that, though I dread to think whom the producers would dredge up for me. Half my friends are dead and most of my lovers are half my age. Eamonn Andrews would be very disappointed in me.'

She had changed the subject, but I could tell she understood exactly how I felt. She was simply doing her thing: carrying on carrying on.

I decided I should do the same.

Chapter Twenty-Nine

Whatever queer things you choose to have around you are nobody's business but your own, and let nobody tell you different.

The I Hate to Housekeep Book,
Peg Bracken, 1962

By the end of the month my business was up and running.

I had paid £500 to an Internet whizz-kid to create me a website, www.iwanttohomemake.com, from where I could sell my aprons. Customers could choose the fabric and style they preferred by clicking on swatches of fabric and diagrams of aprons we'd scanned in. It had been up and running for three weeks, and thanks to a journalist contact mentioning the site in the *Evening Standard* shopping pages, I was starting to see a steady flow of orders. Once I'd made the apron up, which now took an hour in total, I wrapped it in tissue paper and posted it off, complete with my business card and a complimentary bag of jelly beans. I was checking my new orders, sitting with my laptop at my kitchen table, when an email from Dylan popped into my inbox. I nearly died with shock.

> I'm back from the States to an email from you. Yes,
> I'd love to come to dinner. I'm working a lot, but if
> you can do Saturday evening, I'll come over at 8pm.
> What's your new address?
> Dylan

I grinned stupidly, reading the message over again. Since Imogen had sent that email on my behalf, I'd convinced myself he was never going to reply. Now he had, and not only was he coming to dinner, he said he'd 'love' to come to dinner.

I picked up my wine glass and drank, smiling, fighting the urge to jump up and down with excitement. I tried to imagine him here, sitting at the kitchen table with me, looking up at the many photographs I'd framed and hung of friends at various stages of eating. Every one of them made me laugh. But hang on – what if he'd been in California with Sylvie? Hadn't Hanna said something about him mentioning Sylvie at the hen party? Surely he wouldn't accept a dinner invitation if he was still with her, though, would he? That would be tantamount to infidelity in her book.

I pushed back my chair and opened the fridge. I pulled out the only thing left in there – a tub of olives and feta cheese floating in olive oil – then carried them through to the living room with my wine glass in my other hand. Questions raced round my mind. What would I cook for Dylan? What would I wear? What would we say to each other?

I ran my eyes over the room feeling worried. Because I'd been so busy making aprons, I hadn't spent much time redecorating. I'd done the basics – put on a fresh coat of paint, removed stinking old carpets to reveal gorgeous tiles downstairs and wooden floorboards upstairs – but I didn't want to rush. I wanted to hold out for things I really liked, to make the place feel really like my home. So far, I'd bought an old garden bench with iron legs, from a car boot sale, that I planned to make cushions for and have in the sitting room, alongside three mismatched bucket chairs an antique dealer in Brick Lane was selling off cheap. I'd found a wooden hatstand that I loved in a junk shop, but that was currently swamped by fabric. Oh, and lamps – I'd fallen in love with lamps and now had more lamps – the louder the lampshade the better – than anything else. I'd cheered the kitchen up with a dresser that I'd cluttered with chintzy cups and saucers, and in the bathroom I'd gone for a seaside theme. I'd spent one entire evening, while quietly crying through ER, sticking shells on to jars to make them into toothbrush holders, and I'd dug out several old hardback adventure storybooks, which I'd lined up along a shelf above the bath. It was like being ten years old again, but this time I was enjoying myself.

Slowly, my flat was coming together, but there was still a long way to go. I knew Dylan wouldn't care or even notice. But I wanted to give him the right impression of me. I wanted him to see what I was really about, that I was someone he might actually want to get to know better – not the tearful, morose girl he'd met at Rosendale's and caught out in her M&S underwear.

I remembered something Sadie had said when she came over: 'When you see him again, invite him over, but do it the old-fashioned way.' But what was the old-fashioned way? Tying a ribbon in your hair to brighten up your man's day? I didn't want to look like Minnie Mouse, though bows were very 'now' in Topshop! I picked up Violet's book from the shelf, where it sat underneath the photographs of my peculiar family. I lay down on the sofa, tucked a cushion under my head and flicked through it, hoping for some insightful advice from yesteryear. I ran my finger down the list of chapters until I found the pages dedicated to entertaining. I read:

> Tablecloth or place mats? If you use place mats, stick to
> the oval and rectangular shapes. Anything more fancy
> can make a table look too busy.

What were fancy shapes, then? I shook my head in wonder.

> If your guests are coming in the summer, don't put
> them off by having ants march through your kitchen.
> Use lemon juice on surfaces and they won't come near.

But what about wasps and flies? Didn't they like lemons? Then I found the list of Top Tips:

> Plan the menu days ahead. (*I could do that.*)
> Choose a menu that doesn't involve last-minute
> cooking. (*Takeaway?*)
>
> Clean the entire house a day ahead so you don't have
> to wear yourself out on the day of the party. (*A little
> too strenuous*)

Have cocktails waiting for your guests, so you don't spill anything on your outfit when they first arrive and you're nervous. (*Or go to a pub?*)

Give your bathroom a quick clean just before the party in case a child or errant husband has used your toilet and not flushed. (*Child? Husband?*)

There were pages and pages of advice, some of it genuinely useful, much of it laugh-out-loud funny. I turned the pages until I reached the final blank page in the book, on which Violet had written a list entitled 'odds and mends' in black pen. I read her words.

When entertaining, have candles on the table. To stop unsightly dripping, put the candles in the freezer first.

When you start to look old in the bathroom mirror, change the lighting.

Use the bath to pickle walnuts in large quantities.

When inviting guests, leave out orange and lemon peel to freshen the air.

Sellotape is a great lint remover, especially for cat or dog hair.

*If you want to impress a dinner guest
(this is how I won Aaron, God bless his
soul), serve a soufflé (sweet or savoury),
there's nothing better or more mouthwater-
ing. I miss him so much.*

My eyes misted over. I closed the book. Poor Violet. She'd been so young when her husband had died, yet she remained unswervingly loyal to him for evermore. I remembered her telling me that she'd been so nervous on their first date at a local dinner dance, she'd had to spit out her mushroom vol-au-vent into a napkin under the table. She'd been left alone to bring up Ava, then Charles had died and Ava had disappeared to Sydney and Violet had had to become a mother to me. Jesus, my family! I didn't exactly come from a long line of happy and successful romances. But maybe I could prevent history repeating itself? Perhaps now I was out of Philip's and Simon's clutches, I could have a go at finding what Violet and Aaron and Ava and Charles had once set out to have – happiness. Was it such an impossible goal?

I walked back into the kitchen and poured myself another glass of wine – I know you're not supposed to drink alone, but it felt pretty great to me. I looked in the cupboard and picked out a half packet of chocolate chip cookies, those lovely chewy ones as big as your head. Slotting them under my arm, I walked out through the patio doors into the garden. It was late in the day, but Columbia Road was very much awake. I had hoped for a bit of peace but the upstairs neighbours, Andrew and Simone, were having yet another screaming match at their window. I rolled my eyes and sighed. This was the one downside to my new place – the acoustics were such that I could hear everything they said, as if I had earphones plugged into their apartment. I tried not to listen in, but anyone within a mile radius couldn't help but hear. I gleaned that Andrew suspected Simone of having an affair, but she was emphatically denying everything, howling at the top of her lungs that she loved him.

I sipped my wine, watched butterflies land on the buddleia bush and listened to the neighbours trying to kill each other. From the comings and goings at their flat, I suspected Andrew might be right about the affair, but who was I to make such assumptions? Maybe Simone ran a male modelling agency.

I bit into a cookie and wondered if I should make soufflé for Dylan – cheese or chocolate or both? After a short silence, I heard another sound coming from the neighbours' window that seemed to prove they'd made up. They were embarrassingly loud lovers. I stood up to go back indoors and find my earplugs when Simone shouted out: 'Oh Jim, Jim!' I froze to the spot. There was a sudden silence, then Andrew screamed at her, 'What the fuck did you just call me?'

Oh dear. I dashed inside, slammed shut the French windows and clicked on the kitchen light. I stood still in the kitchen for a moment, trembling a little. I wondered who Jim was. I scrunched up my face, remembering Simon's slip of the tongue all those months ago. Was this a sign? There I was, daring to think about new beginnings, but endings were always there round the next corner, ready to slap you in the face, really hard. I took another bite of cookie and had a thought: when one love ends, does another always begin? Here's hoping.

Chapter Thirty

Take fifteen minutes to rest so that you'll be refreshed when your husband arrives. Touch up your makeup, put a ribbon in your hair and be fresh-looking. Be a little gay and a little more interesting. His boring day may need a lift.

Housekeeping Monthly, May 1955

The doorbell buzzed and my heart leapt. I checked the clock – Dylan was ten minutes early.

I was so nervous my hands were shaking and I felt hot all over. Quickly, I put cornflowers in an old-fashioned glass medicine bottle and lit two large red candles with a cigarette lighter, narrowly missing a stray curl. I set them down either side of the fireplace, turned off the main light in the living room and clicked on my standard lamp, which threw out a satisfying amber glow. I stood in the doorway and imagined Dylan seeing the place for the first time. Were the candles too much? Did they scream massage parlour? Oh God. The door-bell buzzed again, this time for a lengthy few seconds.

'Coming!' I called. 'Just be one minute.'

My heels clattered on the stone tiles as I ran to the front door, checking my make-up in the mirror on the way: cherry-red lipstick, pink cheeks, light touch of mascara. The thought that Dylan was, what? – four inches away – made my bones fidget. I had just put my hand on the door when the doorbell buzzed again in four angry bursts.

'OK!' I said, frowning. 'I'm here.'

Be calm, I told myself as I straightened my back and opened the door. And there, in his acrylic best and whiter-than-white trainers as big as yachts, stood Simon.

'What took you so long?' he said. 'I thought you were deliberately ignoring me!'

My eyes were as wide as dinner plates.

'Simon?' I said in a whispery voice. 'What—'

'Hello,' said Simon, pulling a sorrowful bunch of roses from his rucksack. 'I jogged here, so they got a bit crushed,' he said, thrusting the flowers into my hand before striding into the hallway, his eyes scanning the poster-size street map of London I'd framed and hung from the picture rail and resting on a collection of old brass skeleton keys I'd tacked to the wall.

He walked through the flat, popping his head into each room as if he owned it. He kicked off his trainers and peeled off his jumper to reveal a black T-shirt bearing the neon-pink slogan 'Recyclers do it twice'. I raised my eyebrows – Simon was still in the running for The Most Insensitive Man Ever award.

'Smells good,' he said. 'What's cooking? Love the floor, Jules.'

Simon didn't seem to register that I was standing there motionless and speechless. I cleared my throat.

'Simon,' I said. 'What are you doing here? I'm expecting a friend to arrive any minute.'

He looked nonplussed by my question.

'I texted you earlier,' he said. 'I assumed you wouldn't mind me coming over. We were together for, what, four and a half years?'

I rolled my eyes, crossed my arms over my chest and followed him into the living room, where he picked up a sewing book from the bookshelf. He inspected it as if it were an alien.

'Yes, I did notice that,' I said sarcastically. 'But we've hardly spoken in months, have we? Anyway, I didn't see your text and, as I said, I'm expecting someone. Could we make this quick, whatever this is?'

We were standing in the bay window in the living room, overlooking the street. My eyes swept up and along the pavement, searching for Dylan.

'I'm cooking,' I said to remind myself. 'I must remember to take the soufflés out. So, Simon, what is it you wanted?'

Simon gave me a waspish smile. He took off his glasses, moved closer to me and looked at me intently.

'Oh, Juliet,' he said. 'I've missed you.'

He held out his arms and lunged forward to cuddle me. I was so completely surprised that I didn't have time to step away before he pulled me close to his chest, and because he was so familiar, for one confused nanosecond I rested my head on his shoulder. At that moment, I saw Dylan standing outside in the street looking up at the window. I jerked my head up as he saw me see him. He stood still for a moment, a confused expression on his face, then turned and walked quickly away.

'Fuck!' I said, shoving Simon away. 'Get off me, you idiot.'

Violently swinging open the front door, I ran out into the street.

'Dylan!' I called after him. 'Dylan, come back!'

I watched with relief as Dylan stopped and turned back to face me. I half ran, half walked towards him, unable to keep a smile from my lips. He was smiling too. But just as I approached him, blinking at his lovely face, Simon appeared at my shoulder like a parrot.

'Dylan, what are you doing here?' Simon said crossly. 'Could you give Juliet and me a little time to talk? We've got a lot to resolve, if you catch my drift.'

I spun on my heels to face Simon.

'What are you talking about?' I said. 'I invited Dylan over here for dinner. You're the one who turned up uninvited. Why don't you go?'

'Come on,' Simon said. 'Hear me out. I wanted to talk to you in private, but if you want me to tell the world that I'm still in love with you, that I made a mistake, then I will. I just don't think this chump will be too pleased, and did you know you had paint in your hair, Dylan? At the back there, behind your ear.'

I stood open-mouthed at Simon's declaration. Dylan said nothing, just stared at Simon with a slightly amused expression.

'I don't feel the same, Simon,' I said quickly. I noticed my neighbours gawping at us. 'Sorry. Could you just go?' I said to

Simon, trying to smile at Dylan apologetically, but my eyes were filling with tears.

Simon adopted his stern teacher face. I instantly wanted to roar with laughter – I don't know how his pupils took him seriously.

'Now listen here,' he said. 'I've been working up to this for weeks. I've been through hell wondering what I should say to you, so do you realize what this means to me?'

'Um – ' I said, shaking my head in shock.

'I'm actually asking for you to come back to me,' he said, as if bestowing the greatest honour upon me. 'We can re-rent our flat, if you like? I liked that place.'

It was too bizarre. I opened my mouth to tell Simon he was delusional when Dylan spoke.

'Juliet's just bought a flat,' Dylan said – his first words.

'Yes, I know that, you jerk,' Simon said. 'But we used to rent this great place. Newly renovated, nice and clean. We bought a load of furniture for the place, didn't we, Juliet? What did you do with all that stuff?'

I thought about the table and chairs Simon had ordered from IKEA, entirely devoid of personality.

'In the skip,' I said. 'Look, this is too bizarre, let's go inside. Simon, you'll have to go.'

'I'm not going anywhere,' Simon said, squaring up to Dylan. 'He can go.'

I was mortified. What was he doing?

'See you then, mate,' Simon said, pushing his forehead so close to Dylan's he was almost kissing him. I watched Dylan's face pale as his patience ran out. He pushed Simon in the chest and Simon, outraged, pushed him back. Dylan swung his fist and punched Simon in the jaw. Simon roared in shock, then retaliated by punching Dylan in the nose. People walking past on the other side of the road stopped to stare, their hands up to their mouths in horror.

'Hey, he's bleeding!' I shouted, watching blood spurt from Dylan's nose. 'Stop it! For God's sake, this is ridiculous!'

Windows snapped open and heads popped out of doors as Dylan and Simon continued to scuffle and shove each other. This was better than *EastEnders*! This was real life!

'Oh my God!' I said as a strong smell of burning drifted from my open front door out into the street. 'My soufflés!'

I turned towards my flat and saw smoke billowing from the kitchen window. The curtain I'd so lovingly put up was in flames.

'My flat!' I shouted, running towards it, vaguely aware of a siren close by. Coughing, I covered my mouth with my hands and made my way through smoke towards the kitchen.

'Outside, now!' a firefighter said, appearing by my side.

'It's only my soufflé,' I mumbled, sloping off back into the street, where Dylan and Simon stood looking like two naughty schoolboys. Dylan's nose was bleeding and his shirt was torn, while Simon's cheek was glowing bright red and the neck of his T-shirt was stretched wide. We watched as the fireman used an extinguisher to douse the burning curtain.

'Don't you have smoke alarms?' Simon asked me. 'That's basic health and safety.'

'Shut up, Simon,' I said, cursing myself for not checking the existing smoke alarms. 'Just shut up.'

Minutes later the fireman came back out, holding my blackened, smoking soufflé dish.

'I think it's cooked now, love,' he smirked, before giving me a lecture about smoke alarms. Apparently Simone had called them after smelling smoke, but if she hadn't been in, the whole flat might have gone up in flames.

'I'm sorry,' I said sadly to everyone. The fireman was doing a good job at making me feel like a fool. Tonight was really not going to plan at all. Now I had to get rid of Simon, unless Dylan had seen enough already and decided to return to California.

I led them back inside to get away from the nosy neighbours, then turned to face Simon.

'Look, ' I said. 'I'm sorry, but I really do want you to go. I—'

I didn't finish my sentence before he picked up his jumper and rucksack.

'I'm going now,' Simon said. 'But only because I think you've changed, Juliet. You're not who I thought you were.'

I had to stop myself from picking up a frying pan and whacking him over the head with it. He's only being Simon, I told myself. He loves to have the last word.

After Simon had made his exit, Dylan and I stood together in the kitchen, appraising the fire damage – a burned curtain and a black wall. The worst thing was the smell – once up your nostrils it wouldn't go. I had too much to say to speak, so I busied myself with pouring us each a glass of Chablis. My eyes pulled towards his like iron filings to a magnet. When they did meet, his were curious and shiny, mine flighty. Tiny fireworks went off in my heart, making me incredibly nervous. The smoke had mostly dispersed now, leaving nothing but my burned-out soufflé dish to show for dinner. I gulped down my wine in one, unladylike swig.

'Shall we got out for Chinese?' Dylan asked. 'Sound good? What shall we have?'

'I love crispy duck pancakes,' we said in unison.

'Snap,' I said foolishly, but Dylan grinned.

He smoothed the menu out on the tabletop with his hands, running a finger down the list of dishes.

'So,' I said. 'How was California? How were the waves?'

'Good,' he said. 'Lots of white teeth, though. Enough to give you nightmares, all those American teeth.' He gnashed his teeth together jokily.

'How's your nose?' I asked, watching it morph into a bulbous purple lump. He lifted his hand to it and winced.

'Painful,' he said, sitting down on a creaky chair. 'Do you have any ice?'

Rattling my hands around in the tiny freezer compartment of my fridge, shoving packets of emergency fish fingers and a half-empty tub of chocolate ice cream out of the way, I located an ice-cube tray. I popped the ice out into a tea-towel and, while he sat on the chair, held the bundle up to his nose, with one hand gently supporting the back of his head. He sat as still as the stocks, his ear almost touching the buttons on my blouse, while I stood as close as I dared. I felt sure blue bolts of electricity were shooting out of my body and into his. I started to tremble – what was wrong with me?

'There's something I ought to tell you,' Dylan mumbled from under the tea-towel, 'before we go any further.'

'Further?' I said innocently. But my stomach dipped. What hideous secret did he have to reveal?

'Yes,' he said. 'You know what I mean. Don't try to deny it.'

'What do you need to tell me, then?' I said, moving the ice

away. 'I know – you're marrying Sylvie, or, worse, you're madly in love with Hanna.'

I sat down on the chair next to him and poured myself another glass of wine. He shook his head slowly.

'Neither,' he said. 'Sylvie's history and Hanna's terrifying. It's something else. You see, you've bought this great flat, you're obviously doing well for yourself, but I – ' he sighed – 'I haven't got two pennies to rub together. My place in Tower Hamlets is grim. If we . . . if anything happens between us, would that drive you crazy? I'm not saying I couldn't buy dinner or anything that drastic, but for the next few years, I'm going to be pretty bloody skint.' He sighed again.

I frowned and shook my head. I didn't care about how much money he had, but I didn't understand why Dylan was so broke. He worked so hard in TV and had a responsible position – where did his salary go? Dylan read my mind.

'It's my kid brother, Joe,' he said. 'He got himself into a load of debt a few years back, taking on too many credit cards and taking out unsecured loans on his flat in Tower Hamlets, the one I'm in now. Last year he had a breakdown, just couldn't cope any more with the constant phone calls from debt collectors and visits from bailiffs. He went to pieces, so he moved up to Edinburgh to live with our mum. I promised I'd help him pay off his forty-thousand-pound debts, and that's why I work two jobs, trying—'

'That much?' I gasped. 'How on earth was he allowed to borrow it all?'

'You know what it was like before the recession,' Dylan said. 'Those credit card companies literally shoved credit down your throat, irresponsible cowboys.'

'And you have two jobs?' I asked. 'Is that why you kept dashing off?'

'Yes,' he said. 'I do live editing stuff at evenings and weekends whenever I can to earn the extra cash, but even two jobs hardly pay off the interest on the loans. What I really need to do is sell his flat in Tower Hamlets, but no one will touch it because of all the financial problems associated with it. It's all a bit of a mess. That's how I got this.'

He pointed to the streak of white in his hair and smiled apologetically at me.

'Wow,' I said. 'Do you really think it's your responsibility to take on his debt? Can't he do anything to help, or is he in too much of a state?'

Dylan shook his head.

'He's not capable of sorting this one out. He's my brother,' he said. 'I couldn't live with myself if I didn't help him. If I don't help Joe, no one will. I can deal with not having much cash for the next few years, but I know it can cause problems. It was a massive issue for Sylvie.'

'I'm not like Sylvie,' I said, as quick as you like. 'And I think that what you're doing is pretty fucking scarily amazing.'

We shared a look – he knew I was remembering what he'd said on the beach in Cornwall.

'I know you're not,' he said. 'That's why I like you. But my situation isn't ideal. In a perfect world, I'd be living in Cornwall, and I could throw you over my shoulder and take you down there with me. Or, maybe after everything that happened down there, you wouldn't like that?'

'I love Cornwall,' I said. 'But you're right, it does hold some difficult memories for me ... I think everything's changing so much now, though.'

'One day – ' Dylan grinned – 'I'd like to make Cornwall a happy place for you.'

I smiled at him and he smiled back. If anyone could do that, Dylan could.

'So what did you think when Joy told you I'd been bitten by an asp?' I said, breaking into a grin.

'I phoned London Zoo press office asking them to confirm her story, and they thought I was a madman,' he said, laughing. 'I like her style, though – very imaginative. She didn't settle for anything mundane.'

Our knees were almost touching. I confess I wanted to jump on him there and then.

'And so here we are,' I said, suddenly shy. 'Blood-stained and drunk, with charcoaled soufflé for dinner – not that I'm hungry.'

'Juliet?' Dylan said.

'Yes?' I replied.

'Shall we go outside?' he asked. 'My nose can't take the smell of smoke – it's throbbing. I think a blast of cool air would help.'

'Come on then, nose,' I said, unlocking the French windows, and we walked out into the garden, sweetest smelling at this time of night.

Dylan sat down in the middle of the overgrown grass and patted the ground next to him. The air was ambrosial with lavender, honeysuckle and moss. It was dark now, the thrilling sounds of late London rolling across the night sky.

'Sit down,' he said. 'I think I . . .'

I sat next to him and leaned into his shoulder. Then, what I'd been quietly hoping would happen happened. Under the bone-white moon, we kissed. And I was struck by a halcyon thought: This must be it. This must be home.

For the time being, anyway.

extracts reading groups
competitions books new
discounts extracts extracts
competitions events
books
reading groups
new
new books discounts
events books
extracts
new books reading groups
interviews
events extracts
discounts
new books events
events new
discounts extracts discounts
www.panmacmillan.com
extracts events reading groups
competitions books extracts new